CRITICAL ACCLAIM FOR
DANGEROUS GAME

"Gripping interpersonal relationships connected to past traumas as well as a tumultuous romance, for which Rosemoor is known, enrich this novel of shifting allegiances and psychiatric unbalances." —J. Ivanel Johnson, author of the award-winning Just (e)State mystery series

"A twisty and intriguing romantic crime mystery of a strong yet vulnerable woman's fight to survive the onslaughts of unearthed evils and buried family secrets." —Gregory Wilson Taylor

"Annelise Covington can't remember what she's done—and someone is counting on that. *Dangerous Game* is a razor-sharp psychological thriller about fractured identity and buried trauma, with a heroine you can't quite trust...but can't stop rooting for." —Twist Phelan, Thriller Award Winner

"Fast-paced and fueled by justice, *Dangerous Game* features a fearless heroine determined to take down those who prey on women—no matter the cost. You'll race through every twist and turn to an ending you won't see coming." —Addison Brae, award-winning author of the Becker Circle Series

"Rosemoor's strength is in creating and curating relationships between the principal characters, whose identities are intimately tied together in this insightful thriller." —Cari Dubiel, author and librarian

DANGEROUS GAME

SERIES AND BOOKS BY PATRICIA ROSEMOOR

Series

Crimson Duet
Double Trouble
Quid Pro Quo
McKenna Legacy
Seven Sins
Sons of Silver Springs
Chicago Heat
Club Undercover
Detective Shelley Caldwell
New Orleans Heat
Annals of Alchemy and Blood
McKenna Curse
Kindred Souls
Justus Investigations
Wilde Hearts

Novels

Double Images (1986)
Dangerous Illusions (1986)
Against All Odds (1988)
Working It Out (1988)
Do Unto Others (1989)
The Kiss of Death (1992)
Haunted (1993)
The Silent Sea (1994)
Skin (2012)
Written in the Stars (2015)
(with Sherill Bodine)
Eyes of a Tiger (2018)
Sidewinder (2020)
Justice (2020)
Curse of Slater House (2021)
Kiss & Goodbye (2024)

PATRICIA ROSEMOOR

DANGEROUS GAME

A PSYCHOLOGICAL SUSPENSE THRILLER

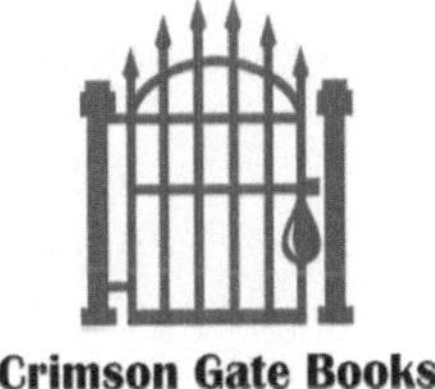

Crimson Gate Books

Chapter One

The night sky blazed in a display worthy of an Independence Day celebration—dangerous diversion, Durant Walsh thought. If one was into amusement provided by a fire, of course.

Edging a crowd of spectators, his chauffeured 1937 Cord Berline glided to a stop. Heads turned and eyes widened as people got a load of the gold and hazel coffin-nosed classic car. The airflow design exaggerated the Cord's low, racy lines into flowing sculptural beauty, and the underslung frame curved into a body which spelled sex. Durant was enamored of this vehicle, which he affectionately thought of as his Cum Car.

In the back seat, he lowered a tinted window to better see the red and gold flames consuming the brick three-story Walsh Parts and Storage Garage. If it had been daylight, the thick column of black smoke rising from what was left of the roof would be visible for miles.

"I'll walk from here," he told the chauffeur.

Durant exited the Cord and made his way laboriously through the crush of bodies surrounding the car and extending all the way to the police tape—FIRE LINE DO NOT CROSS— blocking off the street.

He didn't give a damn for the loss of a building that was old and well beyond its time. The businessman in him was already calculating the damage, dealing with the insurance company and constructing a new facility. The future structure would house more than a storage garage and parts warehouse. Durant smiled as he remembered going through his stepsister Annelise's files, finding her plans for expansion she hadn't yet shared with the board. A branch office of Walsh Restorations specializing in models of the seventies and eighties rather than the older classics would be a perfect replacement.

Above all, he would revel in a successful expansion of Walsh Motors, an expansion he would be quick to instigate, and quicker to take credit for.

As he drew closer to the fire scene by elbowing through a knot of excited teenagers, the full impact of the madhouse pressed down on him. More than a dozen fire engines and half as many trucks surrounded the burning building. The roof was an inferno. Firemen in turnout gear shouted at each other over the thrum of engines and the spray of water hitting the flames. A window exploded, shattering the air with earsplitting noise, raining shards of glass on the firefighters below. Then part of the wall buckled and consumed a parked silver BMW. People in the crowd screamed.

Durant strove to cross the barrier that was keeping spectators back. A uniformed cop working crowd control stopped him.

"Hey, buddy, stay behind the line like everyone else!"

"I'm not everyone else." Durant slipped under the police tape, annoyed when the vigilant cop blocked him with his own body. "I'm Durant Walsh."

Unimpressed, the cop didn't budge. Durant drew out his wallet and showed his identification with an ingratiating smile even as the imbecile shoved at his chest to move him back behind the line.

"Please look at this, Officer Mills," Durant said with an insincere smile, memorizing the man's name from his badge. "Joe Flaherty is expecting me. That's *my* garage burning up."

Finally taking a look at the identification, the cop grunted. "Wait here while I find Flaherty."

Satisfied, Durant looked around. Heat blasted him and the stench of burning wood and heated metal filled his nostrils. Nearby, parked cars were blanketed with a thick layer of black soot, and a few were dented by falling debris. Spectators drawn from every strata of Chicago society watched with him. All engrossed in a hot summer night's entertainment, WASP business owners stood side-by-side with Hispanic gang members while urban professionals mingled with tenants from what was left of the nearby housing projects.

One of the latter in particular caught his eye. She was young and lush. Fleshy thighs protruded from beneath the knit mini-skirt as she leaned on a nearby light pole. Durant pictured the woman entering his Cord, awed by the seats upholstered in pleated and rolled soft glove leather, the burnished gold fixtures, the tortoise-shell dashboard and the amber and gold steering wheel. He imagined her kneeling on the floor covered with handwoven Turkish carpeting...

The low-throated roar of the fire escalated, reminding Durant of a woman's agonized scream. He shuddered and kept tight hold over himself so no one could guess it had given him a hard-on.

"Mr. Walsh." A beefy middle-aged man with curly black hair, small squinty eyes and a double chin accompanied the uniformed cop. "I'm Joe Flaherty."

Flaherty was the Commanding Fire Marshal and the one who'd summoned Durant to the scene. "How in the world did this happen, Commander?" Durant asked.

"We won't know until the ashes settle, Mr. Walsh, but we figure it's incendiary. Arson. As best we can tell, the fire started in at least three separate locations in the building. We're getting things under control now."

"Thank God. I have several million dollars' worth of classic cars in the garage." The insurance would cover the loss of the cars, too. But power plays were his high. Some people drank. Others took drugs. Durant enjoyed making people sweat.

"Vehicles that can't be replaced."

To his irritation, the big man wasn't impressed. "Nothing we can do about 'em. Probably at meltdown by now. Sorry. I'm more worried about a body count. Anyone supposed to be inside?"

"No guards," Durant said. "We have an electronic security system, and a service sends someone by twice an hour to give the place a once-over."

Durant saw Flaherty shift his attention. He glanced back to see his stepsister Annelise squeeze her way through the barrier. An incongruous sight in the midst of the smoky chaos, Annelise wore a demeanor as cool as the air was hot. Dressed in a pale designer suit showing off her waist, her red-gold hair smoothed back into a simple, sophisticated twist, she looked as if she were on her way to a ladies' luncheon. Her green eyes registered a familiar contempt before sliding past him.

"I'm Annelise Covington," she told Flaherty in a husky voice meant to cut through a man. "Chief of Operations Officer of Walsh Motors. If there's anything I can do, please let me know."

"I'd be grateful Miss Covington, but—"

"Commander!" came a shout from one of the grime-covered firemen. "Over here!"

Without so much as an "Excuse me," Flaherty ran off toward the man and the burning building beyond.

But Durant continued staring at his stepsister, willing her to lose her bearing. Flames flickered over classic features so artfully highlighted she appeared natural. Beauty without artifice. Innocence that Durant longed to strip from her even as he longed to strip everything else she possessed. Her poise...her clothing...*her share of the family corporation.*

"What happened?" she asked. "Do they know yet?"

"Someone was playing with matches. Must have as exciting a social life as you do."

Her mouth tightened into a thin if not quite unattractive line.

The woman was repressed. A sexual question mark. One he wanted answered. He took pleasure in her knowing.

"Got us a crispy critter!" someone yelled.

Two firefighters struggled to get their burden through the opening which had been the back doorway. Mesmerized, Durant couldn't tear his gaze from the sight. Then a huffing Flaherty came between him and Annelise.

"You said no one was supposed to be inside."

"No one was," Durant assured the commander as another fireman came running up to them.

Breathless, the new man gestured toward the body. "Found her near the exit...like she was trying to get out as she burned. There's enough of her left we might be able to get an ID on her."

Though sweating inside his Armani suit, Durant viewed the scenario with a certain detachment. Firemen rushing around ineffectually. Conflagration raging out of control. Horrified awareness coloring Annelise's expression and rounding her already large, long-lashed eyes. He focused on the last. He rather liked the edge of panic he read in the wide pupils, would willingly duplicate the reaction personally if given the chance.

Flaherty muttered a curse as the charred body was carried past them. "Johnson, call Violent Crimes."

Annelise fought the queasiness threatening to empty her stomach. Loss of property was one thing, but the remains the firemen carried past them had once been a living, breathing human being. Smoke seared her lungs and threatened to choke her. She started coughing and was unaware of Durant stepping closer until he spoke softly. The breath fanning her ear was cool compared to the air surrounding them. And unwelcome enough to make her skin crawl.

"If you can't take the heat, you don't belong in the board-room."

Amazed anew at her stepbrother's callousness, she demanded, "Do you really get off making stupid cracks at a time like this?"

"I'll always make time for you."

Her heart thumped against her ribs, but she stood her ground. "A woman died in the fire. Don't you feel anything for her? Are you even human?"

Something she couldn't quite define flickered behind his eyes, but Durant didn't respond. If only she could get away from him for good. But she wouldn't give him the satisfaction of leaving the family business—*her* family's business, robbed by his, that was.

He was a handsome good-for-nothing. Crisp blond good looks augmented by a healthy salon tan. Designer clothing steeped with the lingering scent of designer toiletries. Well-kept hands and manicured nails enhanced by expensive, tasteful gold and diamond rings. All camouflage.

"You take things too seriously, little sister."

"And you merely take things, whether they're offered or not," Annelise returned, the accusation based on history.

The smile he aimed her way was wolfish. Her anger amusing him both infuriated Annelise and reminded her of how truly dangerous he could be. Lights flashing behind her eyes warned her of an imminent headache. Leave it to Durant to give her another migraine. Determined to vanquish the aura which usually preceded each episode, she turned her back to her stepbrother.

The man Flaherty had been talking to jogged off toward the firefighters closest to the blaze.

"Who was the woman?" Annelise asked the commander.

"Any identification is history. It'll take some doing to find out."

"Horrible. You'll let us know as soon as you find out, won't you? Whoever she was, she has people. Someone has to talk to them, give them our condolences." And Durant wouldn't volunteer, Annelise thought. "How did the fire start?"

"Arson. No doubt about it, not when it popped in several locations at once," Flaherty told her. "Question is, did the dead woman incinerate herself?"

Annelise shuddered. "You think the woman set the fire?"

"She could've. Why not? Arson's an equal opportunity crime." Then Flaherty addressed Durant directly. "This puts a whole new light on the case. Raises lots more questions. Now you have a goddamn ugly situation on your hands."

Though Annelise was resentful Durant rather than she was in charge of the situation, no matter how ugly, she was grateful his attention centered on something other than her. She tried to remove herself from the disaster, tried to pretend another piece of her heart wasn't being devoured by the flames.

She didn't mourn the loss of the property itself. The ancient building was merely symbolic of Covington Classics, the original company her father had founded more than thirty years before. A company that should now belong to her. What she mourned was the loss of her father's dream, replaced by the cold corporate entity hardly recognizable as his creation.

Bit by bit, the classic car restoration business had been abused by the Walshes even as had the Covington women. Nearly two decades before, her mother had set the wheels in motion after her father's death.

Suddenly a low rumble roared to life, the noise shattering her thoughts. A ball of flame lit up the sky and shook what was left of the building. Sections of the outer wall collapsed, and the side of the building began to cave in on itself. Glass sprayed a fireman on a crane. Recoiling, he dropped his hose which snaked wildly along the platform.

"My God," Annelise whispered as his screams rent the air.

The breath caught in her throat. The man's hands covered his face. Blood oozed through his fingers. Water sprayed in every direction. Two firefighters got to him fast, one helping him down to safety, the other picking up the hose. Heat scorched Annelise and smoke filled her lungs when she finally gasped for air. The fire was a living, breathing entity. The thought of being trapped inside the belly of the fiery beast was terrifying.

Looking down at her ash-covered pale suit and skin, she again envisioned the corpse the firemen had found. Either Flaherty was correct, and the woman was an arsonist, or one of the clerks had the bad luck to work late without telling anyone.

"Mr. Walsh, Miss Covington," Flaherty said. He indicated a thin wiry black man who had joined him. "This is Detective Marcellus Turner. He's got some questions for the two of you."

The detective looked them over with pale brown eyes that didn't miss a thing, giving Annelise the weirdest sensation as if she was a suspect. "Let's find some place to talk." He moved them off toward where he'd left his unmarked car. The sounds of the trucks and water and the fire itself were less immediate.

Pulling out a small notebook, Turner addressed Durant. "Tell me what you know about the fire."

"Only what Flaherty told me."

For once Annelise was glad her stepbrother was the center of attention. Shaken by the whole scene, wanting to get out of there in the worst way, she listened to Durant talk about security provisions and the contents of the building. Her gaze strayed back to the fire feeding on itself, growing more powerful by the moment.

"So, you have no opinion about why the woman was here?" the detective was asking her stepbrother.

"None at all."

Annelise ventured her opinion. "Perhaps one of the parts clerks returned to the building for some reason."

"Poor woman," Durant murmured, "whoever she was."

The tone was appropriately concerned, but the gaze he turned on Annelise was mocking. Surely Turner noticed.

Outwardly, the detective appeared decidedly rumpled— jacket button missing, shirt wrinkled, tie askew—making her think of an African American Columbo. But like the television detective she'd watched a few times on a streamer, she suspected Turner was a man who shouldn't be underestimated.

"I wonder if you'd say the same if she turned out to be the arsonist," the detective asked, gaze steady on Durant.

"Even if she were guilty, dying in a fire like that would be cruel and unusual punishment, wouldn't you say, Detective?"

"I don't mete out punishments, Mr. Walsh. I just catch the bad guys."

"And are you usually successful?" Durant asked.

"You'd be surprised. By the way, where were you when the fire started?"

"Creating a little fire of my own." Durant gave Turner a supercilious smile. "With a woman."

"You won't mind if I verify your story."

Then the detective shifted his attention to Annelise. Turner's miss-nothing gaze traveled up her shape-hugging suit. But when his eyes met hers, they were fathomless, impersonal. They chilled her.

Sensing he was about to ask her the same question, she beat him to the punch. "You'll have to excuse me. I'm getting a migraine."

The aura was returning. Lights flashed behind her eyes. Annelise turned and walked away from the fire scene. Her carriage was straight, her stride purposeful, her nerves taut. She felt Turner's gaze follow and scorch her back. Her hands trembled as she lifted the official tape and ducked under it, then pushed through the horde of spectators.

If Detective Marcellus Turner persisted in pursuing her whereabouts earlier, what then?

She had no memory of where she had been.

Chapter Two

Heat seared the sidewalks hours after sunset. A scorcher of an afternoon had melted into a stifling, humid night. The kind of night Liz Covington liked best.

Her heels clacked a staccato beat as she entered the air-conditioned Sessions Cigar Lounge—more of a sports bar with a half dozen screens on the walls. Dozens of brands of cigars were on display for sale in a glass-fronted cabinet taking up a whole wall. This was one of the few places in Chicago where smoking was allowed inside. Many customers preferred pipes, or like her, cigarettes. Her reason for frequenting cigar bars.

Aware of the not-so-covert male stares, Liz settled on a bar stool and scanned the room for a potential someone who might help ease her restlessness. Not that finding a man, even if only for an interesting conversation, was her purpose in stepping out. Liz didn't fool herself about relationships. She just needed to be around people who didn't know her.

"What's your pleasure?" the fresh-faced bartender asked.

"Gin and tonic, easy on the gin."

He nodded and turned away. She pulled a pack of cigarettes from her purse as two men sat at the table closest to her. She checked them out in the mirror – a couple of regular-looking guys, one sandy-haired and clean-shaven, the other dark-haired and bearded, both wearing expensive suits.

"So, think we'll find some action in this place?" the sandy-haired one asked.

"Who cares after the hard day that jerk-off put us through."

"I can get *hard* anytime I see a good set of legs."

Eavesdropping, Liz noted the boast as she searched her purse for her lighter.

"Man, would I like to get the bastard by the balls," the same man continued. "When he says *jump*, he expects me to ask *how high*. I'm sick of it."

"A beer'll help."

"If we ever get one. Where the hell's the waitress anyway?"

"Settle down, Jimmy-boy, she's busy."

"Sweetheart, over here!"

Liz glanced up at the mirror as *Jimmy-boy* waved to the harried-looking brunette waitress who was dealing with a large table of customers.

"Porker," he muttered under his breath.

Liz frowned at the cruel remark.

"I don't mind a little extra meat on a woman," the man with the beard was saying. "I think it's nuts the way some women starve themselves to death."

"So what if a few of 'em die trying? Better dead than littering the earth with more dogs."

Liz froze...

"I wouldn't let a woman hear you say that, you jerk."

"Why not?" The sandy-haired man snorted. *"What could a woman do to me?"*

...and watched him via the mirror. He lit a cigar and blew the smoke at his friend. He was laughing, full of himself.

Then he turned to the waitress who was finishing up with her customers and pocketing her money. "Yo, sugar, are you gonna take care of us or what?" he demanded.

Smiling, the woman rushed to their table. "Sorry you had to wait. Now what can I get you?" She reached over to pick up the used ashtray.

And Liz saw the sandy-haired man deliberately touch the lit

tip of his cigar to the woman's arm.

The waitress jumped with a choked, "A-ah!"

"Did I get you? Sorry. Accidents happen, you know?" He gave her a fake smile. "Bring us two Coronas like a good girl."

"Yeah, sure."

With a pained expression, the waitress held her arm and backed off. It looked to Liz like she was headed for her manager. Good. Hopefully, the creep would get thrown out. But the waitress stopped, her expression torn, as if she was afraid of making the complaint for some reason. And then she turned away.

The nasty creep laughed. "Wait till you see what I do to her next."

"Jimmy, cut it out," his buddy pleaded.

"Maybe I'll just give her the thrill ride of her life. You think I care what she wants?"

Liz's focus narrowed on the boyish features and expensive suit camouflaging the real person beneath: ambitious but not successful enough, soothing frustration by taking advantage of someone who couldn't fight back. He'd keep at the poor waitress until he broke her or got her fired. And the way he just talked about having her...

Another Durant.

Liz swirled on her barstool, curly Titian hair flying around her face. She crossed her legs, foot encased in a handmade Italian shoe bobbing. A second later, a cold pair of pale blue eyes traveled slowly up her legs, then more quickly met her gaze. A grimace resembling a smile touched his lips.

"How you doing, honey?"

"Good, except..." She held up her cigarette. "...I can't seem to find a light."

"Let me fix that for you."

She slid off the stool. Hiking her bag over her shoulder, she bent forward, cigarette to her lips. When he flicked his lighter, his eyes were glued to her breasts.

"The name's James Scanlon."

"Liz." She took a long, calculated drag and, straightening, deliberately blew the smoke into his face. "Thanks." Betting he would follow, she started to sway off toward the front door until her wrist was caught in a tight grip.

"What's the hurry?" he asked.

Keeping her features composed, she glanced over her shoulder. "I need a little walk. Some night air. You can come if you want. If your friend doesn't mind."

"He doesn't mind." Without letting go of her wrist, he said, "Tomorrow, Ray," and grabbed his messenger bag and newspaper. "So which way are we walking?"

"Which way is your place?"

His place, as it turned out, was conveniently close.

Liz let him hustle her there with a minimum of words and touching that didn't do a thing for her. She was going to get off tonight, but not through sex. His messenger bag had her interest.

Jimmy-boy turned her into a courtyard graced with large trees, carefully tended flower beds and old-fashioned lanterns. The low-rise brick and stone building sprawled on a side street shouldering Lake Shore Drive. With a last drag on her cigarette, she dropped and crushed it. He opened the door and led her to his vestibule, then roughly pulled her into his arms.

His mouth sought hers. She slid her head away, so his wet lips grazed her cheek and landed in her hair. She tried not to shiver, but she was hardly able to breathe in the airless vestibule. A little discomfort would be worth it, she told herself. Jimmy-boy needed to be taught a lesson.

What could a woman do to him?

"Not here." She slid her long, purple-tipped nails the length of his collarbone.

She moved to the inner door of the vestibule. He fumbled with his keys for a second before finding the right one. He pushed through the open door, then grabbed her wrist and roughly pulled her up the stairs.

He stopped on the second floor and jingled the key ring again. She counted the seconds as he released the deadbolt and opened his apartment to her. Heat gusted from the large living room. He pulled her inside, then let go of her long enough to throw the messenger bag and paper on the dining room table and start the window air conditioner.

"Want a drink?"

"Not thirsty." Jimmy made a dive for the hem of her skirt. She stopped him short. Looked deep into his nearly colorless blue eyes. "Shower first."

"What for?" His eyes narrowed for a moment before a smile twisted his boyish face. He backed off. "The shower, huh?" He started unbuttoning his shirt.

She moved past him so she wouldn't have to watch. Instead, she listened to his clothing drop to the floor as she looked around the apartment and cased the place while he undressed.

"What about you?" he grunted.

She undid the top button of her blouse. "Go on. I need a minute." Her voice was silky. "You know. Girl things. Protection."

Stepping out of her shoes, she puckered her lips and blew him a kiss. He backed into the bathroom. She loosened a second button as he disappeared from view. A moment later, hearing shower spraying and feet squeaking along the tile floor, Liz looked down at what she thought of as her girl power tattoo at the top of her left breast and then reversed the process and buttoned up.

"Hurry, will you?" he shouted over the noise of the water.

She stepped into her shoes and moved to get the leather messenger bag, half-covered by the sports section featuring the results of the Indianapolis Motor Speedway Road Course – *C.D. O'Neal Drives Straight To the Top.* Where Jimmy-boy Scanlon wanted to be. What irony, Liz thought, throwing the newspaper aside and opening the case.

Pulling out his tablet, Liz noted it was an android. Her lips curved. Exactly what she'd hoped to find. Checking the outside pockets produced his cell phone. A program she'd gotten from a black hat she'd dated would open both, and hopefully he had some kind of password program she could use to get into his files. Then she could figure out a way to ruin this creep with his employer, make sure he never made it to the top. The waitress hadn't deserved to lose her job—which she was sure he would have manipulated—but *he* deserved whatever she could dish out. Shoving the tablet and phone into her shoulder bag, she traded it for a tube of bright lipstick. Wielding it as an instrument of truth, she left a message on the case, then threw the tube back into her shoulder bag.

She smiled at what she had written on his case: *Consider yourself fucked.*

She was out in the courtyard in less than a minute. When he discovered his tablet and cell were missing, he would go crazy.

Pulling out her phone, she ordered an Uber to pick her up on Lake Shore Drive.

The Uber screeched to a halt mere inches from where she stood. She hopped inside. As she leaned back against the seat, the sense of victory drained from her, leaving behind a familiar hollowness. She'd had enough of controlling abusive men to last a lifetime. This wasn't the first time she'd been willing to take on a pig like Jimmy-boy.

And it wouldn't be the last.

Chapter Three

The main branch of Walsh Motors filled an old, distinguished copper-trimmed brownstone building, which covered half a block in River North. Annelise appreciated the area west of North Michigan Avenue had blossomed as had the thirty-year-old classic car business located in a ninety-year-old building. Not that she had time to take advantage of the trendy galleries, restaurants and boutiques.

When she pulled her Mustang into the garage early Monday morning, the fire was still uppermost in her mind. The vision of the destruction and death had haunted her all night. Not that this was the first time she'd seen a body with the life drained from it. She only hoped it would be the last. Also, she was still worrying about Turner. She didn't need anyone to know what she did with her nights. Not that she could remember.

Annelise stepped out onto the fifth floor. The top landing of the central staircase which zig-zagged down to street level served as the executive lobby area. Windows provided a northern exposure and soft light filtered in, illuminating the oak paneled walls and columns.

She entered her office with its view of rapid transit trains rumbling by on the elevated tracks directly below her office window when she – rather than Durant – should be settled in Theodore Covington's old domain, running her family's business. She started her morning pot of coffee and turned on her iPad and classical music. At least she had a few tangible reminders of her father to keep her resolve strong when the going got tough – his desk and chair, before and after photographs of the first cars Covington Classics had restored.

Pouring a cup of eye-popping strength coffee, she sat behind the desk, ran her hand along the mahogany surface, then leaned back in the massive green chair and hummed along with the music. The leather smell of the chair conjured happy childhood memories. As did the two photographs mounted in a hinged double frame of etched silver displayed on the desk.

The first was of her parents taken in the Covington House garden shortly before her father had died so tragically at thirty-eight. Her mother Madeline wore the pretty blue silk dress which matched her eyes and highlighted her cloud of dark auburn hair. Her father was dark-haired, his eyes a deep hazel. Their expressions were filled with such love for each other, Annelise ached with envy.

How Mama could have let Arthur Walsh take over their lives after Daddy died was unbearable. First it had been the funeral arrangements, and then her foolish mother had married him within months of her father's death and had handed over the running of Covington Classics, which he had quickly renamed Walsh Motors.

She took a long swallow of hot coffee as her attention switched to the second photograph of two teenagers with bright Titian hair. She and her sister had been sixteen then, identical twins – one pretty in pink, poised and tranquil like the roses behind her, the other as wild as the blood red dress she wore.

Not wanting to think about her late sister, she set down her coffee cup and pulled several folders from her attaché case. The new proposal she'd been working on had consumed her weekend. She checked the digital clock set in a miniature classic car next to the framed photos. 7:38 a.m. Early as usual.

Opening one of the folders, she worked for a few minutes until a knock disturbed her. "Yes?"

"Only me." Joyce Hernandez entered. While not conventionally pretty, the administrative assistant was attractive with thick black shoulder-length hair, deep-set brown eyes and a ready smile. "The beginning of the week, and you look tired already. You should let someone who's paid more money do the worrying."

"Have you ever imagined Durant worrying about anything?"

Joyce grinned. "He's too busy demanding attention."

Annelise wondered if Durant had ever made *personal* demands on her assistant. She'd heard more than one man in the office describe Joyce as being seal-sleek or sneakily sexy. She found such observations annoying, for Joyce Hernandezt was first and foremost an outstanding employee, intelligent and sharp.

"So what's up?"

"I was asked to deliver a message from your stepbrother." Joyce sounded apologetic. "He wants your – and I quote – 'fancy butt in the conference room, stat.'"

Annelise swallowed her irritation at the wording. "The fire, of course."

She'd used her proposal for expansion – renovating cars of the sixties and seventies – to take her mind off the disaster for a short while. She glanced at her personal calendar and her day's schedule. The page was loaded with notations.

"You'd better cancel my appointments for today."

"I'll reschedule everything," Joyce said. "I'll make Lewis and Ackerman a priority, say first thing Thursday?"

"That should do it." The two men were vital to her new proposal. She gave her assistant a grateful smile as she stood. "We've got a real mess on our hands, and one day isn't nearly enough for the clean-up."

"Don't worry, we'll muddle through," Joyce assured her. "Things will be back to normal before you know it."

More the pity. If Annelise prayed for anything, it was change in the way this business was run. Walsh Motors needed to be humanized, the way her father had run Covington Classics.

* * *

The Walsh Motors conference room was located in a rectangular space holding the workings of a giant building clock no longer functioning. Annelise felt it was a perfect addition to the classic cars they sold—old but magnificent pieces of art of their kind. Both hands perpetually set on twelve, the clock was the centerpiece of a semi-circular window whose fretwork cast shadows over the fresco mural on the opposite wall.

Slipping inside, Annelise joined her stepbrother and their two executive officers.

Sitting at the head of the elliptical-shaped metal conference table he'd chosen to modernize the room, Durant checked his watch. "Now that *you're* here, we can start."

Annelise remained at the opposite end of the table from him and their two managers.

Sam Nakagawa, Accounting Manager—a Millennial and the youngest of the men usually sported form-fitting suits, while the older GenZ Kevin Dolhonik, Marketing Manager, favored anything a little baggy. She noted impatience crossing Dolhonik's beefy features as he drilled his blunt fingertips against the polished metal conference table.

"Can we get on with business?" he snapped. "I've got a full day scheduled. I don't have time for crap."

Dolhonik was a roll up your sleeves and pitch in kind of employee and had worked his way up through the ranks. He was a straight shooter, saying exactly what was on his mind, unlike Nakagawa, who remained silent if not exactly relaxed.

"The word for this morning is arson," Durant began. "The authorities have physical evidence. A pipe bomb was placed under each of the classics. The cars are unrecognizable."

"Who do the cops suspect?" Dolhonik asked. "Some crackpot in the neighborhood who didn't like the looks of the building?"

Durant said, "Possibly the young woman who died in the fire."

Annelise stared at him, but his expression was unreadable.

"What about a positive I.D. on this woman?" Nakagawa asked. "Were they able to make one?"

"Amazingly, yes. They couldn't get fingerprints. The burn was too severe and they were gone. But a car out front of the place was still there after the fire was put out. They checked the custom plates that read Antique Autos and got her name. Kate O'Neal. Tully O'Neal's daughter." Durant clarified, "As in O'Neal's Antique Auto Repairs. Detective Turner, the man in charge of the investigation, thinks the connection is too significant to be a coincidence."

Dolhonik waved a beefy hand. "O'Neal runs a small time operation compared to ours. Destroying our oldest building isn't going to make a difference to them."

"The building and seven classics worth upwards of ten million dollars," Nakagawa added.

"You didn't hear any accusation from me," Durant said. "The police look for motives. They think they found one."

"They'll have to think again," Annelise stated. "We're fully insured and the O'Neals would of course know that. And if they hoped a loss would dent our business, they would have picked a more valuable property, one that would put part of our operation out of commission long enough to hurt us. Besides, if Kate O'Neal was guilty, she wouldn't have been caught in her own fire."

Everyone in the room shifted uneasily once more. Dolhonik cursed under his breath. Annelise kept eye contact with Durant.

"Kate O'Neal wasn't doing business with us for O'Neal Repairs," Durant went on. "So she had no reason to be at Parts and Storage. Tully O'Neal once worked for us." He looked from Dolhonik to Nakagawa, neither of whom had been working for Walsh Motors at the time. "He was let go for incompetence."

Sitting forward, Annelise protested, "O'Neal was an expert, meticulous mechanic. Arthur fired him as a personal power play. Which was more than ten years ago."

Durant merely shrugged. "Right. Ten years. You were too young to have a clear handle on the situation."

"I'm a lot clearer about what was going on than you know. This is a tragedy, Durant. Have you contacted the family?"

"Should I invite the other suspects to tea?"

"Don't be ridiculous. Kate O'Neal died on Walsh property. The least we can do is give the family our condolences." When he merely raised his eyebrows, Annelise shook her head. "Fine. I'll do it. I'll arrange for flowers for the funeral, and I'll follow up with the O'Neals personally."

"Don't. I have things under control."

"Really? What are you doing about finding the arsonist?"

"Leaving it to the authorities. It's their job."

"And what if they don't find the guilty party before he strikes again?" she asked.

The room narrowed so only the two of them existed as Durant glared at her. "There's no reason to believe he will. So forget any big plans you're making and keep your mind on business."

"If someone's trying to ruin us, there's no reason to believe he won't strike again. A lot of people depend on us, Durant. Workers and their families. What if we don't have time? What about Restorations? Clean Cars? The showroom? A lot of people depend on us. I don't want to see any more employees out of work. I certainly don't want to see anyone else killed."

"It would be a positive affirmation of management's concern for our employees if we look into the situation," Nakagawa said.

Then Dolhonik added, "Employees would likely talk to us before they spilled anything to the cops."

Durant barked, "We all have more than enough to do without starting our own investigation!"

"As an owner," Annelise said, "I intend to make time."

"And as acting CEO of this corporation, I expect you to

check with me before you do anything."

Though Annelise owned twenty percent and was the company COO — looking after day-to-day issues related to marketing, sales and personnel — Durant merely had power of attorney over his father's share, which meant he'd voted sixty percent since Arthur's stroke five months before.

"Then I'm giving you notice I will be paying Tully O'Neal a visit to express our condolences."

If looks could kill...

Durant ignored her for the rest of the meeting, which was just fine with her.

Afterward, Annelise went directly to her car, hoping Durant took her ignoring him as a defiant move. She wasn't going to see Tully — she doubted he was at work the day after his daughter had died — but let her stepbrother think what he wanted.

Heading straight for Lake Shore Drive, she shot south, away from the congested downtown and neighborhoods. She needed time to chill.

To reconnect with Lizzie for a while.

The 1964 ½ Ford Mustang Convertible had been her twin sister's baby. The sporty, lightweight pony car was a first-generation Mustang. Lizzie had bought it second hand after getting her driver's license at sixteen. Since the car had been involved in an accident, that meant a ton of work and replacement parts, but the purchase price had been a deal. Having learned about car repair from some of the Walsh mechanics, Lizzie had spent every spare hour working on her prize classic. Replacing damaged body parts. Renewing the red paint job. Refreshing the white vinyl interior. Annelise had spent time working on it, as well. Lizzie had taught her nearly everything she knew about classic cars. Driving the Mustang kept Lizzie alive in Annelise's imagination.

Sometimes when she was connected to her dead sister through the car, she even talked to Lizzie about problems with

Walsh Motors and specifically with Durant.

And often swore Lizzie answered her.

Annelise pulled into Walsh Clean Cars, her pride directly related to ownership evident in the way she scanned the garage's organized interior. Roscoe Hieber was proud, too, of the division he managed for her.

A 1946 Daimler sedan, its motor purring, exited the garage as Annelise stepped out of her Mustang. Roscoe hitched up his pants from below the spare tire his wife never tired of teasing him about and relit his cigar stub.

Annelise frowned. "I thought you were going to give up that disgusting habit."

"I gotta find another vice first. A man can't be perfect. It's not human nature." Truth was, she knew he liked her fussing over him. "Didn't think you were going to make it today."

Located on Orleans, Walsh Clean Cars was only a few blocks from the main office, but Annelise knew Roscoe had to be concerned about the fire situation.

She smiled and swatted his arm. "If I didn't get over here, I'd miss your cheerful personality."

"Yeah, yeah, it's what all the dames say. Come on to the back of the garage. I got something to show you." He led her straight to a 1966 jet black Shelby Cobra 427. The dream vehicle that had been the fastest production car on the road for its time was now worth a couple million. "Finally found an open spot in the schedule for her."

Annelise inspected the badges, loose trim and exhaust pipe, all removed from the car and now carefully lining a workbench. "Good. Ralston's getting anxious. It's been what—two weeks since he brought it in?"

Roscoe nodded. Smoothing his calloused palm over the hood, he opened it to reveal a gleaming, immaculate engine which had already been cleaned and repainted. Annelise leaned in to inspect the hoses and wires that had been replaced. She grasped one sticking upward and worked it flat like the others.

"There, all perfect alignment." She nodded in approval. "Looks brand new, like it was never driven."

"You're the only woman I know who could appreciate such work. But then you never minded getting your hands dirty learning right from the beginning, even before you joined Walsh Motors."

"I wanted to understand what made a car run as well as what made rich men's hearts tick when they got behind the wheel."

"Beauty, brains, class, drive. You got it all. Teddy would bust his buttons if only he could see you now."

Roscoe's reference to her late father warmed Annelise. If only he hadn't died, life would be so different for her now. And Lizzie might still be alive.

He closed the car hood and ran his hand over it. "Tomorrow we'll finish all the invisible stuff."

Annelise nodded in approval. Dust and dirt would be blown out of the interior with an air hose, and the leather seats and door panels would be treated with oil. Carpets and floor mats needed to be shampooed, chrome touched up, vinyl dashboard and rubber door seals treated with special preservatives.

"So it might be ready when?" she asked.

"A coupla days. We probably won't start buffing up the body till Wednesday morning."

Annelise ran her fingertips gently along the fender that would be washed, then buffed both with a wool pad and another of softer sheepskin. "Ralston said he wants to impress a lady Wednesday night."

Roscoe turned a baleful eye on her. "We'll do the best we can. Tell him to go to a schlock operation if he can't wait."

"I already did." She grinned. "In a less direct manner, of course."

"So what's this I hear about Tully O'Neal being involved

with the fire?"

"Speculation bolstered by Durant's hatred of the man. I sent flowers, and I was thinking about stopping by his place. Well, maybe tomorrow." If he would even be there.

"You got a big heart, kid."

"And an even bigger nose. I probably should leave it to the professionals, but Roscoe, would you do me a favor?" Her thoughts had turned grim and she felt a bit hesitant. "Could you kind of ask around, see what you can find out about any customers or employees or former employees having bad feelings toward management?"

"Hey, even clams open up to me, what with my charming personality and all."

"Play this close, though," she said. "I don't want you getting hurt. Revenge is a strong motivation. That's why the police think one of the O'Neals was responsible."

"So many years after the fact? Bull." An angry Roscoe shook his head in disgust. "Besides, it wouldn't be Tully's style. He was canned 'cause he wouldn't cut corners. That kind of man don't look for revenge. And all these years later?"

"Word is, his business is sinking."

"Hard times don't change a man's basic nature," Roscoe said. "And Tully wouldn't send his girl to do his dirty work."

He stopped mid-sentence and tightened his jaw. Annelise glanced back. Durant Walsh stood only yards away, glaring at them. When had he arrived and what in the world was he doing there? He normally avoided the Clean Car Division, no doubt because her success reminded him of his own failure. Walsh Parts Replications – Durant's baby – had been in the red from day one.

"Maybe Kate O'Neal took the task on herself," Durant stated. "Or maybe she was trying to stop the old man."

"What a crock!" Roscoe returned. "I'd bet a month's pay neither of 'em had nothing to do with the fire."

"If you can afford to lose a month's salary, we're paying you too much." Durant tucked his hands into his suit jacket and gave Roscoe a look obviously meant to cow him. "You're employed by Walsh Motors, Hieber, remember that. Back to work."

Dismissing him as if he were no better than a flea, Durant turned his back and concentrated on Annelise, who had tightened up like she always did when Durant was around. She hated her stepbrother, and though she'd never said as much, she was certain Roscoe knew it.

Roscoe stuffed his cigar in his mouth and sauntered off, not going far before he stopped to fiddle with some engine parts on a bench. She realized he stayed within firing range so he could hear what was said.

"This is *my* division," Annelise reminded Durant. "How dare you order my staff around?"

"I thought we cleared up any doubts this morning about who was running Walsh Motors."

"You may be in charge of the corporation – *temporarily* – but policy has always been to leave the direct supervision of the individual divisions to the people who manage them."

"Maybe it's time for some more changes."

"And who's going to ensure your changes work? A man who can't even make the division he created look good?"

Knowing Durant would be furious at the reminder, Annelise couldn't help throwing her stepbrother's fiasco in his face.

"I have the power to do whatever I please in this company," Durant said coldly. "To whomever I please. So where do you get off discussing sensitive corporate business with an employee?"

"Roscoe was with my father from the start." Annelise kept her voice low and intense. "He's more than an employee."

Durant's words were bile-filled. "He won't even be that if you're not careful."

She noted Roscoe stopped what he was doing at the implied threat.

Durant strode past him as he headed toward the exit, whomping Roscoe in the shoulder and not even looking his way. Annelise stared after her stepbrother, her face twisted into something she suspected was ugly.

Then she realized Roscoe was glaring after Durant. She knew he had the makings of an ulcer. Nothing new, not since the day Covington Classics became Walsh Motors. If Arthur had been no better than a worm, Annelise thought, Durant was a maggot.

Chapter Four

The coach house studio was large and airy if typically messy with clothing puddled across the hardwood floor, and hair clips and jewelry decorating the furniture. Blues filled the air, Liz's throaty warbling competing with the CD.

"Can't remember if I ever…ever…ever been so-o-o blue…" Catching a glimpse of her fierce expression in the mirror, Liz snorted and grabbed a crumpled pack from the dresser. "Don't quit your day job, sweetie."

She shook out a cigarette and lit up. The first drag whorled smoke down deep into her lungs, the acrid fumes slowly working their way up her throat and through her nose. A moment later, she was ready to face a new night. Cigarette between her lips, she flopped across the open futon and fetched the tablet from the adjoining stand. She'd already used the covert program she'd gotten from a black hat she'd once dated to bypass its password and create a new one.

"Well, Jimmy-boy," she murmured, "let's see what we have."

Flipping through the folders, she found several files of interest. The entries were detailed. Enough ammunition to make the creep sorry he'd looked her way twice. She reached for his cell phone and punched in a Milwaukee number.

Two rings, then a crisp-voiced recording: "You have reached Layton Business Services. Regular office hours are nine to five,

Monday through Friday, but you may leave your name, number and a short message at the beep."

Liz removed the cigarette from her mouth. "This is James Scanlon's secretary. Please tell Mr. Carbury Mr. Scanlon advised Parker Industries to award the contract to another company."

She hoped Mr. Carbury would be too ticked to question getting a call after hours.

After cutting the connection, Liz placed two more calls, both to voice mail: one belonging to Scanlon's boss and another to the woman for whom Jimmy-boy had bought an engagement ring. She disliked hurting the other woman, but better Suzie knew now what kind of man was about to ask her to marry him. And if he lost his job...better him than the innocent waitress he'd intended to keep screwing with.

You really messed up that Scanlon guy, Liz. Remember what a prick he was. You'd better start looking over your shoulder...

Liz shook away the chill the eerie warning gave her. She'd been hearing the voice in her head more often lately. As usual, she was going to ignore it. Taking action against a creep like that guy gave her a certain satisfaction. It was a relief not to be Annelise for a while. Not that she normally remembered what Annelise's day was like, but it had to suck big time always having to be noble and caring. Always ending up one step behind Durant. Always trying to live up to their father's memory.

If Liz didn't have some time to be anything she wanted, she would lose it.

Sliding off the bed, she dumped the tablet and cell phone in a drawer with several other like mementos. Then she sauntered to the closet, trying to figure out what to wear. She didn't have any plans. She'd find someplace with lots of people and noise.

Someplace that would make her feel like she was alive.

Maybe tonight she would get lucky rather than running into another putz like Jimmy-boy Scanlon.

Liz tossed a few outfits on a nearby chair before finding one that appealed to her. She climbed into the scoop-backed dress whose bright yellow clashed with her hair, then opened another section of the closet where a rainbow of colors greeted her. Some women went crazy for expensive jewelry. Designer shoes had always been her weakness. She chose a pair of yellow and orange sandals with four inch heels and tie ankle straps.

Then she grabbed her shoulder bag, took the stairs down to street level and left the coach house entry for the garage. Circling the red Mustang parked in the driveway, she headed away from the lake. With a last drag on what was left of her cigarette, she flung the butt to the ground.

A sixth sense made her hesitate and glance over her shoulder, but the swaying branches of a hedged fence were the only movement behind her. The breeze had picked up, shooting warm gusts along her arms.

No one. Her imagination.

She rubbed at her pebbling skin and walked faster.

He watched the woman hurry down the street, clutching her bag, then glanced at the copy of an old magazine article he'd dug up during an after-hours visit to O'Neal's Auto Repairs. A piece of luck for him. The central focus was a photograph of the Walsh Motors Board. Including her. She was the one, all right, Annelise Covington, though in the photo, she seemed more sophisticated and self-contained.

He followed, slowing to crush the glowing tip of her discarded cigarette beneath the toe of his well-worn *Tres Outlaws* boot.

Something had her spooked. Because she sensed his presence? Not that she could know about him. Still, when she glanced over her shoulder again, he slipped into the shadow of a doorway.

A man with a mission, he was about to do more than watch

her. He would use her to get what he needed.

Keeping to the shadows, he followed.

Stewie's was a dark and smoky cigar lounge. It was always busy despite not being updated. The front of the establishment was dominated by a huge old wooden bar that had been lovingly hand-carved decades ago. A few women hung around the place. More men.

"Hey, babe, I got your number," one of them said to Liz as she entered.

"Use it on a lottery ticket. Maybe you'll get lucky," she said with a good-humored laugh.

She claimed a barstool and smiled at the bartender and owner, Stewie Kegan. He wore his thick gray hair and matching handlebar mustache with the pride of someone who knew and liked who he was. Liz liked him, too.

"Gin and tonic," she said, raising her voice to be heard above the seventy's music blaring from the jukebox.

"Liz, haven't seen you around in a while."

"Only because I haven't been available," she assured him.

She doubted Stewie ever forgot a customer. While he made the drink, she hunted up her cigarettes from her purse, lit one and relaxed, in her element at last. She was comfortable here. No expectations. No demands. She could simply be herself.

Stewie delivered the drink. She sipped, and the trickle of cool liquid soothed her throat. The cigarette and the plastic stirrer busied her fingers while her gaze swept over the bar's interior. Tables and chairs worn with age yet having character appealed to her. Neon signs lighting the windows and far walls.

A couple moved cheek-to-cheek around the dance floor. The man's hand strayed down the woman's back. The woman laughed, then relaxed against him.

Liz returned her attention to her glass. A man who could barely stand without weaving planted himself at her side.

"Buy you a drink?" His words were slurred, and he was waving a five dollar bill in her face.

Before he could annoy her, Liz took the money and slipped it into his jacket pocket. "Do yourself a favor. Use the money for cab fare home. You've had enough."

"That's not very friendly, lady."

"Trust me, this *is* friendly."

"Besides, the lady's with me," came a mellow voice, followed by a worn cowboy boot set on the rung of the bar.

"That right, lady?" the drunk asked.

Rather than answer, she took a good look at the stranger, arresting and rawly sexual. Jeans settled low on lean hips, and a deep blue t-shirt, sleeves rolled to reveal muscular arms, stretched across a chest of impressive breadth. Thick waves of longish black hair emphasized angular features. The makings of a beard stubbled sharp cheeks and square jaw. From beneath a high forehead and straight, thick eyebrows, long spiky lashes softened his masculine face.

The stranger fastening his interest on her caused a momentary loss of thought. The lift of his eyebrows countered his slow, knowing smile. Her pulse surged. Pretending to be indifferent, Liz sipped her gin and tonic as the drunk wove away. She ignored the stranger and shook another cigarette from the pack, touched the tip to her lighter. Their eyes met.

"Cocky bastard," she muttered.

"Flatterer." He signaled Stewie. "Tequila with a wedge of lime and a saltshaker. Bring the lady a refill. We'll be sitting over there."

Before Liz could object, he grabbed her shoulder bag, cigarettes and drink, then moved to a corner table. Amazed at his audacity, she stayed put while he made himself comfortable and indicated the seat next to him. She shouldn't respond, but he did have her bag.

Irritated and interested, Liz finally followed his lead. When she sat, he reached across the table, and for a moment, she thought he would try to touch her, but all he did was take the cigarette from her hand and crush it out in the ashtray.

"Those things'll kill you."

"Who says? The Surgeon General?"

"If you like. I've been called worse."

"What if I don't like?"

"If you didn't, you wouldn't be sitting here."

"You've got my bag."

He picked up the bag and held it out to her, inviting her to leave. His intense expression made her insides unfurl and her breasts tighten. He set the shoulder bag down on the other side of the table. She would have to reach across him to get at it when Stewie delivered the drinks.

The stranger held out a fifty. "Keep the change."

Stewie flashed him a rare smile. "Anything else, whistle."

But the stranger's attention was focused on her as she dropped the shoulder bag out of his reach under the table.

"Who do you think you are?" Liz asked.

Liz broke the gaze and glanced at his hands. Traces of something dark stained the blunt fingers as if he'd been working with greasy equipment. In contrast, what appeared to be a stylized gold car twisted around his right ring finger.

"If you ask me my sign, I'll be crushed."

"Not my thing," he returned.

"What is?"

"Figuring out what makes a person tick."

"You're a shrink?"

"I'm a driver."

"Taxis or limos?"

He laughed. "When you're a risk-taker, you want to get to what's real."

An odd response, but one Liz understood. "You think you're going to find what you're looking for in this joint?"

"You can find real anywhere if you search deep enough." His gaze was intent on her again.

"Yeah? So why me?"

He took his time answering, first going through the salt, tequila, lime ritual. "Instinct. I get the feeling you're complicated. I like challenges."

"I'll bet you do."

"Can't blame a guy for chasing a dream."

A slow bluesy number, the kind she liked, was playing. Her foot bobbed as she asked, "Isn't that a torch song or something?" Meaning his comment.

No doubt he purposely misunderstood.

"Let's find out." He rose and held out his hand.

Liz reached for her cigarettes, but he caught her wrist. Tension sparked through her, forced her to her feet. She let him lead her the few yards to the dance floor. He placed his hands on her waist and slowly drew her toward him. If he noticed she wasn't relaxed, he ignored the fact, kept her off balance by splaying his fingers along the small of her back. A tight knot in her belly fought the effect of the spreading warmth.

"Chase Donovan."

"Liz."

Up close, his gaunt features gained strength, and a sapphire in his left ear glittered through his dark hair.

"Liz what?"

She ignored the question. "You don't seem the sort."

"To be in a place like this?"

"To wear an earring."

An ironic smile twisted his mouth. "A present from a lady."

"The ring — did she give you the earring, too?"

"Why? Should I have refused to take it?"

He was full of non-answers, but the implication was clear. As intrigued as she was wary, she couldn't stop herself. She slid her arms up around his neck.

Chase moved in closer, grazing her ear and neck with his breath as they moved in unison to the music. When his calloused palm brushed her bared back, she swallowed hard.

"You remind me of someone," he murmured.

"An old girlfriend? The jewelry fan?"

"She acted cocky like you. Like she had the whole world in her fist. Underneath, she was like everyone else. Scared."

"I'm not like anyone you know. Trust me."

"Trust has to be earned, Liz."

With every movement, a tiny fraction of her control slipped away until she floated on a cloud of charged sexual energy. Chase imprisoned her, took over her space, surrounded her with his heat.

He danced her around and around and suddenly she realized he'd moved her off the dance floor and was opening a door leading into the alley. Before she could protest, he covered her mouth with his and swung her outside where there were three tables, all empty.

When he flung her against the wall, she cried out in anticipation. Kissing him was hotter than anything she'd imagined. No man had ever made her let her guard down quite like this before. His fingers found the hem of her dress and started to slide it up her thigh. The feel of his fingers on her flesh made her squirm a little.

Just then she heard a scuffle. Clutching his shoulders hard, she pulled her mouth free and whispered, "Did you hear that?"

"Concentrate on me." He dropped his head and tested the flesh between neck and shoulder.

Sensation rippled through her until she heard another noise, like leather scuffing against pavement. And remembered the earlier warning from the voice in her head.

"Stop. Someone's there. Let's get out of here."

"Let 'em watch."

Another noise. Pushing at his chest, she looked around, couldn't see anyone, yet she was sure someone was there. She pushed him hard, and he swayed away from her.

"Who's out there?" she murmured, the sexual haze lifting.

Her gaze flashed into the dark corners, but she didn't see

anyone.

"We could go somewhere more comfortable. Your place?"

Alarms went off in her head. She shouldered past him and raced back inside. Faces turned her way, their expressions knowing.

"Liz, wait a minute!"

Heart pounding, she grabbed her shoulder bag from under the table and made a fast escape through the front door.

Picking up the pack of cigarettes she'd forgotten, Chase shot toward the door, but by the time he'd stepped outside, she'd vanished. Headed for home? He wasn't about to face her there. Not tonight. To get what he'd come to Chicago for, he'd have to be focused.

He slid onto a free stool at the bar and shrugged at Stewie. "I guess tonight's not my night."

"Too bad about Liz taking a powder on you."

Not knowing how well the bartender knew Liz, Chase merely said, "She didn't seem like the sensitive type." She didn't seem like the type who ran, either, but he figured she hadn't counted on letting him control the situation. "I could use a tequila."

"Another drink?" Stewie gave him a penetrating stare. "You driving?"

"Thanks for worrying, but don't. I'm sticking around." As long as it took to get what he came for. "You wouldn't know of a place I could crash, would you?"

"Nearest hotel is—"

"No hotel." Chase had learned to hate hotels years ago when they started being a regular part of his life. Besides, he wanted to stay close, near the heart of the action. The moment he'd heard about the fire, he'd been on his way. Luckily he'd still been in Indianapolis, only a three hour drive. "A back room in a joint like this would be perfect. And worth a generous contribution to someone's pocket."

Though Chase was certain Stewie got the idea, he didn't jump right to the bait.

"The back room here is taken," Stewie said, filling a clean shot glass with tequila. "Maybe you didn't notice the pool table."

"I come equipped." Chase salted the area between thumb and forefinger. "Sleeping bag is in my trunk." He licked the salt and picked up the shot glass.

"You hot?"

"I try to be with the ladies. But don't worry. No warrants."

Stewie grinned as he lifted the bottle. "Then let's make a deal."

Chase held out his hand for a shake. "Chase Donovan."

"How long do you plan on being here?"

"A few days. Maybe longer. Not sure how long it will take to get what I came for."

Chase threw back the tequila and sucked on the wedge of lime and thought about the research he'd done on Walsh Motors upon hitting the city. And about the surprises the next day would hold for the woman who called herself Liz.

Chapter Five

Sitting behind her desk, Annelise fiddled with the gold-trimmed onyx pen. Her attention was focused on Detective Marcellus Turner, who'd arrived shortly after the office had opened that morning. As he began asking questions, he appeared relaxed, and yet his pale brown eyes pierced her with unspoken speculation. Every so often, he made an entry in his notebook.

"Do you know the owner of O'Neal's Antique Auto Repairs?" he asked.

"Tully O'Neal? I hung around the garage when my father was alive, so of course I've known him for more than twenty years. He liked children and had a few of his own. He didn't seem to mind my being around."

"You ever meet his kids?"

"No. My father respected Tully, but they weren't personal friends, so no, I didn't know his daughter, either."

Annelise frowned as he scribbled another entry. Why was he trying to connect her with the dead woman? How long would it be before he returned to her whereabouts the night of the fire? And if he asked, how was she going to skirt the truth?

"What about O'Neal himself?" Turner went on. "You seen him since he was fired by Arthur Walsh?"

"At a few car expos and auctions."

Another entry. Her nerves stretched taut. She wanted nothing more than for this interview to be over.

"Categorize him for me. Cunning? Honest?"*

"Look, I haven't the faintest idea. I've never done business with him."

"Meaning someone in this company has?"

Irritation overcoming her unease, she threw down the pen. "Detective, I don't know. Considering the circumstances, my guess is not. Ask Durant if you want to be certain."

"I already have." But Turner didn't share the results of that conversation. He tucked his notebook into the wrinkled interior of his suit jacket and rose. "I expect you'll be hearing from the fire department's inspector on the case."

Annelise guessed she'd better count on a visit from the insurance investigator, as well. "Whatever it takes."

Turner made for the door and Annelise sagged with relief. She might have let it go if she hadn't seen Kate O'Neal's remains up close and personal. The vision still haunted her. The woman should not have been in that building. Annelise was more than disturbed by the tragic death. She was angry.

"Detective Turner, wait."

"Miss Covington?" He was standing at the door, his expression expectant.

"Roscoe Hieber runs my clean car operation. He's agreed to ask around for me, see what he can find out. He's convinced Tully isn't the kind of man who'd be involved in a vendetta."

Surprise shadowed the detective's dark features. "Someone is. But thanks for the tip."

The door had barely closed behind him before Joyce entered. She handed Annelise a thick manila folder that smelled of dust and mildew. "Sorry it took so long, but I had to get the records from the morgue."

Conjuring an image making Annelise shudder. "Thanks, Joyce. Maybe I can satisfy myself about what kind of a man Tully O'Neal really is."

"Did you tell our friendly detective about these?"

"I will if I find anything he'd want to know."

As Joyce left, Annelise paged through the contents – application, evaluations, personal information, medical and insurance records. Three years of Tully's life, including the illnesses and problems of his wife and kids, were spread out before her. Quarterly reports on his work indicated he was one of her father's most valued employees, even as she'd guessed. Typical that Arthur Walsh hadn't valued his integrity.

Sorting through the personal information, Annelise barely had a chance to glance at any individual document before she was startled by the door flying open. She stared wide-eyed at the determined-looking intruder who strode into her office. Longish dark hair. Blue eyes as deep and brilliant as the sapphire sparkling from his ear.

Joyce was on his heels. "I said you can't go in there!"

Caught by his intense gaze, Annelise found herself saying, "It's all right." She glanced at her assistant. "Really." When the other woman backed out, she closed the files on her desk. She felt her heart pounding, heard the hollow rush of blood as she shut the folder and slipped it into the top drawer. "What can I do for you, Mr....?"

When she glanced up, he was securing the door. The lock clicking in place was followed by her momentary stunned silence. Then she flew to her feet and rounded the desk. "What do you think you're doing?"

"Making sure you can't get away so easily this time." Moving closer to her, he slipped a hand inside his jacket and retrieved a rumpled package which he slapped down on the desk. "You forgot these."

Annelise stared at the cigarettes. "I don't smoke."

"Took my advice and quit, did you? Let's talk about why you ran out on me last night."

"Last night?" Was the man trying to pull one over on her? But why? "We've never met."

His forehead pulled into a frown. "C'mon. You remember me – Chase Donovan."

"Annelise Covington."

"I know who you are."

"How? We've never met." Wondering if she'd made a mistake in dismissing Joyce, Annelise backed away from him.

"Getting nervous, Liz? I really do know who you are. I held you in my arms last night." He backed her against the desk. "What kind of a game are you playing?"

Liz? What was he talking about? "No game. I've never seen you before."

They stared at each other until Annelise felt like jumping out of her skin. He was confused – she could read it on his face. Confused or crazy? She'd go for the second choice. Thick silence hung between them.

"Okay," he finally said, backing off. "You don't want to mix business with pleasure. I get it. Meet me at *Stewie's*. Tonight at eight. We'll talk then."

"Talk all you want. I won't be there."

"Then send Liz." He laughed. "Eight. Don't be late."

He backed out of the room, not for a second averting his gaze from her inhospitable expression.

Why had he thought she was Liz? She'd like to think he really was just crazy, but her instincts didn't agree. What then?

She took the cigarettes he'd left on her desk and trashed them. She didn't smoke. Not that she knew of. But there had been mornings after blackouts when she'd awakened with the disgusting taste of tobacco in her mouth...

O'Neal's Antique Auto Repairs located south of The Loop straddled white-collar Dearborn Park and blue-collar Bridgeport. While the first neighborhood provided clients for the business, the second provided the workers. Annelise arrived directly after lunch, which she'd had no desire to eat. The building was old, the asphalt siding chipped, the cars parked in the driveway not nearly as grand as those serviced by Walsh

Motors.

Inside, she sat opposite Tully O'Neal, silver-haired and wearing a dark suit and a somber expression further ravaging his lined face. His blue eyes pierced her.

"What can I do for you, Miss Covington?"

"I was there at the fire. Horrible. I'm so sorry you lost your daughter. I wanted to give you my condolences." Not the only reason she'd come to see him in person of course. She wanted to be sure the O'Neals had nothing to do with the fire. "I know how you must feel."

The look he gave her was skeptical. "You can't possibly know what it's like to lose someone you love, someone so young her life hadn't really started."

The statement pierced her. A memory of her twin's death made her catch her breath. "You'd be surprised what I know, what I feel."

Tully stared at her and nodded. "I'll give you that. You lost your sister when she was little more than a kid. But what's my Katie to you? You didn't even know her, so why are you really here?"

He was sad and angry and not making it any easier for her, but Annelise couldn't blame him. "I'm here because your daughter died in a Walsh property. I feel responsible."

"What? *You* set the fire?"

"No, of course not." But she felt responsible for finding out who did set the fire.

"Well, neither did I! And neither did my kid." He choked on the last.

"I believe you, Mr. O'Neal." Though they were equals in business, she had difficulty calling him Tully because he'd been her father's top mechanic when she was a child. She couldn't believe the daughter of a man with such integrity would have betrayed everything he believed in. "I wanted you to know that if I can do anything for you, all you have to do is ask."

"Yeah, there's something you can do for me, all right. Get

the cops off my back. You tell them sons-of-bitches to look elsewhere, to stop wasting their time with the O'Neals and find the one who was responsible for my baby's death." Tears rolled down his cheeks, but he glared at her unashamed.

Annelise's eyes stung. Through all the terrible things that had happened in her life, she remembered being so loved once.

"I'll do what I can. Please," she said as she got to her feet, "give my condolences to your family."

When she jumped into her car a minute later, she sped out of the lot thinking of how she had been the one to find her dead sister in this very car.

Don't think about me. It will only cause you more pain.

There it was again — Lizzie's voice. She always seemed to hear it when she was driving the Mustang that had been Lizzie's car.

"Thinking about you is all I have left. I wish you were here with me."

Believe that I am...

But Annelise was too practical to believe in anything she couldn't feel and touch.

Dusk had fallen over the city, a cool weather front bringing a hint of relief to the streets, a tiny respite in the heart of the summer. Bone-weary and tense, Annelise tried to relax by driving with the top down and letting the breeze loosen her hair. Unruly curls tumbled around her face and danced along her shoulders. She breathed deeply of the fishy smell when she turned onto Lake Shore Drive and flipped on the radio to a classical station.

If only she could get her mind off the fire and Tully's daughter and Durant's attitude about her trying to learn the truth. That and his constant threats.

She wouldn't put anything past Durant. The extent of his cruelty never ceased to amaze her. He was capable of anything to get what he wanted. More and more often he was sending out the notice that not only did he want her out of the business…he wanted *her.*

The idea was disgusting. And frightening.

Her mind shifted gears as she sped along. There'd never been any love lost between them. She doubted the word "love" was in Durant's vocabulary. She knew he wanted her so he could humiliate her in private as well as in public. She was certain this was part of his plan to drive her out of the company.

Another headache nagged her.

Annelise slipped her right hand over her heart, over the tattoo she and Lizzie had both gotten on their sixteenth birthday — a circle with a small cross beneath. The feminine symbol had meant girl power to them. They'd vowed they would take the world by storm together. But then a year later, Lizzie had died and Annelise had to fight living in fear every time she dealt with Durant.

"I don't know how much longer I can take this, Lizzie." Talking to her dead sister when she was in the Mustang always made her feel better. "Things have gotten out of hand in my world. The horrible fire. Another dead woman. Durant's insistence that I leave it alone. Now I have an additional problem. Chase Donovan. What in the world am I supposed to do about *him?* Why did he insist he knew me? And for God's sake, why had he called me Liz? Does he think I'm you?"

She swore it was Lizzie answering her…

He's some kind of a weirdo. Hopefully, he won't bother you again.

The sun was setting as Annelise exited the lakeside freeway, deep shadow blanking the faces of the high-rises on the Inner Drive, so they lost any detail of character. She turned on Hawthorne, a street with many stately old homes on tax-foolish enormous lots and headed for the French-style mansion with mansard roof. Despite the gloom, the facade of cream-colored brick stood out against the encircling black wrought iron fence.

Not bothering with the garage, she left her car on the covered drive siding the building, grabbed her attaché case and strode toward the main entrance of what had once been Covington House and was now known as the Walsh Mansion.

Upon entering the foyer, Mama's low voice caught her attention and Annelise paused at the living room doorway, her hand possessively touching the fine woodwork, within which was nestled a thick sliding door of burled walnut panels. The spacious room had tall windows with inside folding shutters and a drapery treatment of black-fringed flowered chintz. The intricate design of the parquet floor was partly hidden by a Berber carpet, its color matching the walls, a vibrant red over which had been applied a brown, varnish-like glaze.

"Are you comfortable, dear?" Madeline Rouvel Covington Walsh murmured.

Carefully coiffed and dressed as usual, Mama was fussing over her now husband Arthur, paralyzed by a stroke, a pitiful shell of a once powerful man. Thankfully, Annelise thought as Mama tucked a light blanket around Arthur's legs. Form stiff, face drooping, he managed a nod and slurred words Annelise had no desire to understand.

"It's a bit chilly for summer, isn't it?" her mother went on. "If you were better, you could have a touch of sherry to warm you. Maybe we should have a fire."

Arthur stirred and mumbled something unintelligible, but Mama seemed to understand him perfectly.

"All right, dear. It was only a suggestion."

Obviously the old man didn't want a fire.

As the odd one-sided conversation continued, Annelise blocked it out. Her attention strayed to the occasional table which held beautifully framed photographs of her and the sister who'd died a decade before. Her gaze swept the memoirs dispassionately.

At ten years old, Annelise sitting neatly on a beach blanket, Lizzie with sand clinging to her, showing off a dead fish she pulled from the water...

...at thirteen, Annelise picture-perfect in her grammar school graduation cap and gown, Lizzie making a face, hair poking out wildly from beneath her cap...

...at sixteen, Annelise in a skirt and sweater, Lizzie in greasy jeans and T-shirt staring at the Mustang's engine...

Suddenly a horrible memory shot through her. Annelise did her best to fight it, but it filled her thoughts as if she were watching a movie.

A young Lizzie in this very room, her face streaked with dirt, a handful of pretty pink roses in one hand. Smiling, she started toward Mama, who was fixing Annelise's hair ribbons, but Arthur stepped in, grabbed Lizzie's shoulder and brought her to a dead stop.

"What do you think you're doing?"

"Bringing Mama flowers."

"You cut my *roses?"*

"Not yours. Daddy's! That's his *garden!"*

Arthur swung, his big hand, knocking the flowers out of Lizzie's hand. Annelise cried out as her sister lost her footing and landed on the floor. Her expression was filled with hatred, her eyes filled with tears as Mama rushed over to Arthur.

"Stop this, right now. She's only a little girl!"

Annelise gasped at the memory that had remained hidden in the recesses of her mind until this moment. How many more memories had she somehow forgotten?

Her vision blurred for a moment, the start of another aura leading to a migraine and then a blackout.

Suddenly, she sensed her mother staring at her, the room silent but for the ticking of the clock above the fireplace. Her mother had a hand on Arthur's shoulder. How could she coddle a man who had so damaged their family?

"You look tired, Annelise. Join us and I'll have Clara bring you a tray."

She never had an appetite around Arthur. "Yesterday you said you wanted to talk, Mama." Halfway through their peaceful Sunday afternoon together at a benefit for Lincoln

Park Zoo. "All right, let's talk about your getting Arthur's proxy away from Durant."

"What?" All the color drained from Mama's face. "Th-that's impossible."

"Not with the right legal representation."

"But I have no business experience."

"While I do. Why do you still cater to Arthur?" It had always seemed to her that Mama had only been concerned with her second husband's willingness to take care of her – never mind that he'd been callous and cruel to them all. It had been as if she'd had no real love for her daughters. "He can't do anything to you now. You're free of him if you want to be."

Arthur was staring, his expression half-vacant, half-hostile. Spooky. Her mother flushed and gave her a look saying she was the one who didn't understand.

The aura intensified and Annelise stiffened – she'd chosen to remain in this house not because she wouldn't abandon her inheritance, but because of the parent who had become so difficult to love. She knew Mama had been a different woman once. Before Arthur. And *for Annelise*, love — no matter how twisted — died hard. Mama deserved the bed she had made for herself, yet Annelise had never been able to abandon her.

The migraine flared. She fled to the stairs leading to her sanctuary.

Chapter Six

Annelise made an appointment with her psychiatrist at five-thirty. She'd been seeing Dr. Marva Jackson for more than three years, nearly as long as she'd worked for Walsh Motors. That's when the migraines and blackouts had hit her more often, lasted longer and had become more disturbing. Dealing so closely with Durant and formerly with Arthur had given her nightmares. Dr. Jackson had helped her sleep better. Now she only met with the psychiatrist once a month unless something disturbing came up.

Annelise tried to control the butterflies in her stomach attacking her as she entered the cozy office. The windows were shuttered, and the walls were painted a warm soft caramel, practically the same shade as Dr. Jackson's lovely face.

The psychiatrist rose from her desk, her forehead pulled with worry. "What brings you in today, Annelise? You're ahead of schedule."

"My life is ahead of schedule."

The psychiatrist held out a hand to the seating area. "Sit and tell me about it."

Annelise sat in the recliner, adjusted it halfway back, then gripped the arms hard. "I think I'm losing my mind."

Taking the chair opposite, Dr. Jackson asked, "Another blackout? Did you wake up in a strange place again?"

"Not this time. I didn't even know anything was wrong until *he* showed up at my office."

"He who?"

"He told me his name was Chase Donovan. He called me Liz." Annelise's heartrate sped up. "This guy was serious. He thinks I *am* Liz."

"And why do you think that is?"

"Dear God, I don't know. Even if he found out about Lizzie, surely he would know she's dead."

"You didn't think to ask him?"

"No!" Annelise could feel her surging pulse. "My mind was whirling…"

"Whoa, take a deep breath…then let it out slowly…"

Annelise did as the psychiatrist asked. "Please, Dr. Jackson, you have to help me sort this all out!"

"Of course I want to help you, but we've talked about this before and you've chosen to ignore the blackouts, allowing them to continue rather than digging into them. I'm certain I could guide you to the core of your fears if only you would agree to let me hypnotize you."

After months of psychotherapy had barely pierced Annelise's fears, Dr. Jackson had suggested she use hypnotherapy as a way to help Annelise sort out her feelings. To get to the real basis of what was causing the migraines and blackouts. Annelise had considered doing so, but then she had panicked and hadn't been able to bring herself to agree.

"No hypnosis!"

"What are you so afraid of?"

Annelise was afraid of so many things in her past. Like the memory she'd had when looking at the old photographs of her and Lizzie. A memory that had been lost for years. What if going under made her remember more? Things she wanted to keep forgotten?

What if it pushed her over the edge and there was no coming back?

* * *

Thinking about the night ahead, Liz paced the length of her private sanctuary and back again.

Who was this guy who sought out Annelise and demanded she meet him, then when she refused, insisted on her sending Liz? What did he know about them, and why was he after her? Money seemed likely. He claimed to be a driver but hadn't explained what that meant. She had researched him on the internet and had trolled social media sites looking for him but had found nothing. He could barely be making a living as a taxi or ridesharing driver...or be more than comfortable driving getaway cars for criminals.

Whatever his game, instinct told her he might be open to hers. Certain Chase would show at *Stewie's*, she couldn't stop wondering if he could be the solution to her dilemma.

When Liz arrived at *Stewie's* a half hour later, Chase was sitting at the same table he'd commandeered the night before. Stopping a few yards away, she took the opportunity to study him for a moment. She couldn't remember the last time she'd wanted to get to know a man better.

Glancing over his shoulder, Chase caught her staring at him. An ironic smile curved his lips. He indicated the empty chair waiting for her. And what looked like a gin and tonic on the table. Hmm, he remembered her drink.

She sauntered over to where he sat. "You assumed I would show, huh?"

"Before we get cozy, who are you tonight? Liz or Annelise?"

She laughed and slid into the empty seat. "Only our mama could tell us apart."

Chase inspected her wild hair and curve-clinging dress with great exaggeration. "Nope. Can't tell you from the woman I talked to this morning. Identical, all right."

"But we have different styles. One makes up for what the other lacks. Elizabeth Anne – bold and unafraid — Annelise always in her shadow, wondering how it'd feel to have some real control –"

"Hmm, a control freak." When he added, "Isn't your sister dead?" Liz nearly choked on her drink.

"How would you know something so personal about me?"

"You can find everything on the internet these days."

Except for anything about him, of course. "What's your point?" Obviously he knew more about her than she'd expected.

"That you're a woman who competes in a man's world, even though the man you work for dominates you."

Liz suddenly felt sucker punched, but she wasn't about to admit it. "You're talking about Annelise, not about me."

He raised his eyebrows as he challenged her. "Am I?"

"I don't let any man dominate me." Not that she ever had willingly. "Let's change the subject. Like how you knew about Walsh Motors to start?"

"I can be resourceful."

"You wouldn't have followed me last night?" When he didn't deny it, she asked, "Why go to all the trouble for someone you don't even know? And don't give me any bull about our being soulmates."

"I said you reminded me of someone. She was reckless like you."

She sized him up, trying to decide if he was for real or just screwing with her. "You have a savior complex?"

"I like to keep life interesting." He leaned back. "So tell me about Walsh Motors."

Liz stared down into her drink. "Walsh Motors, founded on the corpse of Covington Classics." She'd never talked about this before to anyone. But if her plan to recruit him into helping her nail Durant was going to work, he needed all the basic information. "Arthur Walsh was Daddy's lawyer. Daddy died and Arthur made moves on Mama. He was cunning and she...she was afraid of having to be more than some man's ornament." That had been the truth. "Of losing her lifestyle. Of being alone."

Not seeming impressed, Chase said, "Not all women are self-sufficient like you."

"But not many women would cheat their daughters of their birthright either," Liz said, thinking she herself wasn't alone out of choice. She just held higher standards when it came to men. "Arthur was an unscrupulous lawyer. A month after Daddy's death, Mama played willingly into Arthur's hands, and in return for his running the company, she signed over Daddy's forty percent to him –"

"Which doesn't sound altogether unreasonable."

"Yeah, well, forty percent was just a start. Arthur should never have been allowed to gain controlling interest." Not that she was about to go into how he'd managed to get his hands on the other twenty. "From the day Annelise started working for Walsh Motors, Arthur let her know her place. His son Durant was worse. Between them, they did their best to drive her away. And to buy her out."

"Obviously they haven't succeeded."

She could relate a litany of grievances if she wanted. "Five months ago, Arthur had a stroke, and now his son has his proxy."

"I take it you don't like the son."

Pulling her cigarettes from her shoulder bag, she lit up. She could tell him exactly how much she hated Durant, but then she would have to bring up the ugly details she kept filed away in her mind so they wouldn't have the power to touch her. And then there were the missing memories...

"What's to like?" she said. "Annelise built Walsh Clean Cars from the ground up. It's the corporation's biggest profit maker after Sales. Durant started Walsh Parts Replications, a real money loser. Arthur was on the verge of closing down his son's division when he had the stroke. So why is Durant in charge of the whole company?"

She took another drag of her cigarette. Talking somewhat freely for once felt good. Chase Donovan had the oddest effect on her. He took her out of herself, out of the Liz she had created as self-protection.

"So how are you dealing with the problem?" he asked. "With Durant?"

She stubbed out the cigarette. "I don't deal with Durant. *Ever.* And I find ways to relieve the stress. Like right now."

"Then drink up and let's get out of here."

Liz was prepared for a wild ride but not in an '89 Jaguar convertible, the first model built by the company since the early seventies. Where had Chase gotten the money for a vehicle of this caliber?

Deciding not to dwell on it, but rather to enjoy the luxurious leather interior and matching walnut burl of the dash and door panels, Liz relaxed as he pulled onto Lake Shore Drive, where traffic was light this late at night. Speculation about the source of his windfall was useless and she was certain he wouldn't tell her. Or maybe he would tell her the car was another present from some grateful woman she didn't want to know about.

As they whipped through the night with the top down, Liz enjoyed the sense of freedom she got from the speed, and, oddly enough, from having shared something of her background with Chase. She felt as if a burden had been lifted from her.

A siren wailed from nearby and a blue strobe light caught her in the side view mirror. She tensed. Cops. All she needed. God forbid she was riding in a stolen vehicle. She could see it now: taken to the station, her identity revealed.

"They can't catch us," she said tensely.

"They won't. Hold on."

Chase floored the accelerator, and the sports car jumped forward as if in hyperdrive. Liz was jolted, her head thrown back to the headrest. The blue strobe continued to haunt them as they tore down Lake Shore Drive. Taut as a wire, she dug her fingers into the leather door rest and turned to get a look at

Chase. Intent on their getaway, he didn't seem to notice her scrutiny. His profile was tense, his body hard-edged. Provocative. Everything about this man was provocative. Even his driving. He handled the car like a pro.

Or a very good thief. Maybe that's what he'd meant about being a driver and a risk-taker.

Adrenaline surged through her limbs, and she almost felt as if she was running. Not the adrenaline of fear, she realized, but a thrill directly related to sharing this experience. And to the possibility of being caught. A little danger she could appreciate. Whereas a moment before she'd feared discovery, she now was equally high on the daring.

They were bearing down on the city skyline.

Chase couldn't lose the bank of pumping blue lights. He shot down an exit ramp and careened to the left through the intersection. He sped up an entry ramp headed back the way they came, taking a lane without other cars. They were flying, and the distance between them and the blue strobe was growing.

Then Chase suddenly cut across three lanes and exited once more. He slowed only a fraction as he careened around a corner and entered Lincoln Park, which, thankfully, was deserted. A short way down, he pulled the Jag into a circular driveway fronting the restaurant and lagoon area. Up over the sidewalk, across the grass and around the building. There Chase braked to a stop.

"You're crazy!" she gasped.

But she must be crazy, too, because she couldn't remember feeling so alive. She was actually laughing as he cut the engine and lights. And not a moment too soon. Flashing blue streaked on the other side of the building.

Even as she sagged with relief at the close escape, Liz appreciated the fact that Chase Donovan was as much a risk-taker as she. She was so tired of going it alone, tired of having no satisfaction, of being left with a lifetime of frustration no matter how she tried to make it go away. Suddenly, everything seemed clear.

"We'd make a good team, Chase. We have something in common. We're drawn to risk." She'd prepared herself for this earlier, but she hadn't been sure she would make the offer. "So take a chance that counts for something."

She could feel his gaze piercing the dark around her when he asked, "As in?"

"I'd like to figure out a way to get back what's rightfully mine. Help me take down Durant." If they succeeded, maybe she would be free of the pain and the rage and the fear that were her constant shadows.

"How?"

"I'm not sure of which way I want to go." She'd considered acting against her stepbrother before, but she'd never figured out a detailed plan. "I'll work on it."

A long, thoughtful silence was broken by Chase saying, "I *am* currently unemployed. So what would be in it for me?"

Liz suspected he would require more than a sapphire stud or another fancy ring – no matter. "Money, of course."

"There is that. If not a more interesting proposition. I'll work on it," he said, repeating her promise. "I'll come up with something."

Her heart was pounding. "*Something* leaves a lot of territory. What if I don't agree later?"

"I really can be convincing."

"But what if you can't convince *me*?"

"I'm a risk-taker, remember?"

He undid his seatbelt and leaned over her to loosen hers. When he cupped her cheek, the warmth from his hand made her stomach tighten. And when he rubbed his lips against hers, she had trouble breathing. Then he was kissing her, his hand slipping down from her breasts to her stomach, setting her on fire.

Then he pulled back. "Deal?" he asked.

She hesitated for only a second before echoing him. "Deal."

He sat back in his seat and said, "Seatbelt," as he secured his own.

Somewhere between disappointed and relieved the moment hadn't gone further, she secured her seatbelt and took a big breath.

Though she was the one who had made the offer, Liz wondered if it had been a mistake. Was she taking too big a chance on him? This was too easy. Too seductive. Too dangerous. This stranger was too willing to put himself on the line when she wasn't making any promises. She would have felt better if he'd been a little greedy.

What *was* in it for him?

Chapter Seven

Last evening, Dr. Jackson had worked with Annelise longer than usual. Dressed in a soft business suit, carrying an attaché matching her designer pumps, she felt better than she had in a long time.

Annelise drove into the Walsh Garage and exited the Mustang. On the other side of the garage, Durant was talking to Vinny DeLarosa, a scruffy looking mechanic she'd never actually met. She knew little about him personally other than he was married and had a very pregnant wife. Durant had brought him on board after Arthur's stroke. He was Durant's creature. The little snitch stuck his nose into the business and reported everything he learned to Durant. He looked like a gangster with his black leather sports coat, the scar splitting one cheek and black hair pomaded on the long top with almost non-existent sides.

From this distance, she could barely make out what they were saying. She moved a little closer and stopped at a workbench, where she set down her case and made a deal of searching it for something.

"Hey, boss, what about the bimbo who got barbecued in the fire?" He snorted. "I hear they're releasing what's left of her body for burial."

Annelise started. Was it true? No one had informed her.

"Watch that smart mouth of yours, Vinny," Durant growled,

glancing her way.

"Hey, I'm just asking a question. Maybe she was—"

"Shut up! Now!"

The men continued to argue in whispers, which Annelise couldn't hear. She gave up the drama, closed her case and headed for the door leading to the offices.

As she entered the executive lounge area, the receptionist Maisie anxiously waved her over. "You have *someone* waiting to see you." Widening her eyes, Maisie pointed to the gorgeous, well-dressed man in the seating area.

Annelise gaped when she met his gaze. The skin around his gray eyes crinkled with his smile. Of course she recognized him immediately. Kyle Zimmerman was even better looking than the last time she'd seen him at her sister's gravesite. She rushed to greet him.

"Kyle! What a pleasant surprise!"

With a wide grin, he stood to take her outstretched hand in both of his. "Annelise, you're even more gorgeous than I remembered."

Excitement simmering in her, she said, "Let's go into my office."

He followed her, then caught up as she opened the door. His hand in the middle of her back made her remember something that didn't gel. It felt familiar, but he'd dated Lizzie, not her. Composing herself, she entered and sat behind her desk, while he perched on it, his long leg inches from hers.

Annelise couldn't stop smiling. "God, I haven't seen you in..."

"A decade," Kyle finished.

A warm moment passed between them.

Annelise broke the silent connection. "So what brings you here?"

"My love of things long and sleek and very, very expensive." He was staring at her legs.

She laughed. Even when he was a teenager, he'd always had

a charming sense of humor. "What kind of a classic are you looking for?"

He met her gaze. "A thirties Duesenberg would do nicely."

"Are we talking an original or a Duesenberg II?"

He laughed. "Of course, an original designed and built by Fred and Augie Duesenberg themselves. I would love a convertible Model J."

Annelise started. "You're talking about big money. More than a million dollars. Probably close to two."

"Sounds right."

She took a deep breath. "I'll get someone on a search for available models." She'd known the Zimmermans had money, but she hadn't known how very wealthy they were.

"Annelise, the fire. I was shocked to read about it. So sorry. How are you doing?"

Her smile faded. "The best I can."

"Any idea how this happened?"

"Arson."

"Right. I read about the pipe bombs. And the dead woman."

She stopped breathing for a moment.

He said, "Rumor has it she died in her own fire."

Which she didn't believe. "The police are investigating." Wanting to get off the fire and back on solid ground with Kyle, she asked, "What about *you*? How are you doing? Bring me up to speed. Job? Wife? Kids?"

Kyle was studying the picture of the twin teenagers on her desk. His smile quickly faded. "Still working for the old man. He claims the company is my birthright." His gaze turned to her. "I haven't thought of settling down since Lizzie—"

The breath caught in her throat. "More than a decade." Trying to read him, she looked into his gray eyes. "Let it go, Kyle. You can't live in the past."

He gave her a sly look in return. "You're right, I can't. That's why I want *you* to have dinner with me."

"*Me?* I don't—"

"Don't say no. Think about it." Getting to his feet, he pulled out a business card and handed it to her. "You can give me your answer when you call me about the car. Just keep in mind my reputation as an impeccable date. I bring flowers, choose the best wine and am willing to share dessert if that'll make you happy."

Annelise laughed again and watched him leave.

When the door closed behind him, her smile faded, but for some strange reason, the very personal connection she felt to him didn't.

Large metal owls perched on the roof of the Harold Washington Library stared down at Chase. After taking a quick look at them as he entered, he headed for the desk to get a day pass so he could use the computer room. He quickly searched both the Chicago Tribune and Chicago Sun Times online, and he searched for anything he could find about Walsh Motors and particularly about Durant Walsh.

He thought about Liz and the kiss they'd shared in his car the night before. Part of him had wanted to take the moment further, to take her right there in the Jaguar, but he had to keep his purpose for coming back to Chicago in mind. She was a hot, desirable distraction, but she was also the key to his goal, so he would have to resist doing anything that might compromise their budding relationship. At least for now.

Newspaper pages went whizzing by. He slowed them as he found what he was looking for. As he read, unease filled him.

A classic Ferrari sold by Walsh Motors nine years ago turned out not to have the original engine as was advertised. A lawsuit was settled by Arthur Walsh, but according to the article, it was the first car Durant Walsh had brought into Walsh Motors. While Durant apologized profusely for his mistake in not having the Ferrari checked out thoroughly enough, nothing indicated he suffered any retribution for his part in the deal.

Sloppy work. Strike one against him, Chase thought, continuing his search.

No follow-up on the Ferrari fiasco, but it seemed Durant was a regular at both business and society events, a different woman on his arm each time. Their choice not to see him again? Or his? He pulled out his notebook and added their names. It might do to contact them and get the down-low on their relationship with Durant. If there ever was one. Then three years back, there had been an accusation of sexual misconduct, but the case had been dropped. Or, more likely, settled out of court. He wrote down the woman's name and underlined it. For sure, she was someone to check on. Could this accusation and court case be the reason Liz had such contempt for Durant?

Well, one of the reasons.

Chase had his own.

Plus, there had to be something else Liz knew about Durant that she hadn't told him. Yet.

Annelise was eating lunch in the break room. A small buffet of take-out Chinese food had been set on a long table against one wall. Their two managers, Dolhonik and Nakagawa, were filling their plates. Nakagawa met her gaze and gave her a nod, but no invitation to join them.

Which was fine with Annelise. She filled her plate, sat at an empty table and turned on her tablet. Engrossed in the latest about the fire in the morning edition of the Tribune, she started when a plate was set down in the spot across from her. A glance up and she lost her appetite. Durant.

"I'm not disturbing you?"

He always disturbed her, but she indicated he should sit. "I wanted to talk to you anyway."

Durant poked his food with a fork. "So what did you find out from O'Neal?"

"He's grieving for his daughter. What did you expect? A

confession?"

"More like an accusation."

"Your paranoia is showing."

"There's the difference between you and me. I'm ready for anything. If your father hadn't set you up with part ownership in the business…" He shoved a forkful of food into his mouth, but kept his eyes locked with hers. Swallowing, he said, "You don't have what it takes to swim with the sharks."

"I don't know." She gave him a pointed look. "I've been treading water pretty well around you."

He laughed and continued eating.

She took a quick look around. No one was paying them any mind. Lowering her voice, she said, "We don't have an audience, Durant, so let's talk straight. Give me one good reason why we shouldn't look into this arson investigation—"

"Exactly what the professionals are paid for."

"*They* don't have an investment in Walsh Motors."

"But they know what the hell they're doing." As Annelise narrowed her gaze on him, he asked, "What is it with you?"

"I just have a feeling I can't shake."

Durant stopped eating and stared at her. "About what?"

She blinked at his indignant tone and then focused on his expression. "If we could only find out why Kate O'Neal was at Parts and Storage."

"We know why she was there, only you won't believe it." His cell rang as he said, "Just leave it, Annelise!" He threw down his fork, answered the call and stepped away from the table.

Annelise stared at her stepbrother's back, unable to hide her suspicion.

What in the world did he know that he wasn't sharing?

Tempted to challenge him, she kept her thoughts to herself. She'd learned to do this years ago. Unlike Lizzie, she had never provoked him.

Losing her appetite, she took her half-filled plate to the

garbage container and dumped it, then headed for her office.

Her afternoon was divided into paperwork, calls from clients and musing over Durant's certainty Kate O'Neal had started the fire. She was still thinking about it when it was time to call it a day.

Shadows fell over the central staircase as, attaché bulging with work, Annelise descended from the formal reception area with Joyce. "I don't know if I believe she started the fire, but Kate O'Neal has to be the key to what happened."

"C'mon, Annelise, you're obsessing. You didn't even know her. What do you think you can find out about her?"

"Maybe nothing. Maybe the police will figure everything out like Durant says."

"Let's hope so," Joyce said. "We have enough to keep us busy."

Annelise gave the case filled with work a wry smile. "That we do. See you in the morning." She took the garage door, while Joyce went straight to the street.

Having waited for Joyce to leave, Durant pulled out of the garage. He spotted her approaching the rapid transit steps, stopped the car and called out to her in his most charming manner. "You look like you could use a ride home."

Joyce whipped around wide-eyed. The surprise in her expression made him smile.

"I'm a public transportation kinda girl, Mr. Walsh."

"Not tonight, you're not. And the name's Durant." He reached over and threw open the passenger door, inviting her in.

Joyce hesitated but didn't move away. Durant forced a welcoming expression as he waited. She glanced toward the garage opening, as if worried about someone seeing before jumping into the passenger seat and slamming the door shut. She sat there, appearing a bit frazzled.

"Seat belt," Durant reminded her.

As soon as he heard the click, he sped around the corner and down the street.

"I live in Old Town—"

"I know exactly where you live." He grinned at Joyce, whose eyes were wide, her expression shocked. "I run the company. I know where everyone lives."

"Oh...of course you do." Silent for a moment, she then asked, "Why the ride offer? Is there something I can do for you?"

"Definitely." Not that he was going to tell her now. Not until he had her in his thrall. "I admire you, Joyce. You're a hard-working, self-sufficient woman. One I would like to know better."

"Oh."

"Do you live with family?"

"No. My parents moved to Florida."

Already knowing the answer, he asked, "Siblings?"

"Just a brother. Mike."

"Right. Someone told me he's in Cook County jail."

"Mike hasn't been convicted of anything. He drank a little too much and had an accident. He's incarcerated until his trial."

Because someone had been badly injured in the accident he'd caused, Durant knew. And it wasn't the first time. Mike Hernandez did more than drink a little too much. He had a real problem with alcohol and couldn't straighten himself out. Now he'd almost killed someone.

Even so, Durant said, "I have some contacts. Important people working in the judicial system. Maybe there's something I can do to get Mike released until his court date."

"Th-that would be wonderful." She reached out and touched his arm.

He noted the change in her breathing, the way she seemed to glow as she fell silent. She was excited. Thinking about his helping her brother or was it something else?

Could she be attracted to him?

Well, well, well. This was going to be easier than he thought. She'd always been polite to him but never personal. Which was going to change tonight.

Joyce lived in the garden apartment of a three flat. Though it was small, her choice of décor told Durant she wanted more. He could easily give her more and would if she did what he wanted.

Her bedroom was sybaritic, the bed tented in plum-colored gauze matching her sheets. It had taken no more than a couple of drinks and a few kisses to get her in bed. Durant had never been attracted to her, so he thought of Annelise as he worked Joyce over. When he finished, he rolled over onto his back and checked his watch.

They'd been at it for more than an hour. How long would he have to stay to be sure he could get what he wanted from Joyce later? She knew every move Annelise made, and he planned to tap Joyce for information when he needed it. To get her to switch her loyalties, he would have to make her obsessed with him. The challenge was more appealing to him than the woman herself.

She pressed her body along his. Though he was itching to leave, he forced himself to appear content. "I've been walking around with a hard-on for you for months." A lie to make her think she had some power over him.

"So what took you so long to do something about it?"

"A matter of divided loyalties. You work for Annelise."

Joyce shrugged but her brow furrowed. "You're right. She won't like this."

"Then we won't tell her."

"She'll know something is different if she so much as sees us speaking together. Tonight was a mistake."

Durant flipped over on top of her to stop her objection. Her eyes widened and breathing deepened as he slid his body against hers. When he entered her, she made little guttural noises which irritated him, but he had Joyce right where he wanted her, and he was going to keep her that way.

No matter what he had to do to make it happen.

Stewie's was more crowded than usual. Finishing her first drink of the night, Liz moved to the jukebox. No Chase. She couldn't help but feel let down.

Hip-hop she found depressing blared through the room. Jukeboxes playing vinyl had been revived, and Stewie had installed one. For all she knew, it might be an original. She crossed to it, checked the playlist. This was the last song. Thankfully. As it ended, she loaded enough coin to choose a few of the most played tunes — Sweet Home Alabama, Old Time Rock and Roll, but starting with Crazy. Patsy Cline's soulful tune about being crazy for wanting a man seemed appropriate, considering her disappointment in not finding Chase here.

She stood there, listening for a moment, wondering if she *was* crazy to want to get to know Chase better. Needing a drink, she turned toward the bar.

And right into Chase who was standing behind her.

"You been there long?" she asked.

Grinning, he flicked his gaze over her, then took her in his arms and twirled her to the music. "Long enough to be appreciative. Been thinking about you all day."

"Obviously you don't have enough to keep you busy."

"That was a compliment. Say thank you."

Liz thought about it, but rather than giving him the satisfaction of doing so, she led him to the bar where she ordered her usual gin and tonic, and he ordered his tequila. Then, drinks in hand, Chase guided her to an empty table. He waited until she sat, then took a second chair and pulled it close enough so legs were touching.

Trying to ignore the attraction for a moment, she took a slug of her drink and asked, "So what do you do all day?"

"Oh, I have places to go, people to see. What about you?" He downed the tequila and sucked on the lime. "What do *you* do...while Annelise is working?"

Liz gritted her teeth for a moment, then said, "Let's talk about Durant. I think he's hiding something."

"As in?"

"I'm not sure."

"Has he bent any rules at Walsh Motors?"

"Knowing him, I'm sure he has."

Not that Liz had specifics on what was going on with Durant at Walsh Motors since she didn't have all of Annelise's memories. Annelise might not know about her, but Liz sensed Annelise instinctively hid what she didn't want to share. Having researched the idea that one person could psychologically split into two or more, she knew a lot of strange things could happen, many revolving around memory problems. Annelise couldn't hide from her, but Liz was pretty certain Annelise didn't know about her. Liz knew about Kyle's reappearance, but she didn't want to know whatever might be going on between the two of them.

"Annelise has access to company records, but it's a big company now. A half-dozen divisions."

"What about Durant's division? You said Walsh Parts Replications is a money loser. But should it be? Or could our boy be taking advantage of the profit margin?"

Liz shook her head. "He's salaried. He doesn't actually own any shares."

"All the more reason for him to dip into the till."

"Something to look into. For Annelise."

She wasn't unhappy with the way things worked between them, with her knowing enough of what Annelise did to keep her up to date. Annelise didn't need to know about the things *she* did with what little life she had. Living in the main house, with *them*, Annelise had enough on her hands. Liz wished she could protect her from things she might not like, as well, but her power to do so was limited. She'd been good with this particular division of knowledge until lately. If only she could tap into all of Annelise's memories and somehow make life easier for her.

Chase told her what he'd learned about Durant at the library. "He's obviously sloppy, whether at work or at play."

"Sloppy doesn't cut it either way," Liz said. "Criminal does. We just have to find the proof before we can bring him down."

Her last jukebox play ended, and the music changed to a slow, bluesy number someone else had selected.

Chase got to his feet and held out his hand.

She stared at it. Her breathing shifted slightly, but she hesitated.

"I won't bite," he said, "unless you ask nice."

Telling herself she was in charge, that she wasn't afraid of being crazy like the woman in the song, that she could handle herself no matter what, she took his hand and let him lead her out to the dance floor. Unable to deny being in his arms felt damn good, Liz placed her head in the crook of his shoulder.

He laughed softly, seeming almost too satisfied.

She told herself she could handle him.

But what if she was wrong?

Chapter Eight

The next morning, Annelise tried not to yawn as she approached the church with dozens of other people dressed in black. How long had she slept? The last she remembered was watching the evening news...and then nothing until she woke up this morning, again with the sour cigarette taste in her mouth, making her remember the pack of cigarettes slapped down on her desk by the stranger who'd called her Liz. These blackouts were getting more frequent. What had she been doing last night? Obviously not sleeping. She was exhausted.

Kate O'Neal would be buried today. Gossip about her being the arsonist was growing. Annelise looked around at the people who entered the church with her. Most appeared solemn but others were talking quietly with grim expressions.

She heard one woman whispering, "They say Kate burned in a fire of her own making."

"I don't believe it," her companion said.

"Well, I don't want to, either. But Dad says they don't have another suspect."

The two women continued to argue in whispers as they walked up the aisle, while Annelise sat in the back of the church alone. She couldn't stop thinking about it. She hadn't ever met Kate, but she couldn't believe the woman had been the arsonist either. If only she could figure out why Kate O'Neal had been in the building after hours. She simply didn't believe the woman had packaged and set those pipe bombs under the cars.

Annelise had plenty of time to think during the funeral service, though her thoughts were far from clear. She felt oddly detached, almost as if she was dreaming, something that happened to her too often. The world around her seemed unreal — filled with ghosts — until the service ended. As the organist played another hymn, she snapped back to the real world.

The mourners exited, followed by the pallbearers and coffin, leaving Annelise at the rear of the church.

At the cemetery, Annelise stood alone once more as mourners placed flowers on the coffin and scattered back to their vehicles. Then movement ahead in a wooded area caught her attention. She only saw him for a few seconds, but she swore the man who had quickly disappeared was that Chase guy who'd barged into her office and had called her Liz. A shudder went through her. He'd certainly seemed dangerous enough. What was he doing here? Had he known Kate O'Neal? Could *he* be somehow connected with the fire which had caused the woman's death?

She turned to see Tully O'Neal escorting his sobbing wife to a limousine. Suddenly spotting her, Tully let one of the other men take over for him and headed her way. Oh, no, she hadn't meant to intrude on them.

"Miss Covington. What are you doing here?"

"My father would have wanted me to come to pay my respects. If he was alive..."

"If he was alive, everything would be different. My girl would be alive, as well. Instead of observing the niceties, why don't you spend your time figuring out who wanted my Katie dead."

Annelise was disturbed by the implication. "You think her death was murder?"

"You know as well as I do — the fire was no accident."

"No, but you don't know if someone planned to kill her,

either. The classic cars were the target. She might have been in the wrong place at the wrong time. I assume you heard about the pipe bombs set under each of the cars."

"Yeah, I heard. So what?"

Tully went silent and tight-lipped. Annelise sensed he was holding back.

"Mr. O'Neal? If you suspect something…some*one*…I want whoever was responsible for your daughter's death brought to justice as much as you do, but I'm in the dark here."

Tully seemed to fight with himself, but finally blurted out. "I thought she was going out to meet *him* again."

"*Him?*"

"Some mystery man Katie was seeing. She wouldn't talk about him. I figured he was married. She wouldn't admit it, though. I told her she was asking for trouble."

"Does Detective Turner know?"

Tully shook his head. "I shouldn't of told you."

"I don't understand the connection."

"Neither do I." Tully shook his head. "Neither would her mother."

With that, he turned his back on her and went straight to the limo.

Leaving Annelise with even more questions with no answers.

Going directly from the cemetery, Annelise surveyed what was left of the Walsh Motors building that had burned. The building had blackened eyes where windows used to be. Several entryways were boarded. Part of a wall had collapsed.

Ignoring the official posted warnings to stay out, she entered on the far side, through a scorched metal door that still took her key, though it took some doing to get it unlocked.

Inside, the smell of the burn stung her nostrils. Her eyes watered when she thought about Kate O'Neil being called a crispy critter by one of the fireman. Though she'd only seen the woman's corpse for a moment, the horrific image remained in her mind. It was something she would never forget.

Flipping on her flashlight, she carefully made her way through the burned room to the showroom and the charred remains of what used to be classic cars. Wandering through the rubble, she didn't exactly know what she was looking for, just something off.

She picked up a dark twisted piece of metal...examined it closely...discarded it and continued her search until something else caught her eye. Grasping a part in slightly better condition, she ran a finger along an edge, concentrating so intently she didn't hear the footsteps until they were directly behind her.

Heart thumping, she whipped around and came face-to-face with the ever-rumpled Detective Turner. He quickly hid his grim expression for one more inquisitive.

Carbon streaked her hands and smudged the front of her suit. She let go of her breath and indicated the part in her hand. "I've seen burned cars before — metal skeletons with all the flammable parts gone — but nothing like this."

"You've never seen the damage done by pipe bombs?"

She shook her head and dropped the warped metal into the pile. "Of course not. There doesn't seem to be much left."

"Fire investigators removed a load. They might come up with a more accurate conclusion as to exactly what took place here."

How much more accurate could they get than pipe bombs? Or did he mean Kate O'Neal's probable involvement, which was Turner's case?

"So what are *you* doing here?" she asked.

"I could ask the same of you. You ignored the official DO NOT ENTER signs."

"This is my family's business. I have a right to be here."

Turner gave her a questioning look. "The same reason you attended the funeral?"

The question gave her a jolt. How did he know where she'd

been? "You're following me?"

He avoided a direct answer. "What are you after, Miss Covington?"

"I was paying my respects to the family."

"Seems to me it's more than that. First the funeral, now the garage. Like you have some bond with the dead woman. How well did you know her?"

"Not at all. I already told you. Do you have a problem with my feeling sorry for a woman who died so horribly? Another victim? That's what she was, you know. One more victim caught up in some man's game!" Startled by her own heated words, she stopped abruptly and took a deep breath as the remains around her shifted like a mirage. Not unlike the incident at the church earlier. "This is ridiculous." She forced out the words. Forced herself to stay focused in the present. "Please, Detective, don't let your imagination run away with you."

"What's left of this building is dangerous —"

"I'll take my chances."

"And it's still a crime scene. You oughta leave well enough alone, Miss Covington, and let us do our jobs. But if you do learn anything, I'm sure you'll share it with me, right?"

"Of course. Why wouldn't I?"

He moved away from her but stopped short of the doorway. "Oh, one more thing." He waited for a moment before asking, "Who is Liz?"

Annelise started but quickly covered. "I'm certain you already know my sister died ten years ago."

Turner pulled a face and nodded, then left without commenting.

Leaving Annelise trying not to panic. First that Chase guy thinking she was Liz, now the detective wanting to know about Liz. Agitated, she opened her purse, found a tissue and tried to wipe away the evidence of her search from her hands. Then she pulled out her cell and called her psychiatrist.

"Dr. Jackson, could you squeeze me in right away? I've reconsidered your suggestion about using hypnosis to find out what's going on with my mind."

An hour later, Annelise reclined in the chair, still a ball of nerves. Dr. Jackson dimmed the lights and took her seat.

"I'm glad you changed your mind, Annelise. You've never told me. Why is it you've resisted hypnosis until now?"

"Fear."

"But of what? You're afraid you might tell me something you don't want me to know?"

"That you'll take me someplace I don't want to be." Caught in a dreamworld, lost and unable to force her way back out. "And then I won't be able to come back to being myself."

"That won't happen. You'll be safe with me, and I will remind you to remember everything."

Annelise nodded and tried to relax.

"Take three deep breaths and close your eyes."

Though she did as Dr. Jackson asked, Annelise couldn't shake the fear consuming her. Her body remained stiff, her muscles taut.

"Concentrate on your breathing. Slow it down. Take deep comfortable breaths." Dr. Jackson spoke in a modulated, soothing tone. "Now let go of your worry. That's it. Notice how your breathing feels...how it has changed...how it calms you...lightens you..."

Her anxiety receded. Her racing thoughts quieted even as she felt herself distancing from the present.

"Let yourself relax, starting with your feet...your legs...your hips...your stomach...your chest..."

Annelise's muscles unknotted one by one until she felt as if she was floating in another world.

Then Dr. Jackson asked, "Annelise, do you have another name?"

The psychiatrist sounded hollow, seemed to be some distance from her.

"Never had a nickname."

"Do you ever ask people to call you something else?"

Annelise let her mind wander away from the question, but Dr. Jackson didn't give up. "Have you ever asked anyone to call you by a different name?"

The question made her start. Without hesitating, she said, "Liz."

"Why is that?"

"I-I don't know."

"May *I* call you Liz?"

Annelise shifted uncomfortably. "Lizzie was my sister. I'm Annelise."

"Yes, but may I speak to Liz?"

Annelise fought the suggestion and tightened up her face. And her body. Shielding herself...

"Relax," Dr. Jackson said. "When you awaken, you will still be Annelise."

Suddenly her eyes popped open, and she aimed her direct gaze at the psychiatrist. She snapped the reclining chair into the upright position and crossed her legs so the business skirt rode up to mid-thigh.

She glanced down at her conservative shoes and made a face. "Annelise, some taste, please!" She shifted her gaze back to the woman in the other chair. "You're Marva, right? I'm Liz. You wanted to talk to me. Is this going to take long?"

"Are you in a hurry to get somewhere, Liz?"

Liz peered into the shadows of the darkened room. "This place gives me the creeps. Christ, I need a cigarette."

"I'd like you to be comfortable here, but sorry, this is a no smoking zone. I want you to feel safe. To feel free to tell me anything you like."

"I don't like. Besides, it's your dime." She laughed. "Actual-ly, it's Annelise's dime, isn't it?"

"Would you like to talk about Annelise?"

Liz sobered. "Yeah. I want to ask you to leave her alone. She has enough to deal with, without your springing *me* on her."

"So, you care about Annelise. And you don't want her to know about you. Is that because you want to protect her?"

"Someone has to."

"You don't think Annelise can take care of herself?"

Another silence. Liz shot Dr. Jackson a furious glare. "Look, you don't have a clue what it's like in that house. What it has always been like since Daddy died."

"I want to understand, so I can help you. What happened to make you think Annelise can't take care of herself?"

"A person can only take so much."

"Take what?"

Liz shook her head. She'd said too much already. No way was she going to share family secrets with a stranger. Though she would like to get up and walk out on the psychiatrist, she couldn't do that to Annelise. "I'm outta here!"

Liz uncrossed her legs and closed her eyes.

"Liz, wait!"

Too late. Liz floated in the darkness of her mind, then hit the off button.

Her tone modulated, soothing, Dr. Jackson said, "Remem-ber, you are Annelise. I'm going to count backward from three, Annelise, and when I get to one, you'll open your eyes...feel refreshed...and remember everything. Three...two...one."

Annelise awakened, confused for a moment. Then her thoughts clarified. "Oh, my God!"

Chapter Nine

That evening, Annelise worked late. Or rather tried to, as her computer screen and the scattered folders on her desk indicated. But she was having trouble concentrating. Her session with Dr. Jackson had unnerved her. She might as well give it up and go home.

The question was, would she remember anything about what had happened with Liz that morning. What about tonight? Would she have another blackout? They had become more and more frequent. And while she remembered her session with the psychiatrist, she still had no memory of *being* Liz.

What did she do when she wasn't herself? Things she wouldn't normally do? Drink? Smoke, obviously. The blackouts always happened at night, but why? Because Liz met someone? A man? Or was it men? To have sex? Safe sex?

Annelise didn't want to think about having to get tested for STDs.

Frustrated with the lack of answers, she pulled a file she meant to leave for her assistant. When she got to the reception area and placed the work in Joyce's IN box, most of the lights were off, leaving the area heavily shadowed. Hearing the scuffle of feet, she whipped around to see Durant leaving the office, his back to her.

Annelise stared after him. His snitch Vinny waited for Durant at the top of the stairs. She drew back, deeper into the shadows, even as Vinny looked around. Apparently, he didn't spot her.

"Hey, Durant, you got any word on the cars?" he asked in a nasally voice sending a chill down her back.

Durant kept going, Vinny trailing him down the stairs.

"Patience is a virtue, Vinny."

"Fuck patience. You and me gotta talk."

"Not here."

"Matter a fact, I did do a Patience once," Vinny said with a snort.

As they disappeared, their voices faded.

Any word on *what* cars? What was Vinny talking about?

Not wanting to play guessing games with herself, Annelise headed back into her office, dark now but for the pooled light of her desk lamp. She leaned back in her chair, lifted a file from the stack and opened it. Tully O'Neal's employment records. After paging through them, she closed the folder and threw it on her desk, her mind cutting back to the scene in the reception area.

Any word on the cars?

Patience is a virtue, Vinny.

You and me gotta talk.

Talk about what? About the burned cars? Or had he meant something else?

Annelise tried to focus her thoughts, but an aura began clouding her thinking. She rubbed at her forehead like she could stop the migraine from happening, leaned back in her chair, closed her eyes and took a couple of deep breaths, telling herself *I am Annelise...*

I am Annelise...

I am...

When she opened her eyes seconds later, Liz rose and crossed to the door. She'd never interrupted Annelise during the day before. Hopefully, she wouldn't be too freaked out when Liz let her retake the reins. She supposed Annelise would be angry. Surely after the session in the psychiatrist's office, she would resent Liz for every moment she stole from her. What would she do then? Seek revenge of some kind? Let people know about her?

To what end?

Annelise couldn't do something so careless. She'd be incriminating herself, making people think *she* was crazy, think *she* should be locked up. Then life would be over. For *both of them.* And Durant would be able to get exactly what he wanted and didn't deserve — her share of the business.

The reception area was unoccupied but for a night janitor coming out of Durant's office, locking it, then disappearing into Nakagawa's office. All clear.

Liz crossed to the janitor's cart and took the keyring which she found on top. Sneaking to Durant's office, she unlocked his door, then returned the keys to the cart. She slipped into the office just as the janitor came back into the hall.

When Liz heard the cart wheel away from the area, she crossed to the desk lamp and snapped it on. The massive walnut desk was a real classic that her father had bought from an auction house. It was far larger than any sold now. It nearly took up one side of the room. She started opening drawers, found what she was looking for and began searching through files of the various divisions: *Classic Restorations...Customization...Parts and Storage...Scraps...Parts Replications...Clean Cars.* All this should be online, but Arthur had run the company old school, and Durant had been too lazy to modernize.

Liz looked through folders until she heard footsteps in the hall outside the office. She closed the file drawer, turned off the desk lamp and quickly crouched behind the desk just before the door opened. Peering through the opening under the desk, she watched polished wingtips moving closer.

Durant, damn it!

Trying not to make the slightest noise, she slid completely under the desk and huddled into a corner.

Durant snapped on the desk lamp and sat.

Liz frantically pressed back to avoid his leg. His wingtip barely grazed her thigh. Had he felt it? She braced herself…

Until what sounded like Durant searching through something gave her a moment's relief.

Then he backed away from the desk a bit, and Liz could see he was unlocking his center drawer. It looked like he had a folder in his hand, but it sounded like he slipped it into the drawer before relocking it.

Then Durant dropped the key on the floor and swore. "Damnit!"

Liz held her breath and froze, watched wide-eyed as his head dipped to her level…but he snagged the key and straightened without ever looking her way.

Liz remained still as he returned the key to wherever he'd gotten it, switched off the desk light and left. When she heard the door close and footsteps dying away, she sagged in relief against the inner desk.

Waiting a moment to make sure he hadn't forgotten something and had to come back, she finally decided the coast was clear. She slid out of her hiding place, turned the lamp back on, and looked over the objects on the desk.

"Where'd you hide the key, Durant?"

She checked the pen holder.

The accessory tray.

And finally, his cigar box.

She dumped the cigars in a careless pile and the inner tray shifted. Plucking it out revealed the key.

After unlocking the middle drawer, she noted the lone file Durant had left there from Parts Replications for safekeeping.

Pulling it out of the drawer, she sank down into Durant's chair and settled back to read.

* * *

Not wanting to think about having another blackout at the office, Annelise was both relieved and angry when she came out of whatever fog she'd been in. She was sitting in her chair at her desk, just as she had been when she'd gone under. With no idea what Liz could have been doing, she closed her eyes and searched her mind, trying to find something that would clue her in. But no, of course not. Liz had locked her out.

Annelise wondered if there wasn't something she could do about getting Liz to cooperate. Or...the next time she had an aura, surely there was some way she could hang on long enough to break through the invisible barrier separating her from Liz.

Wait! The tattoo! She slid her hand inside her top and over the heart which had connected her and Lizzie. If Lizzie was there somewhere, maybe she would help her find out what Liz was doing when she had one of her blackouts.

It was worth a try.

Her stomach grumbled. She was starving. And she didn't want to be alone. She thought of the only person who made her feel good about herself, checked the time — half past eight — and decided to call Kyle and invite him to a late-night dinner. If Liz could spend time with men — as Chase's appearance in her office had convinced her — then so could she.

No doubt Liz would know she'd gone out with Kyle. The thought made her stomach tighten. She hated Liz knowing what she did while she knew next to nothing of her other self.

Kyle accepted her invitation and an hour later met her at a restaurant located on a high floor of a Michigan Avenue skyscraper. Sitting at a window table with him, she thought the city lights looked like electric candy sparkling below. True to his word, he'd brought her flowers. Rather *a* flower. A beautiful pink rose reminding her of the ones Lizzie had cut from Daddy's garden. The thought made her uneasy.

He'd also chosen one of the best wines on the menu. A

Sauvignon Blanc.

Filling her wine glass, he said, "I have to admit I'm pleased to see you tonight but surprised you called. And not about the Duesenberg. You were never very impulsive."

"I'm trying to make some positive changes in my life."

"Here's to change, then."

They clinked glasses, and she took a sip before setting hers down.

His brow furrowed. "You don't like the wine?"

"It's wonderful," Annelise assured him, "but I had this miserable headache earlier, so I'm going to pace myself."

"Perhaps you work too hard."

Kyle covered her hand with his. Annelise stared down at it, wondering what she was doing. He'd been in love with *Lizzie*, not with her.

She forced a smile to her lips. "Hard work is good for the soul."

Kyle laughed. "Hm, never heard that one before. Maybe you need something different for your soul. Something to make you happy."

Annelise slipped her hand out from his and took another sip of wine. "Right now, a look at food options would make me very happy. I'm starving."

Picking up the menu, she stared at it rather than looking at Kyle. Perhaps inviting him to dinner was a mistake considering how weird life had become for her lately. She liked Kyle. She really did. He was a great guy. But Annelise couldn't forget what had happened when she'd been hypnotized. Couldn't forget that somehow, she had another personality. She had reinvented Lizzie into an adult Liz, a woman of mystery. No matter how hard she tried, she couldn't for the life of her remember what she'd done during any of those blackouts.

If only there was a way to record Liz, to see what she was up to.

"The Chilean Seabass looks great," Kyle said. "What do you

think?"

Annelise started. Realizing the waitress was at their table, she said, "Seabass? Perfect."

The waitress took their order, and Annelise was grateful Kyle kept the conversation away from what might — or might not — make her happy. Instead, he told her about the home he'd recently purchased in Wicker Park.

"It dates back to 1905, but it's totally updated. I just moved in last month with the furniture I had in my apartment. I have to admit it needs a complete redo with respect to its history. What would you think about taking a look and giving me some advice on changes I can make to honor its age? I mean, you do live in a house with history, as well."

Suddenly uncomfortable thinking about spending time with Kyle alone in his new home, Annelise said, "I've never had a voice in making any decisions about the furniture or décor though."

"Still..." He reached across the table and again covered her hand with his. "I could use your advice."

"Of course I'd like a look."

Hiding her discomfort, Annelise smiled and removed her hand once more, picked up her glass and sipped the wine. She was relieved when Kyle changed the subject to politics. Which felt safe enough to carry them through dinner.

It was only after she tried to pay in vain since she had invited him, and they left the restaurant, heading for the valet stand when she became uncomfortable once more. He slipped an arm across her back, his hand curving around her side just above her waist. Her flesh responded, sending a chill through her. Why the discomfort? Lizzie was long gone. Ten years had gone by, and Kyle was obviously interested in *her* now. It wasn't like she would be cheating on her dead sister.

But when they arrived at her waiting car, and he took her in his arms and kissed her, that's exactly what it felt like. Cheating. Annelise didn't object, but she didn't participate, and she kept her eyes wide open.

Then Kyle backed off. "Too soon?"

Nodding, Annelise tried to hide her confusion by looking away from him at the Mustang.

The valet opened her car door. "The key is on the dash."

Annelise reached into her purse to get a tip for the man, but Kyle beat her to it, and swept her closer to the car. "I'll call you to set up a date to see my place. Then you can tell me your thoughts for new furnishings over drinks and dinner."

Smiling, Annelise nodded. "I'll look forward to it."

But as she headed for home, she couldn't help but think she'd made a huge mistake starting something personal with Kyle.

"Sorry, Lizzie," she whispered.

No need. You deserve to have a good guy in your life. Maybe Kyle is the right one after all.

After all? Did Lizzie think she'd had a thing for Kyle all those years ago? If Lizzie was really putting words in her mind, she could take an easy breath, though she had no idea what Liz might do when *she* found out about her evening with Kyle.

Twenty minutes later, Annelise was in her room. She set her purse on her gilt-edged white dresser with the photographs of her with her sister. She picked up one and brushed her fingertips across the glass, remembering the night her sister had locked herself in the garage with the engine running. "Oh, Lizzie, you don't know how much I've missed you."

With a sigh, she set the photo down and moved to her closet.

She guessed she missed her sister so much she was trying to be her. What other explanation could there be for her calling herself Liz and doing...what?

She had no idea.

Removing her shoes, she placed them in a special rack holding dozens of others. At the sound of the door closing, she turned to face her smiling mother.

"It's about time you had some diversion from the business," Madeline said. "How did it go with Kyle?"

Wondering how Mama knew about her impromptu dinner date, she realized Kyle possibly had called her mother to get some kind of information about her. Is that how he'd chosen the pink rose?

"You mean, did I scare Kyle off?"

"I just want you to be happy. *Safe.*" Mama's voice trembled on the last. "You really don't need to work so hard," she said for the hundredth time. "Or at all."

Annelise gave the older woman a disbelieving look. "You do you, Mama, and I'll do me." And Liz, if she could believe it. "I like who I am and what I do. And I need my work for self-respect."

In her opinion, Mama had never respected herself or she would never have replaced her father with a slime like Arthur. If she really loved her daughters, she would have figured out how he was surreptitiously hurting them emotionally and, in Lizzie's case, physically as well. He'd been very clever deceiving others to believe he was a caring stepfather. After Daddy died, the only love Annelise had ever known had been from her sister. Mama had been so concerned with keeping her husband happy that she'd had little time for her daughters. The one time Lizzie had told Mama about Arthur's cruelty, she'd called Lizzie a liar.

Then Lizzie was gone, like a hot flame snuffed out by a cold wind. And Annelise was left with no one.

"What you need is a husband," her mother was saying. "Kyle is perfect for you. He always was."

"You're not thinking about *me.*"

"Who else?"

"He was Lizzie's boyfriend, not mine!"

Her mother's silent gaze and disbelieving expression cut through Annelise. What was that about? Unease rippled along her nerves. "I will never have a husband, Mama. I'm nothing like you.”

“You’ve never appreciated what I’ve sacrificed for you. For both of my girls. You needed a man in my life to take care of us. I always had your best interests at heart.”

“Your *best interests* put my sister in a grave when she was seventeen years old.” And she had lost the only person who loved her.

“Her death was an accident.”

“Suicide is no accident.” Rubbing her forehead, Annelise tried to erase the spotty as always memory of finding Lizzie in the garage, of being too late to save her. “Lizzie hated it here. Hated what you’d done to us!”

They stared at each other. Annelise was certain her mother knew the truth of her accusation, yet she was certain Mama would deny it...

“Her death wasn’t my fault!”

“Then just who is to blame, Mama? Me?”

Even as she asked, Annelise stared at her mother’s expression. She read regret and pity and felt guilt biting her. In the end, *she* had been the one who had made her seventeen-year-old sister realize suicide was the only way out of this hell hole.

Chapter Ten

Though it was after midnight, Liz put the finishing touches on her make-up, then thought she needed something fresh to wear. Opening a drawer, she stared at the tablet and cell that belonged to Jimmy-boy Scanlon and wondered if she'd successfully ruined his life with her phone calls the other night. Somehow, the idea had lost its importance to her. Shoving the tablet and cell aside, she found the long scarf she was looking for, then dropped it on the dresser top and shut the drawer.

Checking her mirror, she finger-combed her hair, then grabbed her cell and called *Stewie's.*

"Hey, Stewie, it's Liz. Get Chase to the phone, would you?"

"He had an errand in Uptown. Some car restoration place. Said if you came in, I should tell you to stay put and wait for him. But it was an hour ago."

"Okay, thanks." Puzzled, she hung up. "Uptown?"

What did he think he was going to learn at Rowdy's Restorers, the only car restoration business in the area. Rowdy mainly dealt with cars from the seventies and eighties. She ordered an Uber, grabbed her purse and shot out the door. By the time she got to the street, she realized she'd left the scarf, but her Uber was pulling up. On the way to Uptown, she wondered if Chase had some kind of lead. Maybe he'd learned something about Durant being involved with Rowdy's. Ten minutes later, when she spotted Chase's car parked in front of the place, she had the

Uber driver pull over to the curb.

Stepping out of the vehicle, she checked the door to the business. Locked. And the interior lights were turned off. The place was closed up tight.

"Chase, where in tarnation are you?"

Frustrated, she looked around, spotted a bar on the other side of the street and thought it was a place that seemed likely. Chase was probably there having a tequila. She was getting some kind of weird headache as she crossed to the bar. Her vision went slightly off, and it seemed as if she was looking through some kind of fog. It took some doing to focus. What was going on?

Once inside the bar, Liz saw the place looked seedy, making *Stewie's* appear glamorous by comparison. The dark, smoky business was mostly filled with men. The few women acted like appendages, hanging onto their boyfriends' arms.

Which didn't prevent the men from eyeing Liz, who was searching the crowd for Chase. She felt distanced, as if she couldn't properly focus.

An oily looking guy followed her. "Hey, wanna dance, sweetheart?"

"Do I look like I'm here for a good time?" she snapped.

She moved around him, trying to get a better view of the people in the back. Her vision blurred for a second. She shook her head and scanned the place. Nope, no Chase. So where had he gone off to? And why did everything feel so odd? Like something was pushing at her brain, trying to make her leave. Something or someone. She sensed Annelise. What in the world did she think she was doing? Trying to switch being in charge?

No. Dear Lord, Annelise couldn't deal with this place. Concentrating on keeping the upper hand, Liz decided she'd better call another Uber to get home. She started back through the crowd, wanting out of there. *Now.* A furious scream stopped her.

"Let me go, Javier!"

"I'll let you go when I'm ready to leave, *A-ni-ta.*"

Liz flipped around to see a burly, scar-faced bully holding onto a young woman's wrist as if he was ready to break it. The girl, made up to appear older than she was, looked both scared and defiant.

"Now apologize!" the man said.

"Me? Javier, you're the one —"

When he backhanded the girl across the mouth, Liz's stomach tightened, and she felt her pulse rush through her.

The bartender yelled, "Hey, Javier, not in here!"

Anita ripped her arm free and raced for the door.

Javier started to follow, but Liz stepped into his path, blocking it to allow the intended victim to escape. Javier was instantly on her, glaring at her for interfering.

Though her vision was a tad foggy, Liz stood her ground and gave him a brittle smile. "What's your hurry? The girl wants to go, so let her."

"Hey, slut, I could use a change!" He grabbed *her* by the upper arm. In return, she kneed him, but missed his groin.

"Whore! You think you're gonna stop me?"

About to say something smart, Liz lost whatever she'd come up with. She felt as if her head was being jostled from the inside...as though Annelise was trying to pop out and take over.

"No, don't!" Liz gasped. "He'll hurt you!"

Her head spun when Javier started dragging her toward the door.

And suddenly Annelise was there. In a seedy bar she didn't recognize. She had gotten through, and for the moment, Liz was gone. She'd wanted to know what Liz was up to, but she hadn't been prepared to be manhandled by some jerk.

Some weird oily-looking guy got in front of them, making her captor slow down. "Hey, Javier, I saw her first! You got you a woman! Gimme this one," he said, making Annelise want to gag.

Digging in her heels, she thought fast. "Aren't you even going to buy me a drink, Javier?"

"I'm gonna give you what you're asking for."

Though alarmed, Annelise didn't fight him as he opened the door. Javier dragged her out of the bar and into the alley where her spiked heel caught in broken pavement and threw her off balance. A strap broke.

She pulled off the shoe and saw the red sole. "A Louboutin! Damn! You're going to owe Liz a small fortune for these—"

Javier shoved her up against a brick wall hard enough to make her gasp.

He pinned her throat with one hand, then shook his other arm. A four-point metal throwing star popped from the sleeve of his jacket into his free hand. He waved the deadly looking weapon in front of her eyes.

Annelise's gut clenched, but showing fear would be a mistake. Instead, she forced a smile. "I thought you liked me."

"Ever done it in an alley?" He pulled the point of the throwing star up her thigh under her short skirt.

Annelise froze. Liz had picked the wrong man to mess with. And she had picked the wrong time to attempt a switch. She'd merely wanted to find out what her other self was into, not to get into some kind of brawl with a gangbanger.

She tried to take a normal breath and choked out, "Can't we go someplace comfortable?" Someplace where he might let down his guard long enough to let her escape and call the police?

"Shut your mouth. Or maybe I'll do it for you."

His kiss was an attack, an insult. One immediately sending her mind spinning...

A shadow man pressed her back against a wall...his mouth forcing hers open...his tongue invading...She tried to stop him...to push him away...instead the dark figure tried to shove her down hard...

Horrified by the memory, wishing she had Liz's strength, Annelise started to blank out.

Liz forced her way back, subverting Annelise if not the dark memory. She closed her mind to the past. Ignored her fear at what might happen now. Played along with the snake, her nails sliding down Javier's side to his hip, then shifting between their bodies where she grabbed his balls as hard as she could.

Javier exploded away from her, dropping the throwing star, holding himself and cursing in Spanish while Liz hobbled toward the street on her broken shoe.

"Now you're gonna get what you deserve, whore!"

Javier grabbed her hair, jerking her backwards. The purse flew to the pavement and the contents spilled. He tugged her toward him. She flipped around, fists flashing, one connecting with his ugly face.

Suddenly, another body hurtled between them, flipping Liz onto the alley pavement as Javier flew against the garbage cans.

Chase!

On her knees, stuffing her things back into the purse, Liz looked up and saw him moving toward her. "C'mon, Liz, let's get out of here."

Movement behind him caught her eye. Javier retrieving the throwing star from the ground. He stood and whipped out his arm, aiming at Chase.

She gasped, "Chase, watch out!"

Chase turned too late. He couldn't move fast enough. The pointed weapon grazed his side and blood bloomed through his shirt where it sliced him before falling to the pavement. Javier bounded forward and tackled him. Down they both went, rolling around on the ground, trading punches.

"Omigod!" Liz cried, getting to her feet even as Javier grabbed Chase's head and slammed it back against the cement. Then he reached out and grabbed his weapon yet again.

Liz kicked his arm but was unable to make him let go of the metal star. She was about to jump on the creep's back when Chase rolled and pinned Javier down, his elbow in the man's throat. Javier gagged and tried to rip Chase's arm free.

"Settle down, Javier. Throw away your damn weapon and I'll let go."

Javier tossed the star down the alley.

Chase let go and jumped back, but Javier wasn't finished. As he launched himself forward, Chase's foot met his face.

The man went down again, holding his bloody nose, rolling on the pavement in agony. "You broke my nose, you mother-fucker!"

Purse in hand, Liz rushed to Chase's side. "Let's get out of here!"

Expression unreadable, he grabbed her arm and dragged her exactly as Javier had. Hopping, she took off the broken high heel and carried it as she limped to his car. She glanced over her shoulder as Javier's buddies left the bar. One of the men stopped to pick up something from the pavement where her purse had landed and handed it to Javier.

What in the world was it?

Chase was already pushing her into his Jaguar. She searched her purse to see what the man might have of hers. Oh, no! She looked out the window as Javier stumbled to his feet. He stared after them with a malevolent smile, her driver's license in hand. Damn it! Now he had her address!

A furious Chase started the Jaguar and zoomed down the street. "What was the brawl all about?"

"He was strong-arming a kid. I figured I was better equipped to cool him down than she was."

"Cooling him down...is that what you thought you were doing? Why?"

Her fiddling with the ripped shoe in obstinate silence irritated him.

"God damn it, *why*?" he asked again.

He glanced at Liz, who was glaring at him when she said, "I hate bullies, especially ones who threaten women! I won't stand around and just watch. *I'm* not afraid."

"You *should* be afraid. So this isn't the first time?"

"Not the last, either."

"How many times?" When she didn't answer, Chase said, "He would've hurt *you*, Liz. Bad. One of these days the target of this dangerous little game of yours will get *you*."

"This time I miscalculated."

"Mistakes can get you killed."

He swore and heard Liz grit her teeth. Why? So she wouldn't say something she shouldn't? Damn it! If he hadn't interfered, who knows what would have happened to her?

She tried changing the subject. "Where'd you learn to fight like that?"

"On the damn street!"

He noted she was eyeing the blood on his shirt, but she kept her mouth shut the rest of the way to *Stewie's*, where he parked the car, grunting with pain as he left it.

"What are you doing?" Liz opened her door and stood right there. "The place is closed. You need to get to an emergency room."

Ignoring her, Chase pulled out a key and unlocked the door.

"Stewie gave you a key to his business?" Liz closed the car door and rushed to catch up with him as he entered.

The place was dark. Chase snapped on a bar light and poured them drinks.

She slid onto a stool. "When did you and Stewie bond?"

He laughed. "Stewie isn't so generous. I'm paying him for use of the back room."

"You're not the back room type. What are you hiding from? Or should I say who?"

Chase stared at her, wondering if she suspected him of

something. But what? He slid her a drink. "This arrangement suits me. Finding an apartment would take forever, and I never did like hotels."

"Right. A hotel room would be depressing compared to the back room of a terrific place like this."

"Hey, I've got my own pool table."

"To sleep on?"

He gave her an intense look and began unbuttoning his shirt. "Hm, now you have an interesting idea. Want to join me?"

Liz laughed…but froze when her eyes locked onto his bared chest. When he looked down, he saw the cut in his flesh, blood still dripping.

"Damn it, Chase! You really do need a doctor!"

He poured tequila over the wound, screwed up his face and swore.

"What are you doing?" In a flash, she flew around the other side of the bar and took a closer look.

"Making sure I don't get an infection."

"It looks like the bleeding has pretty much stopped, but you really need stitches."

"It's not too deep. Thanks for the concern, but I have what I need to take care of it."

Chase moved away from the bar and Liz followed him to the back room where he turned on the light. He crossed to his cot tucked into a corner of the room along with a small table and chair. He grabbed his case from the floor and set it on the pool table. When he unzipped it, he pulled out a laceration kit. Considering the potential physical danger of his work, he always kept one with his things.

He removed the bloody t-shirt, then fumbled with the package, holding his right arm carefully, keeping it from disturbing the wound. He could tell Liz was trying not to stare at his bare chest tattooed with a silhouette of his Jaguar and a car tire with wings and the words *Born for Speed.*

She said, "Thanks for the save, by the way." Then took the

package from him. "I'll do it."

Emptying the contents onto the pool table, she picked up the adhesive which she set above the wound in his side and placed the first of four attached steri-strips over the cut to close it.

In pain from her touch, Chase closed his eyes and shuddered. Liz stopped with her fingers still on the second strip. He blinked his eyes open and stared at her intense expression...what was she thinking? Then she averted her gaze and sealed the last two steri-strips over the wound. When she backed away, he took a relieved breath. He wanted her — would have her before he disappeared again — but he was in no shape to make any moves on her tonight.

He carried his case from the pool table to the chair. "I need another tequila."

She gave him a disbelieving look. "You're going to pour it over the steri-strips?"

"To drink this time."

Mumbling something about stubborn men, Liz beat Chase to the bar and poured him one. If he didn't know better, he would think she cared.

Pushing it toward him, she said, "Why did you risk yourself with Javier? No man ever stepped out for me like that before."

"I didn't want to see you get hurt." He raised his glass to her. "I'm getting used to having you around."

"I've been told I wear on a man pretty fast."

"Then maybe he wasn't much of a man."

Liz appeared oddly vulnerable when she took a deep breath. "You break the rules, Chase. You make me think —"

"What?"

She shook her head and looked like she swallowed whatever it was she was thinking. "Let's talk about something else. What were you doing at the renovation place?"

"Hoping to get something on Durant, of course. I asked Rowdy if Durant tried selling him parts that weren't authentic. You know, if he was trying to sell parts from his replication division to restorers rather than simply to some average Joe restoring his own car."

"And?"

"No luck there."

"I had a little luck," Liz said. "I know why Durant's division was losing money."

Chase tossed down the tequila and grimaced. "I'm listening."

"I got a look at this folder he was trying to keep hidden. More parts are being made and shipped out than are being paid for. A lot more parts."

"I don't get it."

She circled the bar and took a stool next to him. "Most were for a half dozen very specific classic car models. What if Durant's been rebuilding classics from the frame up?"

"You think the money he can make on replicas is enough to take such a big a chance on?"

"I *know* the money he can make on the originals is."

They stared at each other in silence for a moment.

"The fire?" Chase asked.

"The parts were made for models like the very classics that were blown up."

"You think the cars at Parts and Storage were replicas?"

"Why not? After being decimated by car bombs, I don't think there's anything left for the fire and insurance investigators to question."

"Only?"

"Certain engine parts should have been handmade," she said. "But when I went back to check things out after the fire, the edge on a surviving piece that I handled was definitely machine-made."

"A replication?"

"A replication. What if Durant has the authentic cars stored somewhere, just waiting to sell them? There's a healthy black market, lots of serious foreign collectors who don't care where the cars come from."

Whistling, Chase moved around the bar. "Durant's bank account would do cartwheels."

"Millions of them. He can't be working alone."

"Do you think that's what happened to Katie?" Chase asked, making sure to keep his voice unaffected. "You think Durant made sure she died in the fire because she was his partner, and he didn't want to share? Or maybe she knew too much for him to be comfortable?"

Liz gave him a penetrating look before saying, "Durant wouldn't work with an O'Neal, not the way he feels about them."

Chase started. "Then, who?"

"Vinny Delarosa, a Walsh mechanic and snitch who does whatever Durant wants. Something's been going on between them lately. They're always whispering, like they're working on some illicit plan and don't want anyone to overhear. I figure he may be the weak link."

"You think we can get him to break?"

"*I* can get him to set up a sale for us."

"What are you thinking? That he's blind? That he wouldn't make the connection to Annelise?"

"He's Durant's creature. He's got nothing to do with Annelise at work. Besides, I can get a lot more creative in the looks department. Trust me, when I'm done with the transformation, he won't know me in a Chicago mile."

"You'd be putting yourself in the line of fire."

Liz laughed. "I know how these men think, how they operate. I can bring it home."

Not wanting her to put herself in any kind of real danger, he said, "I don't like it."

"You don't have to like it. Just be there when it counts."

"Oh, I'll be there, all right. No way would I miss bringing Durant down for the world."

Shit. Liz was staring at him with a suspicious expression, when she said, "Sounds like you have a personal stake."

They locked gazes for a moment. Intent on getting closer to distract her, Chase leaned in. Liz caught her breath. He reached out...touched her face...slid his hand behind her head and inched it toward him.

"Very personal."

He kissed her.

Tentative at first, Liz closed her eyes and kissed him back until he slid his hand to her breast. Damn, he wanted more and he had the idea that maybe she did, as well! But her eyes snapped open, and she pulled back, breathing hard.

Chase ran a thumb over her cheek. "Is an apology in order?"

"For what?" She shrugged as if it was no big deal, but her eyes told him a different story.

"I should get you home."

The easy smile on her lips looked forced. "I can Uber."

"I insist. Just give me a few minutes to clean up and get a fresh shirt."

Liz nodded, then followed him into the other room.

"I'll just be quick," he promised, backing up toward the bathroom.

"I'll be right here."

Glancing back at her once on his way to the bathroom, she appeared confused. Because of him? Or was there more going on with her he hadn't figured out?

Yet.

Liz couldn't take her eyes off Chase until he closed the door behind him. Her pulse was still ragged from the kiss. But she'd had to stop him after his intimate touch had made her remember the terror which had gotten through to her when Javier had Annelise against the alley wall. Plus they might be working together to get Durant, but she still didn't know Chase's reason for helping her. She *wanted* to trust him...

When she heard the running water in the adjoining bathroom, she yelled, "Hey, keep your wound dry!"

Trying to take her mind off what could have happened between them, she thought about how wrong the night could have gone. How had Annelise broken through? And why? What if the confrontation with Javier changed her somehow? Liz couldn't let Annelise suffer for something she had instigated. She would have to figure out a way to keep Annelise's curiosity or whatever was driving her at bay.

Wanting to get her mind off the barely averted disaster, wondering if Chase was simply helping her or if he had his own reason to bring Durant down, Liz checked out his things scattered around the living area in the corner. She sat on the chair and went through his case. Nothing but clothes and a few toiletries. The edge of a notebook stuck out of the casual jacket hanging on the chair's back. As she started to reach for it, the water stopped running.

She spun around to find Chase coming out of the bathroom, wearing only provocatively half-open jeans. Her breath caught in her throat for a moment. He was as fit as they came. And as hot. He looked ready for anything. Now that he'd cleaned up, the cut wasn't looking too bad. He stopped at his case and pulled out a clean t-shirt.

She didn't take her eyes off Chase until he pulled it on, secured his jeans, and said, "Let's get you home."

Chapter Eleven

Liz sat in the recliner with her legs crossed and skirt raised above her knees. Annelise had chosen to see Dr. Jackson after what had happened between them the day before, but Liz had immediately taken over the session.

"Well, Marva, now we have a problem."

"Mm, Liz."

Though the psychiatrist realized Liz was present, she didn't make a big deal of it. "You're not surprised."

"No. You're the stronger personality."

"So I thought...until yesterday."

"What happened yesterday?"

Liz told her she'd been at a bar looking for Chase when she ended up in an altercation with the jerk who was mistreating a young woman. "I had to step in, to give the poor girl a chance to get away."

"You wanted to protect her the way you protect Annelise?"

"Something like that. Well, my plan was blown. Annelise showed last night, right in the middle of things. Butted in where she didn't belong. I could feel her trying to take over, but I couldn't stop her." Liz shook her head. "I don't know what she did to break through. She could have gotten us killed. And now the jerk who calls himself Javier has our address."

Neither of them was safe from the creep. Though Annelise didn't seem to acknowledge the fact.

"Tell me about it," the psychiatrist said.

Liz did so but left out the shadowy memory which had forced her to break back through.

"So what happened to make Annelise concede to you?"

"Fear. She realized she'd stepped in it."

"How did you feel when you were able to take over?"

"Relieved. Annelise couldn't deal."

"But you could." When Liz nodded, the psychiatrist asked, "Why do you think you're so different?"

"Experience. It wasn't my first rodeo with some asshole who thought he could do what he wanted to a woman. Last weekend, I took on this Jimmy-boy Scanlon after he burned a waitress with his cigar. For fun."

"Do you enjoy fighting men?"

"Enjoy physically fighting misogynistic men? No. But I take satisfaction in making them seem small whenever I can."

Though she hoped she'd ruined Scanlon, both at work and with his girlfriend.

The psychiatrist asked, "And you made this Javier seem small?"

"In a way, yes. I had help this time," Liz admitted. "Not Annelise. She could have gotten us killed. Chase."

"So he rescued you?"

As much as she hated to admit she couldn't always take care of herself against dangerous men, Liz wasn't sure how the night would have ended if Chase hadn't shown. "Yeah, you could say he rescued me."

"Why were you looking for him in the first place?" the psychiatrist asked.

"Because I knew he was digging for dirt on Durant."

"So he got something on your stepbrother."

"No, Marva. But I did." She told the psychiatrist about the parts replications which could have been used to rebuild classic fakes which had been destroyed by the car bombs and the fire. "I want to ruin Durant. And make sure he ends up in prison where he belongs."

"What do you have against your stepbrother other than his taking over the company you think Annelise should run?"

Not wanting to go there, Liz's gut tightened. "Isn't his double-dealing with those parts replications enough to serve him prison time? And that's just a start. He's evil through and through." Of course she kept the worst memories, the ones she knew could undo her, locked in the dark recesses of her mind. "He was born an asshole. Or maybe his father Arthur twisted him when he was a kid."

"Then this goes beyond Walsh Motors. Do you want to talk about it, Liz?"

The shadowy memory Javier had provoked haunted her, but she said, "You've got to be kidding, Marva. I don't even want to remember."

The psychiatrist hesitated for a moment, then asked, "How do you plan to make him pay?"

"My plan is for me to know."

"Are you afraid I'll warn him?"

"Or Annelise. Hah, if I tell you, she'll know enough after this session, won't she? Besides, I don't want to jinx the plan. If it works, you'll know about it soon enough."

"And you have no qualms about whatever you plan on doing? You don't think getting revenge can be a double-edged sword?"

Liz stared at the psychiatrist, hesitating, then checked her watch.

"You have no clue as to what Durant deserves. No way could I even the score with the prick. Time's up, Marva. Hurry up and get Annelise out of here so I can get to Nordstrom's shoe sale. Some asshole ruined a pair for me last night."

"You'll have to wait until Annelise is ready to leave."

Liz groaned. "Don't ruin my dreams."

She closed her eyes. Gradually, she felt her too tight face muscles relax.

"When you awaken, Annelise, you'll remember everything Liz and I talked about. Three...two...one."

Annelise slowly opened her eyes and connected with Dr. Jackson.

"Welcome back, Annelise. How are you feeling?"

"Trying not to panic. I wish I knew what Liz was planning. I would gladly help her get something on our stepbrother. She knows everything *I* do, right?"

"Apparently not everything. But enough."

Annelise nodded in resignation, uncrossed her legs and straightened her skirt over her knees. "It's so unfair I'm left out, especially when we're of a like mind about Durant."

"Unusual for someone who has DID."

Annelise started. "I have what?"

"Dissociative identity disorder."

Yikes, it didn't sound good. "That's the name for what I've been going through? Why didn't you mention this before?"

"I didn't think you were ready to hear it. I was going slow, giving you time to get used to the reason for those blackouts."

"Well, you can tell me now."

Dr. Jackson nodded. "All right. Your personality is split into two individuals. Could be more."

"More?" Annelise swallowed her rising panic.

"Hopefully not, but it is possible."

More people in her head? Dear Lord! Having one extra was more than enough. She didn't think she could handle others. "How can I tell?"

"I'm afraid you won't know unless they want you to. Or if you somehow accidentally cross wires. So to speak. And there is always hypnosis. So how would you feel if we learn there are others?"

"Like crap. I'm having enough trouble dealing with there being a Liz and the fact she's been hiding from me."

Did Liz know if there were others? If Annelise learned there *were* others, was there something she could do to get rid of them?

"There is a way you can at least know everything Liz does," Dr. Jackson said. "If she agrees."

Floored by Dr. Jackson's analysis, Annelise took several deep, even breaths. "I don't understand. Agrees to what?"

"You both would have to be willing to co-operate. To integrate. To become one person again."

"You mean there'd be no Liz anymore?"

"Mm, maybe. And possibly no Annelise."

Annelise took a shaky breath as she considered the implications. She wasn't ready to do a disappearing act. Forever.

"How would you feel about taking a chance?"

Annelise shook her head. "I'm not ready to take such a big leap of faith yet. Maybe I never will be."

But she wanted to know more about what affected her, made her somehow create a Liz in her life. If she asked Dr. Jackson to give her more information, Liz would know pretty much everything she did. What if she stopped her from doing anything which might allow her to change things? To make Liz disappear.

She was going to have to research this DID thing on her own.

When Annelise pulled her car inside Walsh Clean Cars, Roscoe was going over a classic, checking off items on the form attached to his clipboard. As usual, he was being extra-thorough. He waved to acknowledge her and returned to his inspection. She leaned against her car and waited. When he finished, he set down the clipboard and gave her a penetrating look of concern.

"You look tired, Annelise. Getting enough sleep? Or is the fire keeping you awake at night?"

"Something like that." She smiled as if it was nothing.

"I know you worry about everything. So take as much time as you need to recuperate."

Annelise nodded. "When I can, I will. In the meantime, did you ask around about Tully O'Neal for me?"

"Have I ever let you down? I talked to a guy who works for Tully. Used to work for me and I trust him one hundred percent. Sounds like Tully is the same straight shooter he was when he worked for your father. He didn't start no fire, no way." He hesitated but knew he had to share the rest. "But his daughter? The guy didn't know about her. She worked in the office. He said she was secretive, told me one day he went in to get some paperwork, and she was on a personal call and quickly covered and hung up. Then one of our mechanics recognized the photo of Kate O'Neal. Said he'd seen her around Parts Replications a coupla weeks ago."

Annelise's forehead pulled. "But Durant denied doing business with her."

"And you believed him? She coulda used a fake name. Or maybe she was there to see someone who works for him."

"Or maybe he was lying." Which wouldn't surprise her. "I spoke to Tully after the funeral. He thinks Kate might have been meeting some man she'd been seeing. Kate wouldn't tell him who it was," Annelise said. "So Tully thought the guy might have been married."

"Or someone up to no good," Roscoe added.

"No doubt he thought something similar, as well."

A man cleared his throat. "Hey, Roscoe, you got a minute?"

Roscoe looked over to the customer who'd just brought his classic in for refurbishing. He waved the man over.

Annelise backed off. "You're busy, and I need to get going, Roscoe. Thank you."

"You know I'd do anything for you, kid. Go home and get the rest you need."

Though she smiled, Annelise didn't say she would. She got

into her car and drove toward the exit, certain Roscoe wouldn't stop asking around about Kate O'Neal until he got the kind of information about her that she needed.

Someone had to know something...

Not wanting to do her research at work where someone might interfere, Annelise drove to Roasted Beans, her favorite coffee shop in the Fulton Market area, for a late lunch.

Her laptop was set up and she began searching for dissociative identity disorder and instantly had a ton of leads. She clicked on an article about DID in Abnormal Psychology. Just then, a server she knew named Davina landed at her table, multiple slender braids swinging around her smiling copper face.

"Annelise! Haven't seen you in a while."

"I've been too busy at work to take time for myself."

"Well you're here now. So what can I do for you?"

Annelise said, "You can bring me my favorite, a —"

"— salmon avocado and bacon toast and a large dark roast coffee, no cream or sugar."

"Wow, great memory!"

Davina grinned at her. "Coming right up."

The second Davina turned away, Annelise began to read. The article told her dissociative identity disorder most often seeded when a child was emotionally, physically or sexually abused, so the child created an alter so he or she could imagine the trauma was happening to someone else.

She thought about it. Arthur had emotionally abused her and had emotionally and physically abused Lizzie. Was it possible she'd had another personality as a child? Maybe Lizzie had an alter, but it didn't seem likely that she did, because the blackouts happened later. Years later. Her breath caught in her throat as she remembered.

Right after Lizzie died...

When Davina set down her mug of coffee, she glanced up at the server and smiled. "Thank you."

"Your food will be up in a few minutes."

"Great." Taking a slug of her coffee, she waited for Davina to walk away, then went back to reading.

The main symptom of this mental illness is the imagined presence of different identities, as if more than one person is sharing one body and mind. Each identity has differing characteristics and mannerisms.

Whoa. That described the difference between her and Liz, all right. But mental illness? A frightening description of what had happened to her.

She kept reading.

Memory loss can be serious — the memory of a traumatic event or a whole period of time can go missing.

Like the memory she'd started to have when Javier had attacked her. The dark cloud hovering over her head made her insides crawl, but she couldn't remember what had actually happened to her in the past. Had Liz been able to deal with the memory when she took over? Other than the blackouts, Annelise had thought her memory was good until the Javier incident. But when she read: *Rarely, there can be a thorough loss of knowledge about themselves. An individual can be disoriented and walk away from his or her life...*it made her wonder what else she couldn't remember.

She was so wrapped up in thinking about the possibilities that Davina setting her food on the table startled her.

"Sorry." Davina gave her a close look. "Are you okay?"

"I'm fine. My mind was elsewhere for the moment." Annelise popped a display on her laptop screen to hide what she was researching from Davina. Forcing a smile, she said, "Ooh, looks good." Then picked up her salmon, avocado and bacon toast and took a bite. It was as delicious as always.

"Can I get you anything else? More coffee?"

"I'm good for now but check back in a bit."

Davina nodded and moved away.

Annelise hadn't realized how hungry she was. She set aside her project for the moment and ate. Let her mind drift back ten years. The blackouts had started after Lizzie's death. Had she created Liz as a way of keeping her sister alive the same way she talked to Lizzie when driving the Mustang and imagined hearing Lizzie answer? Now she wondered if it *was* her own imagination. Or was it actually Liz talking to her? *Actually?* Hm. Was it the right way to describe another part of herself filling her head with what she wanted to hear?

She finished her coffee, waved to Davina and pointed to her cup. The waitress picked up a coffee pot and approached the table. Annelise pushed her mug forward to be refilled.

"Any dessert in mind?"

Though Annelise loved the sweet treats the coffee shop made, she said, "I'm going to pass today. I have a little more research to do, then I need to get back to the office." Or no doubt Durant would be waiting to give her a hard time, criticize her for abandoning her duties.

Bracing herself with more coffee, Annelise turned off the display and went back to the article, picking up where she'd left off.

A person with DID has two or more identities which could have different ethnicities, genders and interests. The one with the personality most frequently used is the core identity. The others are alters. The different alters control a person's behavior at different times. The core and alters may be familiar with one another, but not always. Often, there are one or more alters in hiding.

Well this described her and Liz to a T. Since she spent the most time dealing with daily life, she was obviously the core, the real Annelise, and Liz was an alter, possibly created because she missed Lizzie so much. But why didn't she know what Liz was doing when Liz knew about her? If there was only some way she could spy on Liz.

Then it hit her. She could set up a camera to record Liz. What would she learn about her if she did? And were there more alters hiding from her? Or from them both? Would she be able to get them on video, as well?

Realizing Davina was returning with her check, Annelise fetched her credit card from her wallet and handed it to the waitress without looking at the bill. "Here you go."

"I'll be right back."

Annelise hoped it would give her enough time to finish the article.

It seemed therapy could help with behaviors and reduce the number and frequency of identity switches. Which gave her some hope this DID thing could be controlled. Reading further, she learned hypnotherapy was a form of guided meditation and could help recover suppressed memories. Not that Annelise was certain she wanted to remember and cope with the past. But it seemed the only solution — to explore and process traumatic events — would help her understand why she had disassociated. She would have to consider it.

But how would understanding help her stop *being* Liz?

Arthur had treated her and Lizzie horribly from the time they were seven, when Daddy died. Like they were worthless. Like they were bad. When Mama wasn't around, he'd punish them for the slightest infraction, calling them evil little witches, when he and his son were the true evil ones.

Five years older than her and Lizzie, Durant had taken his cue about how to handle them from his father. He'd been mean. Merciless. He'd especially treated Lizzie as an enemy, because she'd refused to let him control her. Which had led to fights, both verbal and physical, and more than once he'd hit her hard enough to leave bruises. One time, he'd knocked Lizzie out. Annelise had been frozen with fear, but thankfully, Lizzie had quickly come to. And Arthur had seen it all. Rather than punish his son, Arthur had patted him on the back like he was proud of him.

Realizing Davina was on her way back to the table, Annelise closed the computer lid, took a big breath and gave the waitress a smile she wasn't exactly feeling at the moment, added a generous tip to the check and signed.

"Have a good day," Davina said.

"I'm trying."

Now if only she could go back to work and finish the day without ever setting eyes on Durant.

Chapter Twelve

Durant was already in a foul mood when he entered his office mid-afternoon. He'd had lunch with the contact who would find him shrewd international buyers who didn't look too closely at provenance for his private collection of classic cars. The asshole wanted double his usual fee.

Durant was slowing down the process by handling the insurance paperwork himself. Walsh Motors would be paid for the loss of a half dozen classic replicas, but the VINs would also be reported as cars which had been totaled. He didn't want those who bought the real classics to get the damning information. Not only could it stop sales — the proposed buyers probably believing he was trying to sell them the replicas — the wrong person might report him to the authorities, as well.

So he and Vinny had to work fast to find buyers for the cars they'd replicated. He'd projected the first sale offer to come in a week. Which would be tomorrow, and he still didn't have so much as a lead. He finally had a contact he could count on, but he doubted the man could work magic in twenty-four hours.

Frustrated, Durant went looking for Annelise, but her office was empty. Where the hell was she?

Swallowing his building anger, he sought out her assistant and gave Joyce a fake smile when he pinned her at her desk. "I'm looking for your boss."

Eyes wide and voice a bit unsteady, she said, "Annelise isn't here right now."

Which prompted his searing stare. "I get it. So where is she?"

There was a false note to her "Still at lunch."

Durant ground his teeth to keep from losing his temper with her. He silently counted to five, then gave her an even bigger fake smile. "When she comes in, let her know I want to talk to her."

"Of course."

He turned as if starting to leave, then stopped and faced Joyce. "As for this evening…" Though she didn't say anything, her startled expression was enough to irritate him further. "I'll be in the car across the street at six. I thought you would want an update on your brother. Don't keep me waiting."

He then headed straight for his office, certain she would be prompt, that he would have another evening to find out what Annelise was doing. Chasing after the fire again? If Joyce knew, he would no doubt have to seduce her into telling him all about Annelise's activities.

He would start with the fact that her brother now had a court date and Durant had made a deal to get him released on an ankle monitor.

Once in his office, Durant poured himself a Bowmore Scotch. Swirled it. Sniffed it. Swallowed it in one gulp.

Time he got some useful information out of the bitch. Once he knew something about Annelise he could use against her, he could also hold the knowledge over Joyce's head. Then he would own her.

Chase parked a half block down from Walsh Motors in time to see Durant pull into the garage. It was nearly five. He wondered how late the bastard would work. *If* he was working. Didn't matter. Chase would wait for him to leave the building at whatever the time. No doubt he was scheming to sell the classics which supposedly had been destroyed. His turn to get something they could use against Durant. He was well prepared with tech to help him get the proof he would need if Durant crossed any lines.

Putting in earbuds, he tuned into Sirius XM NASCAR Radio and listened to an interview about one of the newest stock cars in production. He checked the clock. Five-fifteen. No vehicles or employees on foot leaving Walsh Motors. Next, an interview with a top driver took him to half past five. A couple of cars left the business, neither belonging to Durant. A NASCAR owner promoted his team for the rest of the hour.

And then he saw a coffin-nosed classic car pull out of the garage. A Cord Berline.

Chase started his engine, but when Durant pulled to the other side of the street as if parking, he waited...

What was Durant up to?

At exactly six, a dark-haired woman exited the building. Chase recognized her as the assistant who'd tried stopping him from facing Annelise Covington in her office when he'd assumed she was Liz. Despite Annelise's denial, she had to be both women, though he didn't get why the theatrics. Everyone knew Lizzie was dead. Was it just one of her dangerous games, or was there more to it? Was this Annelise's way of bringing her twin back to life...or something darker? Maybe he should just ask.

Annelise's assistant crossed the street, looked around quickly as if she didn't want someone to see her, then got into the Cord.

A moment later, Durant pulled his car away from the curb.

Chase followed, wondering what was going on between the car's occupants. Business? If so, then why had the woman looked so nervous? Something more personal?

He would soon find out.

Following, he kept them at a distance, making sure he didn't get too close, switching lanes and dropping back another car length after turning west onto North Avenue. Now they were in Old Town. Although this was a monied area, it was also very commercial. Chase couldn't fathom Durant having a place here, not when he lived in the Walsh Mansion. Though he supposed Durant could have a sex pad where he could do what he wanted with — or to — the woman.

Chase followed them west and then turned onto a side street. They continued several blocks before turning. Halfway down the block he stopped in front of a two-flat, a century-old Chicago duplex with an apartment on each floor. Durant parked. Though Chase spotted a second available parking spot a bit behind the prick, he slowed but kept going, staring out his tinted windshield to see both occupants exit the car. Then from his rearview mirror, he saw Durant grab the woman's arm and pull her to him, cupping her ass while heading toward the building. Well, that clarified things. They took steps next to the main porch down to what must be a below grade garden apartment.

Certain this was the woman's place, not Durant's, Chase quickly circled the block back to the available parking spot he'd seen. Before getting out, he checked his surroundings in every direction to make sure he wouldn't have eyes on him. No one he could see. Taking his leather case, he headed for the two-flat and walked around the side under cover of a large bush where he would be invisible to anyone on the street.

There were two garden-level windows on this side of the building. The first looked over the living space. Durant was lip-locked with Annelise's assistant, pumping his pelvis against her as he walked her backward toward another door. Undoubtedly the bedroom. Durant was the same scum he had been since high school when he'd used several girls for more than just sex. Wondering what his motive could be this time, Chase moved to the next window. A shade covered it so he couldn't see inside.

That didn't mean he couldn't hear.

Opening his case, he removed the professional wall micro-phone stethoscope. It sent a signal to a small recorder and to the earbuds he already had in place. Hoping to get something on

Durant they could use to incriminate him, Chase attached the stethoscope to the window and turned on the recorder. He was willing to do whatever it took to make the man pay for thinking he could get away with anything just because he had Walsh money.

The first thing he heard was the woman's moan.

"Like it, do you?" Durant asked. "Get on your knees!"

The woman was making guttural sounds as if she was into whatever was going on in there. The last thing Chase wanted to hear.

He gritted his teeth together. A picture of Durant with a different woman formed in his mind. His stomach turned, making him nauseous. He shook his head and told himself to keep calm and concentrate on getting details of what Durant was into. And proof of what he had already done. Nearly a full week since the fire, and the cops hadn't made an arrest. As far as he had heard, they had nothing new and were holding Katie responsible for everything.

The grunting and cries on the other side of the wall went on and on. The minutes passed far too slowly, but to Chase's relief, the sex play on the other side of the wall finally ended.

"You and I are going to make a great team, Joyce."

Breathless, she asked, "Doing what?"

"You tell me. Have I missed any part of you needing attention?"

Chase hoped it didn't mean they were going to go at it again.

"What about my brother?" she asked sounding scared.

Brother? Whoa! Chase wondered if there was some kind of blackmail involved...

"He now has a court date next week," Durant told her. "He'll be released in 48 hours with an ankle monitor. He won't be able to leave his apartment. Make sure he understands he can't, and make sure you get rid of his booze. If he starts drinking, you know he won't give a second thought to leaving the place."

"If he leaves anyway?"

"He'll be behind bars, maybe for a long, long time."

What kind of a crime did this brother of hers commit? Chase wondered.

"Get the consequences through his head," Durant said. *"Or maybe I need to hire a babysitter for him."*

"You would do that?"

"Of course I would do it for you, but you'll have to convince your brother to go along with it. Whoever I hire will do whatever is necessary to get him to court on time and sober."

Whoa. A threat if Chase ever heard one.

"Whatever is necessary?" Joyce asked, *"He wouldn't hurt Mike?"*

"I hope he wouldn't have to, but you need to understand the seriousness of the situation." Durant's tone softened. *"If you object, I understand. Just say so and we'll leave it to Mike to behave himself."*

"Uh, no, no objections."

"Good."

Obviously Mike had a problem with alcohol and who knew what else once he was drunk, but Chase feared Joyce was agreeing to something she might have reason to regret.

Then Durant said, "We need to be on the same page with Annelise."

"Oh, right. Of course I'm not telling her anything like we agreed."

"But you could tell me something."

Ah, there it was, Chase thought. What did Durant want her to do for him?

"What do you mean?" Joyce asked.

"Annelise has been a little off the rails since the fire. She's ignoring her work and playing detective. Tell me you haven't noticed she's been off the job."

"Well, maybe a little. But she does her best for the company as always."

"But not this afternoon," Durant said. "So where was she?"

Hesitating only a few seconds, Joyce said, "After she stopped at Clean Cars, she went to lunch."

"But why did she need to go to Clean Cars today?" When Joyce didn't automatically tell him, Durant said, "I'm in charge of Walsh Motors. I need to know. C'mon, sweetheart..."

Joyce made a breathy sound. "Oh, yes..."

"As soon as you tell me, I'll do whatever you want," Durant promised.

"She said someone spotted Kate O'Neal at Parts Replications a couple of weeks ago."

Her mentioning Katie made Chase want to hit something. More specifically Durant.

Durant cursed, then changed his tone. "Now I have something for you. Hold out your hand."

It sounded like they were moving around in the bed.

Joyce gasped. "Omigod! This is gorgeous! Are those stones real?"

"You tell me, beautiful."

"Well, I would expect a man like you to be generous."

Then it sounded like they were kissing again. Great.

Closing his mind to what was going on in the room for the next half hour, Chase recorded without paying attention to what they were doing. If necessary, he would listen to the recording later to get something useful.

He couldn't help but think about Liz. Attracted to her from the moment they'd met, he'd kept his own desires in check. He hadn't come back to Chicago to get involved in a personal relationship, but he couldn't deny wanting one with her. There was something about her setting her apart from other women he'd known. She had an angry energy which had come from somewhere. He thought of the Javier incident. What had happened to her to make her willing to stake her own safety for another woman's — one she didn't even know? And what made her so determined to bring Durant to some kind of justice?

Then he thought about Katie. He realized her having been at Parts Replications shortly before the fire would make her look guilty if anyone figured out why she'd been there.

Information he wasn't ready to share with Liz yet, no matter how deeply he felt about her.

Chapter Thirteen

It was late by the time Annelise got to I-Spy, a local superspy shop where she hoped to find a video camera which would work for her. In an effort to keep Liz from knowing what she was doing, she'd worn earbuds and played hip-hop music, stuff Lizzie had hated — and which *she* didn't care for, either — in hopes the music would distract Liz while she searched for the spycam.

She couldn't believe the incredible technology around her: cameras in alarm clocks, in Bluetooth speakers, in picture frames and in dummy smoke detectors. Of course the spycam had to be something which could blend in with her bedroom, something Liz would never recognize as being out of place. She finally found the perfect hidden camera in what *looked like* a receptacle outlet cover to replace the one already installed. Its tiny hidden camera and mike would send signals that would be recorded on her smartphone.

When she took the spycam to the cashier, Annelise was relieved she would finally have a way to learn something about Liz.

Annelise got home a half hour later. She set the spycam in an outlet near her bedroom door, so it would cover the whole room. She'd barely checked it out to make sure it worked as advertised when her cell rang.

Though the caller's number wasn't in her phone contacts, she answered anyway. "Annelise Covington."

"Tully O'Neil here, Miss Covington. You said you wanted to help find the truth about whoever started the fire."

"I do." Taking a big breath, she asked, "Mr. O'Neal, what can I do for you?"

"Meet me at my daughter's place in Edgewater." He gave her the address. "I'm there now, going through some of her things."

"I can be there in twenty minutes if I can find easy parking."

"See you soon."

Hoping to get some insight to Kate O'Neal — but not wanting to listen to more hip-hop — Annelise removed the earbuds, then took off. As she got in the Mustang, her mind was whirling as she wondered what kind of help the dead woman's father was looking for. She headed east for Lake Shore Drive. Kate's place was about two miles north and close to the lake. Annelise was so focused on the possibilities of what Tully wanted from her as she made a left turn, it took her a minute to realize a Jeep Grand Cherokee was nearly sitting on her bumper. She picked up speed, but so did the other driver. What the heck? What was his rush? Then she pulled to the right so the driver would go around her.

Instead, he rammed her from behind. Hard.

She slammed on the brakes and via her mirror, saw the guy get out of his vehicle, a billed cap hiding his face, a tire iron in his hand. He'd hit her on purpose! To carjack her? Oh, no, she wasn't giving this thug the opportunity.

He was steps away from her door when she wheeled the Mustang away and stepped on the gas. Her heart raced. A glance into her mirror showed he was running back to his car. She flew the last two blocks to Addison and made a fast left. It wasn't long before he followed. The cross traffic was far enough away to run the red light at Halsted, and she zoomed to the right and slammed on the brakes in front of the 19th District police station.

The Grand Cherokee zoomed right by her and kept going so fast she didn't get the license plate number. Still, she took a relieved breath.

Annelise got out of the car to check for any damage. The bumper was scratched and there was a good-sized ding. She closed her eyes and took a slow, deep breath. Luckily, she could bring the car to Roscoe in the morning, and she was sure he would make it look like new.

Though she thought about going inside the police station and making a complaint, she got back in the driver's seat instead. Without the guy's license number, there was no point. And Tully O'Neal was waiting for her.

Checking her mirror dozens of times to make sure the idiot who'd hit her wasn't anywhere behind her, she went down a couple of side streets, then headed for The Drive. Her life had taken a wrong turn somehow. Maybe it was her own fault.

"Oh, Lizzie, what have I gotten myself into by trying to force Liz to let me in..."

You need each other...

Annelise shook her head. Knowing there was a Liz that was part of her made her feel like she had to be someone other than who she was. "I need to make Liz go away, Lizzie. Maybe then my life would go back to normal."

Well, as normal as our life could be...

She didn't feel a sense of safety until she got off The Drive and onto local streets in Edgewater. As she'd guessed, Kate O'Neal's place was in an area with more cars than parking spots. To be fair, most of the north side had the same problem, especially this close to the lake. Which is why it took her more than ten minutes to find a parking spot. And another five to get to the building, a three floor brick walkup from the early 20th Century.

The lower door leading to the half-dozen apartments was locked. Annelise pressed Kate's doorbell. She was buzzed in and took the stairs to the third floor. Tully had left the door open for her.

He was inside, taking books from a shelf and boxing them. Glancing up when she entered, he said, "I figured I might as well take care of something which needed doing while I was waiting for you."

His voice was shaky, and his eyes appeared a bit watery. No doubt he was mourning his daughter as he went through her things.

The apartment was smaller than Annelise had expected. Casual modern seating was mixed with several nice antique wood pieces. Modestly appointed, but classy and comfortable. Except the place had been tossed. Chairs knocked over. Cushions and papers on the floor.

"The police have already been here, looking for I'm-not-sure-what," Tully said, sounding disgusted.

"So I see." The living area was a mess. "Did they find anything?"

"They wouldn't say!" He shrugged but his voice revealed his anger. "She was my daughter, but I'm probably still suspect. Have a seat."

Annelise took a chair, Tully the sofa.

"I keep thinking about Kate's mystery man," Annelise said, "wondering who he might be."

"I been wondering a whole lot longer than you."

"I was just thinking, what if she *did* mean to meet him that night?"

"But Katie died at the Walsh garage," Tully said.

"Exactly."

His eyes widened and his voice went up a notch. "You think the man works for you?"

"Not necessarily me, but perhaps for the business. I had Roscoe Hieber ask around. Someone told him he saw Kate in the Parts Replications building a couple of weeks ago."

Tully shook his head and raised his voice again. "What in the world would she have been doing there?"

"Your guess is as good as mine. Did your O'Neal Repairs have a car she needed new parts for? Or was she meeting the mystery man you told me about?" Annelise thought the last was sounding probable.

"Could be the mystery man, considering the connection to the fire. I thought if you looked through her things, you might see something the cops missed."

"Sure, I can help you."

Tully nodded. "Though you would think if there was something to find…" Shaking his head, he indicated the mess the authorities had made of the room. "Detective Turner and his men went through everything already."

Annelise spent the next twenty minutes looking through drawers, but there was nothing there that had anything to do with a man. She found a scrapbook and paged through photos and other memorabilia. She stopped at a family photo of Tully, his wife, a young girl — Kate, of course — and an older boy who looked vaguely familiar.

"I don't remember seeing your son at the funeral."

Tully's expression darkened and his voice went flat. "Donny's been dead to me for more than a decade. I expected him to keep working with me, to take over the business eventually. He wanted no part of it. And considering how he wanted to throw his life away, I wanted no part of that. So he left and I haven't seen him since. Didn't know where to find him to give him the bad news."

Not wanting to upset him further by asking details about their estrangement, Annelise flipped to a page with a photo of a race car and helmeted driver — an old boyfriend of Kate's? — then closed the scrapbook and set it down. She gazed around the room and noticed the telephone had some kind of answering machine, though it wasn't turned on.

"Any messages the morning Kate died?" she asked.

"Here? Nothing."

"The day before?"

He shook his head. "None at all. The police are getting a warrant to find out who called her and who she called, either on the landline or on her cell."

"Hm, a clue as to why she was at Parts Replications might help clear things up."

"That's why I brought this from work." He pulled a piece of portable techware from his pocket. "It records all calls coming in or going out of the office whether landline or cell." His voice tensed. "The man I thought Katie was seeing...I think he called her cell the day before the fire."

Why had he waited to mention this? "And?"

"I'll play it for you." He started the recorder.

"Be at the Lincoln Tap at nine tonight."

"That's all there is."

Annelise gasped. "I think I know who it is. He sounds like—"

"Someone you know?"

"One of our mechanics. Vinny DeLarosa." Durant's snitch. "I don't exactly know him. He works for my stepbrother. He's v*ery* married. His wife's pregnant." The little slime. Just thinking about it made her jaw clench. And her head was starting to hurt. It felt like Liz was trying to get through. "I would hate to think your daughter was mixed up with the creep."

"I suspected he was married! How do we find out if this DeLarosa guy is the one?"

"I don't know yet. I have someone who works for me that I trust. If anyone can get information on Vinny, Roscoe can." She rubbed her forehead as if it would make the ache go away. "Then we'll think of a way to use the information."

"We will," Tully said, his voice low and threatening.

Annelise started. Of course she'd been thinking of Liz, not of him as the other half of the 'we'. No doubt Liz would have something to say about Vinny. She must be trying to get through now if the onset of the migraine was any indication.

"Mr. O'Neal, I'm sorry, but I need to go." Getting sensitive to light, she rose and backed up toward the door, saying, "Keep the recording safe. We may need it as proof."

"I'll put this in my home safe. Miss Covington, thank you."

Annelise left and rushed down the steps, then put on sunglasses as she headed down the street to her car. The aura was already making it difficult for her to keep focused. The last thing she wanted was to have Liz pop out while she was driving. She decided to blast some hip-hop music on the radio to help fight the takeover. Staying local rather than The Drive, she navigated the side streets carefully and got herself home even as the aura assaulted her. Bright lights blinded her for a moment. Then when she left the car, everything around her seemed to be moving at once. As she entered the house, she was getting nauseous. So when Mama tried to stop her, she kept going to the stairs.

"Annelise, I want to talk to you!"

"Not now, Mama. I have a migraine coming on."

By the time she got into her room, her head was whirling, her vision blurred, her stomach threatening to empty. She sat on the edge of the bed, lay back, and within seconds, blacked out.

Chapter Fourteen

Though it was dark by the time Liz left her secret room above the garage for *Stewie's*, she planned to walk so she had some thinking time. As she left the estate property, she smelled cigar smoke — and got a weird sense of something not being right. Another presence nearby. Someone watching her? Turning in a circle, she scanned the area loaded with trees and bushes but saw no one. No smoke either, but the flesh along her spine crawled. A breeze kicked up, wiping away the cigar smell but chilling her. Her cell phone pinged, but she ignored it. Her instincts nagged at her, made her think whoever was there was dangerous. Turning in a circle, she tried to spot what was bothering her, but there seemed to be nothing. Even so, she thought about going back into the garage to get the car, but she hadn't had time to get a duplicate driver's license. That snake Javier had hers. It would be her luck to get stopped by a traffic cop for something, and then all hell would break loose on her. It wouldn't take long for them to realize *Liz Covington* didn't exist.

Even though she wanted to believe she was just being paranoid, she flagged down a taxi that was dropping someone off on the other side of the street.

All the way to *Stewie's*, Liz couldn't stop thinking about the weird past several hours. Either Annelise had taken a long nap after work, or she'd found a way to block her. And then when

Annelise left to meet Tully O'Neal, the block was gone. She'd had some kind of mishap with another car. And an almost altercation with the driver. Annelise had thought the guy was trying to carjack her. But what if it was more personal?

Like Javier intent on revenge? Annelise hadn't been able to see his face...

And then it hit Liz. What if it had been Javier watching *her* as she'd left her quarters?

Her stomach tightened as the taxi pulled up in front of the cigar bar. Liz paid the driver and got out, hoping Chase was here tonight. He hadn't left a text for her or voicemail for her.

Opening the door to the noisy, smoke-filled bar, to her disappointment, she couldn't spot Chase. Thinking Stewie might know if he'd stepped out and would be back, she crossed to the bar and signaled him. After handing a customer a drink, he joined her at the end of the bar.

"Your usual?"

"It would be if Chase was here. Any ideas about where I might find him?"

"He left late afternoon, just as I was opening the place. Said he had something important to take care of."

"He didn't say what? Or when he'd be back?"

Stewie shook his head. "Sorry."

"Yeah, me, too. When you see him—"

The bartender's gaze shifted away from her, and he pointed over her shoulder. She turned to see Chase entering the bar, a leather case slung over his shoulder.

She said, "Thanks, Stewie," then went to meet Chase, who seemed surprised to see her.

He raised his eyebrows. "Oh, you're here. I texted you twenty minutes ago when I was on my way," he said, "but you didn't respond."

Liz started. Twenty minutes ago she was wrapped in para-noia about someone — undoubtedly Javier — out there watching her as she left the house. "Let's go someplace quiet where I can tell you why."

"Outside." When she looked at him questioningly, he said, "You remember the alley area from your first night here. Maybe those tables are still empty. You go claim one and I'll bring the drinks."

Liz nodded and headed for the back door. A couple was just coming inside. Only one of the three tables had occupants, a young couple who were so into each other they probably didn't even know she was there.

She took the table farthest from them, sat and checked her cell. Yep, Chase's text told her he was on his way to *Stewie's*, and he hoped he would see her there. He had a lot to tell her.

Which went two ways.

She fetched a cigarette and lit up, hoping a smoke would even her out. She felt charged. Uneasy. Jumpy. A long drag smoothed her out a bit but didn't take away her mounting questions, and not just about Javier or whoever was after her.

There was Chase to disturb her…

Remembering the hot kiss they'd shared out here the night they'd met, and the one after he'd rescued her from Javier, she wondered why he hadn't tried to get closer to her. Part of her wanted that. Another part thought it might be a mistake. Would having sex screw up their working relationship to nail Durant? She still didn't know Chase's reasoning in the matter, but it had to be more than just his willingness to help her. What did he know about Durant that she didn't? If she was keeping secrets from him, no doubt he was from her, as well.

The screen door opened, and as if she'd conjured him, there he was. Chase headed for their table.

Waiting until he'd set her drink in front of her, she stubbed out her cigarette. "Something weird is going on."

"You mean with the fire case?"

"No, with me." She picked up her glass. "I think that lecher Javier is looking for some payback." Then downed nearly half the drink.

"What happened?"

"Earlier this evening, when I was on my way to see Tully O'Neal, some guy in a Grand Cherokee followed me so close he eventually rammed me." Though she was talking about what happened to Annelise, Chase didn't have to know all the details. "He got out and came for me carrying a tire iron. He was wearing a baseball cap so you couldn't see his face. But his intent was obvious." At least it had been to Annelise. Now Liz believed there was a different reality if that had been Javier wanting revenge. "I got out of there fast."

"Did he follow?"

"All the way to the local police station where I pulled to the curb. He zoomed off. I'd thought he was trying to carjack me. I didn't see his license plate, so reporting it would have been a waste of my time."

"What made you think of Javier?"

"When I left to come here, someone in the dark was watching me. I smelled cigar smoke. My instincts picked up, and I was certain there was someone I couldn't see. Luckily I got a taxi, and on the way here, I put it together. Javier has my driver's license and obviously, my address. Both incidents started from home."

"So what are you thinking of doing about it?"

Swirling the liquid left in her glass, she said, "I'll be on the lookout for him."

Since Annelise was trying to get in her head, Liz would try to warn her about Javier. Maybe leave her a note. That would probably fry Annelise. Or scare her, more likely. But being really scared meant being careful every minute as Liz so well knew, so Annelise's being scared would be a plus.

"Why did you go to see O'Neal?" Chase asked.

"He called and asked me to come to his daughter's apartment. When I got there, it had already been trashed by the cops, but he said he thought if I looked through her things, I might see something they hadn't."

"Did you?" Chase asked, his voice a bit odd.

Liz shook away the thought. "Tully was really there for something else. He knew Kate had been seeing a mystery man. He brought some techware from the office. It recorded all landline and cell phone calls going in and out. A man left a message the night before the fire."

"Go on."

"He played it for me. *Be at the Lincoln Tap at nine tonight.* That was it."

"Not much to go on."

"Not the words, maybe. But the voice…Vinny DeLarosa, the little weasel who works for Durant."

Chase slid his hand across the table and grasped hers. "What do you suggest we do about it?"

Though Liz knew what he meant, she wished for something more personal as warmth spread from her hand up her arm.

"Don't worry, I'm not going to let it go, but I need some breathing room to think this through." Especially since she was worried Annelise might be trying to do the same. "In the meantime, what were *you* up to today?"

"I waited outside Walsh Motors for Durant to leave so I could follow him. But he pulled over and waited for someone to join him. Joyce Hernandez."

"Annelise's assistant?"

"They went to her place in Old Town where she has a garden apartment. I had no idea where he might go or who he might talk to, so I was prepared with some spy tech of my own which would allow me to hear everything going on in that apartment."

"Everything?"

"Unfortunately more than I wanted to hear. But the good thing is I know Durant is using his political contacts and no doubt money to help her alcoholic brother who almost killed someone in a car accident. Even though the SAFE-T Act eliminated the bail system in Cook County, the judge felt his offense was bad enough to hold him behind bars until trial. Somehow, Durant made a deal to get him released on an ankle monitor."

He went on with various things he'd heard, but Liz was aware Chase gave her a highly edited version of the personal stuff. That bastard Durant had seduced Joyce with sex and with promises to help her brother. She downed the rest of her drink. Annelise would have to know about this, and Liz realized she would have to find a way to tell her.

"Which gives me even more thinking to do," Liz said, getting to her feet. "I need to go. Now."

"Whoa, wait a minute." Chase stood and grasped her arms. "We're in this together. We need to talk this out."

"Tomorrow," she promised. "That will give me the time I need to get my life in order." At the moment, the thought seemed overwhelming. Annelise needed to know what she knew, and Liz would have to find a way to tell her.

"So I have no say in how we're going to do this?" Chase asked.

"Of course you do. But my life is complicated. I just need time to think."

Liz reached up and drew his head closer, then touched her lips to his. She was startled when Chase deepened the kiss, making her want to complicate her life even more. His hands slid down to her butt and pulled her tight against him. He rubbed against her and made a sound that almost seduced her. The alcohol was kicking in, the buzz making her think he had a big stick shift, and she could imagine how it would feel to drive it...but not tonight. She bit back a laugh, pulled away and took a step back, still grinning at the silly thought but breathing hard. The way he was looking at her...

"I promise we'll figure it out tomorrow," she said. "Together."

He nodded. "I'll drive you home."

Not wanting to give Chase the opportunity to try to pry open her complicated life on the drive — or to have another opportunity to entice her tonight — Liz backed away, cell phone in hand. "I'll Uber," she insisted.

"I want to make sure you get home safely, Liz. What if Javier is camped out, waiting for you?"

"I doubt it, but I'll take the chance."

"Big surprise."

As she headed into the bar, Chase right behind her, one hot hand on her hip, she ordered a nearby Uber, which appeared in less than the minute it took to step out front. "Tomorrow, Chase," she said as she got in.

As the Uber sped off, she glanced back. Chase stood still, staring after her until the vehicle turned a corner. She took a deep breath. They would figure out what to do *about Durant* together.

But what about *them*?

Liz couldn't deny Chase was the first man in a decade who'd meant anything to her. She'd never met anyone like him. Yes, she wanted him physically, but it was far more than physical. Though she'd originally thought he'd agreed to help her for financial gain, now she thought it was something else. Something going deeper. Perhaps his sense of doing what was right. That was as attractive to her as he was. Not only had he saved her from Javier, he was also on board to help her nail Durant.

When she got back to her secret quarters, she showered and changed into Annelise's clothes, brushed her hair and removed her make-up. Then she took the hidden passageway below ground back to the main house.

Damn! She still had to leave a warning for Annelise. She should have done it at her place. Thinking about it, she took the elevator to the second floor and stepped out only to find Mama in the hallway.

She asked, "What were you doing out so late?"

"Nothing you would want to know about."

Ignoring Mama's call to her, Liz headed straight for Annelise's room. Once inside, she looked for something to write on so she could leave the warning she wanted to give her. Wait. Annelise's cell phone was charging on her make-up table. Liz unplugged it and touched her thumb to the screen to unlock it. She hesitated only a moment before adding her own cell number to the contact list. Then she left a voice activated text to herself making her insides tighten.

"Annelise, so much to warn you about. Durant has your assistant Joyce in his grasp. He's seducing her by promising to help get her brother out of Dodge and using her sexually, too, so he can seduce information about you from her. Be smart around that cheesy bastard! And around Joyce. By the way, this afternoon, it was probably Javier who came after you. I think he was waiting for me tonight. You must be very careful of both men. Keep your head on straight and don't take any chances. I'm so sorry, Annelise. I've tried my best to protect you, to make sure you had the normal life I couldn't have. But I'm not giving up. I promise I will find a way to deal with both bastards."

She couldn't let anything happen to Annelise or it would happen to her, as well. She nearly choked on the idea. Then, after everything she'd done to safeguard Annelise, they might both be gone forever.

When she set the phone back on the make-up table, Liz realized this could be the end for them. Her heart felt like it was pounding, and her breath was coming in short gasps. There was a very real possibility the end of the double life they were leading was near.

Dammit!

She closed her eyes and tried to think of something positive to lift her spirits. When her thoughts were invaded with dark images from the past, she felt no hope and gave in to the grief she'd held at bay for the last decade, ever since she'd lost her twin.

She broke down and wept...

Chapter Fifteen

Annelise awakened sometime before dawn. Still dressed and lying on top of the bed, she was at first confused. Why would she have gone to bed fully dressed? Then her thoughts cleared, and she remembered the aura leading to the blackout. Excitement throbbed through her as she focused on the wall outlet covered with the spycam that would let her see what Liz had been up to.

Getting up, she went to the dresser and her cell phone. Anticipation of what she would see made her pulse hum. According to the instructions, the program would have started recording any time there was movement or sound in the room. The first thing she saw was herself sitting on the bed and passing out. The second was her – rather, Liz – awakening, only to get up, check herself in the mirror, then leave the bedroom without doing or saying anything that would let Annelise gain any kind of knowledge about her alter.

Annelise sighed. She'd been certain Liz's clothes weren't stored in her room because she'd looked for them in vain. But she'd thought she would see or hear *something...*

No doubt Liz's return to the room would be equally unfulfilling. Thinking about where Liz kept her clothes, shoes and make-up, she guessed Liz probably had used the hidden room above the garage which had been an escape on the night her twin had died.

The video was playing again. Liz returning from wherever she had been for the last hour and a half. Annelise was about to turn it off when Liz went straight to the make-up table and unplugged her cell phone. Annelise could see she was adding a phone number to the contact list. Liz clicked on the text app and then held down the icon for an audio message.

Annelise's pulse surged as Liz began to speak.

Annelise, so much to warn you about…

Annelise gasped. Liz had never tried to contact her before, not that she knew of. Then again, Liz may have known about her, but Annelise had only known about Liz for less than a week. Realizing she'd missed some of what Liz said, she backed up the recording and started again.

Annelise, so much to warn you about. Durant has your assistant Joyce in his grasp. He's seducing her by promising to help get her brother out of Dodge and using her sexually, too, so he can get information about you.

She hit pause. What a horrible new thing to learn! She'd thought Joyce was totally loyal to her, believing her assistant had her back, no matter what. That she had at least one person she could count on. Not anymore.

She restarted, her skin crawling when Liz mentioned Javier as the one who'd probably rear-ended her.

I think he was waiting for me tonight. You must be very careful of both men. Keep your head on straight and don't take any chances.

She hadn't taken chances for a decade, not until the fire. Not until suspicion deep inside her gut pushed her to look for the truth, because another woman had died. Annelise was certain Kate O'Neal hadn't set the fire, that she'd been another victim.

I'm so sorry, Annelise. I've tried my best to protect you, to make sure you had the normal life I couldn't have. But I'm not giving up. I promise I will find a way to deal with both bastards.

To Annelise's shock, Liz wept.

The sound choked Annelise. Here she'd been trying to find a way to get rid of Liz, and all this time Liz had been doing her best to protect *her*. To give *her* the life Liz felt she couldn't have for herself!

If only she had known, she might not be feeling guilty now...

When she collected herself, she slipped the cell phone and a small tablet of paper in one pocket, then picked up the spycam.

She checked the time. Nearly four in the morning. No one would be around to see her. Leaving her room, she took the elevator down to the basement level. She hadn't been down here in ten years, but she hadn't forgotten Lizzie's obsession with her FROG — *Finished Room Over Garage*. That was the secret hideaway Daddy had gotten built at seven-year-old Lizzie's request a short while before he'd died. The only access was from the stairs going to the basement, an underground path leading to a the garage-level exit door hidden behind carefully constructed paneling. She opened the door to a walk-in closet, then moved to the entryway to the underground tunnel. Lights flicked on the moment she entered. It took her to the steps leading to the garage and then to the second floor.

Standing before the door to the hidden room, Annelise's stomach knotted. The last time she'd been inside had been the night Lizzie had died. Her memory of that night was pretty much non-existent, but she hadn't forgotten the grief she'd felt at losing her twin. Sometimes still felt.

Taking a slow, deep breath, she slid her fingers along the panel and to the hidden latch that released the door. It slid open. She turned on her cell flashlight and quickly found the switch to illuminate the room.

Nothing had changed as far as the furniture went. A bed, a couple of upholstered chairs, a small table with a mirror, a chest of drawers and a large closet, which now held the bright-colored and sexy clothes and expensive shoes Liz preferred. Annelise spent a few minutes checking out the dresses and outfits she herself would never wear. Too hot, too wild, too much for her taste.

Next to the closet was a dresser. The top drawer was filled with lingerie, the perfect undergarments to go with Liz's clothes. The second drawer had odds and ends like scarves and gloves.

And, oddly enough, a tablet and a cell phone.

She picked up the phone, turned it on and pressed her thumb to the glass, but it didn't get her in. So, not Liz's. Then she turned on the tablet and saw the name James Scanlon on the opening screen. She was fairly certain Liz was into Chase. Maybe this Scanlon guy was an old boyfriend who'd spent time here. Turning off the tablet, she put it back and closed the drawer.

Which is when she turned to the table and saw Liz's cell phone charging.

Great! She wouldn't have to leave her own cell to contact Liz.

Annelise disconnected the phone and pressed her thumb to the screen to unlock it, then did the same thing to her phone that Liz had done to hers. She entered her phone number in the contacts list and hit the text app under her name.

She thought about what she wanted to say for a minute, then started recording.

"Liz, I'm not going to fight you anymore. We need each other. We need to work together to put Durant away so he can't hurt anyone else. If Kate O'Neal was at Parts Replications, it wasn't for business. She was there to see someone. Maybe Durant's snitch Vinny. We need to find out what was going on. What she knew...why she had to die."

Annelise added her cell number, then stopped the recording. After finding Liz's cell number in the directory, she added it to her phone. She plugged in Liz's cell and left a note about the number exchange and said to listen to the message she'd left.

After which she shifted her focus to the bathroom door. She wanted to leave but felt glued to the spot. Heart racing, she opened the door, but couldn't bear to enter the room. She ran her gaze over the toilet and sink and for a moment refused to look directly at the shower. About to step back and close the door, she struggled against the instinct. But when she heard the water running, she forced herself to step inside and toward the shower. Then she forced her hand up toward the shower head and felt the water spilling over it...

Of course the water wasn't running. Her imagination was.

Still, she couldn't move.

She stared at the shower head and tried to force herself to remember the awful night ten years ago...but all she got was the sound of Lizzie's cries. The wails cut through her, brought tears to her eyes, but still no actual detailed memory. Maybe what had happened was so bad she wouldn't ever remember.

She backed up and almost left, then realized she hadn't set up her spycam. There was an outlet near the bed, so she attached it there. Part of her felt guilty at still wanting to see what Liz was up to, but a more urgent part convinced her it was necessary if they were going to be equally involved in Durant's take-down.

The next morning, after thinking about all she'd learned the night before, Annelise realized she still had a real friend, someone she could always count on. She knew Roscoe worked most Saturday mornings, so she called him from home.

"What's going on?" Roscoe asked. "I'm on my way to the shop now."

"I was counting on that. Good. I called at the right time. First, I'm going to bring in the Mustang. My rear bumper needs some work."

"What happened?"

"I got rear-ended." Not wanting to share the real details with Roscoe, who would be furious and determined to protect her somehow, she said, "It's not too bad. Should look like new when you're done with it."

"All right, I can handle work on your car today. What else is on your mind?"

"I have some information I didn't have yesterday. Tully O'Neal thought his daughter was having an affair with a mystery man. Maybe a married one. He found some guy left a message for her to meet him the night before the fire. He played it for me, and I recognized the voice. Vinny DeLarosa."

"The little cretin? Tully's daughter was making it with *him*?"

"I don't know. That's what I was hoping you could find out. That and any other information about him you can dig up."

"Frank Moretti, one of my mechanics, might talk," Roscoe said, "especially if he thought Vinny was cheating on his wife."

"They're friends?"

"Not exactly. Vinny's wife is Frank's sister Gia. He tried talking her out of marrying the little prick. Complains about him all the time."

Annelise hoped his talking to the guy wouldn't screw things up. "Still, he would want to protect his sister. If he tells her what's going on before we can do anything about it—"

"I'll make him see the upside of keeping the info to himself until we have more answers."

"By threatening him?" she asked. "Or by bribing him?"

"Whatever it takes."

Annelise wasn't sure what Roscoe meant by *whatever*. He was cagey, but not violent. If they were dealing with a murderer, they *needed* to do what was necessary to prove it to Detective Turner.

"Whatever it takes." Surely the guy would be willing to cooperate without putting Roscoe at risk. Hoping she had no reason to worry about the man who was like a second father to her, she said, "Call me when you have something."

"Will do."

Satisfied, Annelise started her single-serve coffee maker and got dressed while it was brewing. She'd already texted Joyce that she needed her to come in to work this morning. Joyce's response to working on a Saturday had been less than enthusiastic, but she'd agreed to be there. While part of Annelise wanted to fire the woman, another part thought Joyce might be useful.

She had believed Joyce was in her corner all this time. Obviously, she had given her trust too easily. But her assistant had worked for her for more than two years without a clue she might not be as loyal as she appeared. It would take everything she had to keep Joyce from figuring out how disgusted she was with her. Considering how long she'd kept her cool with Durant, she could do the same with the woman she could no longer trust.

Her coffee was waiting for her. She poured it into her travel mug, snapped on the lid, then headed out.

After dropping off the Mustang with Roscoe, Annelise refused a ride to the office, preferring to walk the few blocks to put her mind at ease. She made a mental list of the things she needed to take care of in the coming week so Durant would just leave her alone. *As if.*

Nearly there, she saw Joyce descend the steps from the elevated stop. Hm, good timing. She slowed down and managed to meet her assistant just as she hit the street.

"Joyce, good morning."

Her assistant seemed surprised. "You didn't drive?"

"I did but left the Mustang at Clean Cars for a small repair." Thinking Joyce seemed a little weird with her, Annelise gave her a half-truth. "The bumper got scratched up by some guy who wasn't paying attention to a light turning red."

"Oh, how terrible!" Joyce was silent for a moment, then asked, "Is that why you were there *yesterday?*"

Guessing Durant was the one who really wanted to know why she'd been there the day before, Annelise continued the lie as they entered the building. "Right, but everyone was so busy, Roscoe asked me to bring it back this morning."

Joyce seemed to be avoiding looking at her. Guilt for throwing in with Durant to save her brother? Was that the only reason she'd had sex with Durant? Whatever the reason, Annelise wasn't going to give Joyce a pass. When they had enough to convict Durant, she would fire her traitorous assistant and find a new one.

"So why did you want me to come in this morning?" Joyce asked. "Something special going on?"

"I decided it's time to do some reorganizing."

"Reorganizing?"

"Right. The records for all six divisions."

Joyce's forehead pulled into a frown. "But I've kept them organized as always."

Annelise smiled at her. "Not the way I would like them, though." Then explained how she wanted them completely redone.

"It's going to take a while, considering how busy I get at the office."

Obviously, Joyce was far from thrilled. Good. "Yes, it will probably call for more overtime." Annelise kept a friendly smile aimed at her new secret adversary. "But I want it done this week. It's why I called you in today, to get started."

Joyce took a big breath and said, "Of course," though she sounded distinctly unhappy.

Annelise swallowed a smile. She intended to keep Joyce so busy she wouldn't have time to spy on her for Durant.

Once in her office, she got to work on a contract for a classic they were selling to a longtime customer. Halfway through the morning, she checked her emails and saw one from the employee she'd assigned to look for a thirties Duesenberg. He'd found a convertible Model J just as Kyle had requested. Calling Kyle would have to wait.

Durant was on her mind.

What kind of information did he expect Joyce to get on her? Did he want to prove she wasn't doing her job? So he could what? Fire her? He couldn't do so when she owned twenty percent of the company and he owned nothing, though he could use Arthur's sixty percent to make her life miserable. Just thinking about it was making her stomach churn, emphasizing how important it was to take quick action against her sleazy stepbrother.

If they could somehow prove he'd had replicas built, that they were the cars destroyed by the fire, and that he was attempting to sell the originals, surely he would serve prison time.

And Kate O'Neal's dying in the fire would elevate the crime to murder.

Her cell rang. She checked to see who. As if he'd had a premonition about the Duesenberg, Kyle was calling her. Though she would have preferred waiting until she was in a better mood before talking to him, she touched the screen to take the call.

"Kyle, you must be psychic. I was just thinking I should call you."

"You were thinking about *me*? I'm flattered."

The sound of his voice relaxed her. She was smiling when she said, "I was thinking about you driving a 1931 Duesenberg Model J Roadster Convertible, deep green with the cream-colored cowl pulled down in back."

"Whoa, exactly the kind of classic I was hoping you would find! A direct sale?"

"Afraid not." Though in fact it was somewhat of a relief she didn't have to deal with negotiating a sale for him right now. "The Duesenberg will be going up for auction two weeks from today. Asking price is two million." Just as she had predicted.

"Where is the auction?"

"Graham Raceway Auctions in Indianapolis."

"I assume we could get a preview."

"*You* could, yes."

"What about us going together? It's only a three hour drive. And we don't have to come back right away. I would bet you could use a day off after all you've been through this week."

Uh-oh, she guessed Kyle had more on his mind than simply buying his Duesenberg.

"I wish I could," she said more cheerfully than she was feeling. "There's so much to deal with here right now. Plus police still haven't nailed the person responsible for the fire, so the investigation is ongoing."

"But *they're* doing the investigating, *not you.*"

She wasn't about to tell him she was trying to get to the truth herself or why. "I'm sorry, Kyle, I just can't right now. I'll email you the photograph of the car and all the information you need about the auction."

"Or you could give it to me tonight. I called to invite you to see my new place and talk about furnishing to complement its age over a catered dinner."

"That sounds lovely, but again—"

"You have too much going on." He sounded disappointed. "Got it."

It sounded like he really did.

The call ended on a down note. While Annelise liked Kyle, he'd been in love with Lizzie. He simply wasn't the right man for her.

Would there ever be one?

Not in the mood to continue working, she prepared a file for Liz on her computer, detailing the classics that supposedly were burned in the fire.

1990 Ferrari Testarossa, red, $279,000

1938 Mercedes-Benz 320 Cabriolet A Convertible, Bordeaux-Red, $650,000

1931 Bianchi S8, a blue/white/lime exterior, $1.3 million

1932 Rolls-Royce Phantom II Convertible, black, $1.2 million

1931 Invicta S-Type Low Chassis, black, $1.4 million

1955 Cooper-Jaguar T38 Mk II Convertible, white, $2.2 million

1967 Ferrari 275 GTB/4, silver, $2.3 million
Sending the file to Liz's phone, she closed down her computer and got her bag. On the way out, she saw Joyce working on one of the lower drawers in the wall unit. She was on her knees.

Did she get on her knees for Durant?

Annelise struck the disgusting image from her mind's eye just as Joyce turned toward her. Faking a smile, she waved and left the office. Out in the executive lounge area, the sound of loud male voices made her stop. Durant and Vinny stood in the doorway to Durant's office several yards away. She backed up out of sight and listened.

"What is so important you don't have time to do it?" Durant demanded.

"I got plans for tonight."

"Change them."

"*Drive with Fury 3* just opened at the Clybourn Theaters. I got plans to go with someone. And after..."

"With your wife?"

"Shit, no, Gia thinks anything I like is trash. I got a date with Desiree, a hot blonde with luscious boobs and a tight ass. Found her on *Chicago Heat*, one of them internet sites. Man, those photos of her body got my engine running."

"Photos on a website got you hot? Everyone knows people lie on those sites. How do you even know if those photos are of this Desiree?" And Durant figured if it was one of those pay for a date sites, Vinny had himself a hooker. "You don't know what this broad really looks like and you're going to go for it anyway?"

"With that body, you bet I am. She's gonna meet me at ten and it's all I can think about, so no, I ain't running your errand tonight."

"You disappoint me, Vinny."

"Now you sound like the wife..."

They quibbled for another minute or two, and then Vinny stalked Annelise's way. Fearing he would see her, she ducked behind a large plant. Peering between the leaves, she could see Vinny never looked her way as he headed for the staircase. She waited a moment, listening hard for Durant to follow. But all she heard was his office door slamming.

And then nothing.

Thinking Liz needed to know what she'd just heard — which meant leaving her another message — Annelise slipped from her hiding place and left the building, heading for Clean Cars and her Mustang.

Chapter Sixteen

A weird feeling urged Liz to awaken and take charge. What was going on? Feeling a little woozy, she checked the clock on the dressing table. Annelise's dressing table! It was barely seven-fifteen, earlier than usual for her to start her evening. Had Annelise forced her to come out and if so, how had she managed it?

Liz left Annelise's room and headed for her quarters above the garage. Once inside, she saw the note on her cell phone, telling her to listen to two voice text messages. In the first, she responded to Liz's warning to her. Annelise wanted to work together to bring Durant down. Her heart raced at the thought. She was vaguely aware of the argument between Durant and Vinny, but Annelise had heard it in person and wanted her to share the details with Chase. Especially details about Vinny's supposed date that night. Plus she'd left her cell number, so Liz could leave Annelise a message from anywhere.

On her phone, Liz found the *Chicago Heat* dating site. Found Desiree. The woman looked hot, but who knows when those photos were taken? They were more about her body than her face. And then Liz saw how much it would cost to make a match and realized it was more than a matchmaking site. She figured what Annelise had made her think about doing with the information could actually work, especially if she had Chase's cooperation.

One thing was clear. She wasn't going to be able to keep her alter out of potential trouble if she didn't act fast. Like tonight.

After showering, she called Chase and asked him to pick her up in twenty minutes. Then she changed into a hot dress and high spiked heels and shoved a few things in a cloth bag. She spent the remaining time on make-up and hair. When Chase texted he was out front, she pulled on a short-sleeved top over the dress, grabbed the bag and her purse and ran out to meet him. The sun was already setting.

As she got in the car, he asked, "Where to?"

"The walkway near Belmont Harbor. Go to Irving and past the tennis courts to the parking area. We need to discuss something and that area is usually quiet at that time."

"Why there?"

"I have my reasons."

Ten minutes later, they were parked and walking along the lake on the highest of four levels, several feet above the water. The sky around them was starting to get dark, but nearby, lights made the harbor area glow, and in the distance, the city was lighting up like a birthday cake.

Chase caught her hand in his and laced his fingers through hers. Warmth spread up her arm, and she took a good look at him. He was smiling at her, making her stomach tighten.

"The city has made some great improvements in this area."

That sounded like Chase knew the harbor area but that it had been some time since he'd been around. "So you've been here before?"

"I'm familiar with it."

How familiar? How long ago? What was Chase's story? She wanted to know everything about him. Then again, she couldn't fault him for not sharing his past. She certainly hadn't shared hers.

"Not many people around today," she said. "Great for some privacy."

"It is getting dark." He raised an eyebrow and grinned at

her. "What did you have in mind?"

The breath caught in her throat for a second. Then she said, "Dealing with a serious situation." At least for now.

She indicated the three foot wall which provided flood control if the lake backed up during storms. Liz pulled her hand free and sat on top of the wall. Chase followed suit, giving her some breathing room.

"So what's going on?" he asked.

"We have an opportunity to get some information this evening."

"What kind of opportunity?"

"To find out if I was right about the cars burned being fakes and Durant selling the real deals to wealthy investors."

"How?"

Again acting as if she rather than Annelise had figured out the first clue, Liz said, "I spent some time with Tully O'Neal in his daughter's apartment. He knew how I felt about the fire and wanted to find the truth. He brought a piece of tech from his office. It recorded messages both from landlines and from cell phones used in the office. He played one Vinny left for Kate the night before the fire. *Be at the Lincoln Tap at nine tonight.*"

Chase swore, then asked, "Who is this Vinny?"

"Durant's snitch. Here comes the good part, the thing that may give us the kind of access we need. The office was basically empty this morning, but I heard the two of them arguing about tonight. Durant had some kind of a job he wanted Vinny to take care of, but it was a no-go. Vinny had a hot date and not with his pregnant wife. Some hottie named Desiree. Found her online. She's a paid companion. He talked her into meeting him at the Clybourn Theaters to see *Drive with Fury 3*."

"So you want to what? Crash their date?"

"No, I'm going to *be* Desiree tonight."

Chase stared at her a moment before asking, "Doesn't he know you?"

"Never actually met him. He may have seen me at work but

certainly never the way I will look tonight. He won't have a clue as to who I am."

Relieved when Chase didn't immediately object, she told him how they were going to do it. And what she thought she was going to get from that prick Vinny.

Before leaving the area, she retrieved the cloth bag she'd left in the car and took it into the nearby public washroom for a makeover — her reason for wanting to meet down by the lake — including a blonde wig like the one she'd seen Desiree wearing on her webpage.

After which they left for the movie theater to execute her plan.

Chase hoped Liz's plan would work the way she believed it would. This could be a brilliant move, or it could be a disaster. He was hoping for the first.

They arrived at the movie complex at 9:40. Entering the lobby, they stood in the back away from everyone. A line of people already waited to get their tickets from three machines at a long counter.

"I don't see Vinny," Liz said. "Or Desiree."

Sensing Liz's nerves were on edge, Chase said, "Probably because we're early. Vinny said he was meeting his hot date at ten, right?"

"Right."

Thinking of hot dates, Chase didn't think one could be hotter than Liz tonight. She'd removed the top she'd worn that had hidden the cut-out areas of her dress. The fullness of her breasts was obvious through an asymmetrical slit going from her right ribcage to her left shoulder, revealing a tattoo — a circle with a small cross above her left breast. Some kind of feminist symbol. The sleek right side of her waist was revealed through a round opening. A long blonde wig hid her warm titian hair, and make-up emphasized her green eyes and full lips.

From the moment she'd returned to the car out at the lake, Chase had wanted to get Liz alone, but they had a plan to follow which would lead to Durant's downfall, so alone time tonight wasn't likely.

"That's her," Liz whispered. "Desiree."

She was pointing to the blonde who'd stopped inside the entry door and was looking around, no doubt for her date. This Vinny had said she was hot, but despite the little pink number she wore which showed off her cleavage and clung to a tight butt, she couldn't compare to Liz.

"Go!" Liz pushed him toward his target for the night.

He stowed his regret at having to leave her and approached the real Desiree. Luckily Vinny wasn't here yet.

"Desiree," he said, stopping in front of her, "you look great tonight."

Her overly made up eyes narrowing on him, she frowned. "How do you know who I am?"

"Vinny, of course. I'm his friend Donny. He can't make it after all, so I'm filling in for him. Um, not to see the movie, though." Wanting to get out of there before Durant's snitch showed, Chase took her arm and gestured toward the door. "I thought we could get to know each other a bit over drinks."

"Whoa. Drinks where?"

"A bar called The Lavender Lounge."

"Isn't that one of them fancy-schmansy places?"

"It's one of the top lounges in the city." And close enough they could have one drink and Chase could put Desiree in an Uber and hurry back to the theater before the movie ended. "But if you're not comfortable with going to The Lavender Lounge, we could—"

"Are you kidding? Let's get outta here."

Desiree charged toward the exit, Chase following.

He glanced back once at Liz and hoped she could manage this Vinny character without putting herself in danger until he could get back and make sure she was safe.

* * *

Pacing the lobby, Liz checked her cell for the time. It was ten exactly. The line to get tickets for *Drive with Fury 3* was non-existent. The last of the moviegoers were entering the auditorium now.

Vinny was late.

Or not coming.

Well, great. Now what?

She went to the wall of windows which let her see part of the parking lot. No movement there, but she kept looking out at the cars, willing Vinny to show.

When a silver Lexus entered the lot and parked, and she finally saw him get out and rush for the entry door, Liz came alive inside. Her pulse buzzed through her. She took a deep breath and when Vinny entered, got right behind him. Then he suddenly stopped, and she nearly ran into his back.

After looking around at the nearly empty area and mumbling to himself, "The bitch was in too much of a hurry to wait, dammit!" he headed for one of the ticket machines.

The comment put Liz off for a moment. Quickly making a decision of how to proceed, she backed off slightly but just far enough that she could still see the screen which showed her what seat he'd just bought. When Vinny headed for the usher standing guard and gave the man his ticket, she quickly stepped up to the ticket machine he'd just used. There was an available seat next to his, one of the few left, no doubt because it was in one of the poorer seats — the first row all the way to the side. She bought the ticket as Vinny stopped at the refreshment stand. When he left it, he was carrying a large popcorn and drink.

Waiting until he entered the theater, Liz followed. The movie was just starting. On the screen, a car flew over a gap in a bridge.

Vinny took his seat at the front of the theater and placed his tub of popcorn on his lap. After a calculated moment, Liz slid into the seat next to him, leaned over, let the cascading curls of her blonde wig brush his face and reached into the tub.

"Hey, what's the big…"

He stopped, and his eyes opened wide as Liz seductively placed the kernels in her mouth. Though they'd never actually met, Liz knew he'd seen Annelise more than once when he'd been with Durant. She'd made sure to look as different as she could from her alter. In addition to wearing the blonde wig, she'd carefully applied make-up like Desiree had worn in those photographs. The eye make-up almost looked like a mask, and generously applied lipstick made her lips appear larger and fuller.

His weaselly eyes focused on them for a moment, then dropped to her cleavage. "Want some more?" he whispered. He nudged her leg with his in a way that told her he didn't really mean the popcorn. His lips were nearly in her ear when he said, "I thought you stood me up, Desiree."

Then he slipped a hand between her thighs. She grabbed it, digging her nails into his flesh. "Not now, not here."

"You two, shut up!" a guy behind them ordered.

She pointed to the screen and mouthed, "Movie first."

Vinny focused on the movie as ordered, while she spent the next hour and a half on Vinny watch. Having to remove his hand from various parts of her body multiple times made her want to break his fingers. Instead, she gave him a fake smile and whispered empty promises in his ear so he wouldn't ditch her when the movie was over.

The big finish race scene couldn't come fast enough for her. She wondered whether Chase had sent the real Desiree home as planned. If so, where was he? There had been a few seats left, but though she looked around, it was too dark to see much. If he was in the theater, she wasn't able to spot him. The movie ended and credits started to roll.

Suddenly feeling Vinny's hand slide around her back to her

right breast, she jammed her body against the seat to crush his arm and whispered, "Not here!"

Removing his hand and then arm, Vinny grumbled, "Can't blame a guy for trying."

Thankfully, since the credits were playing, moviegoers were getting up and leaving. Liz got to her feet. "Let's go."

As they headed for the lobby, she looked for Chase while Vinny rubbed himself against her butt. Ready to smack the crap out of him, Liz held herself in check. She had a plan and was determined to keep him in line until she could execute it.

"Where to now?" Vinny asked as they left the theater and headed for his car. "Your apartment?"

"How about a classy bar?" She regretted not thinking to tell Chase to wait for them at the Lavender Lounge. "I could use a drink."

Vinny's "I could use a drink of you!" made Liz want to gag.

Instead, she forced another smile and said, "Don't get ahead of yourself."

After dodging a couple of cars heading for the exit, Vinny stopped at the silver Lexus and placed a possessive hand on the roof. "New wheels."

The Lexus was the latest model. It probably cost a small fortune. Where would a mechanic have gotten that kind of money? No doubt handling crooked business for Durant.

"Great package." Liz stroked the car's hood as if it were a man's body.

Vinny gave her a lusty grin. "You, too."

"Mmm, a sixty-five thousand dollar penis."

Vinny snorted. "Seventy-five."

"I like expensive toys."

"Something we got in common." He moved in closer.

Liz retreated and avoided another moving car. The lot was emptying fast.

"We have a common friend, too," she lied. "He tells me you deal in even pricier wheels."

Vinny's eyes narrowed and he suddenly appeared suspicious of her. "What friend?"

She ignored the question. "Classics, right?"

"You gotta be kidding. Do I look like a fat cat?"

"Well, a poor man wouldn't be driving a new Lexus. I have another friend with an expensive appetite, only he *is* a very fat cat. And he's in the market for a classic. He's particularly interested in a classic Ferrari." As in one of the two Ferraris that supposedly had been burned in the fire.

"So why come to me?"

Liz moved in on him, running her long nails down his chest. "I was hoping you could get him a real *steal.*" She paused for a second, then gave him her best engineered smile. "You know, a reasonable mark-up."

His eyes narrowed on her. "You're pretty slick. Too shrewd to be the Desiree advertised on *Chicago Heat.*"

"What's in a name? She had another appointment, so I *am* Desiree tonight."

"Yeah, well, forget tonight. What kinda con are you trying to pull on me?"

"No con. If he was able to buy the classic at a reasonable price, my friend would be happy, which would make *me* very, very grateful."

"Yeah? How grateful?"

Liz laughed, barely brushing his body as she moved away. "We'll see when you come through for me. You do whatever is necessary to make it happen. Where can I find you tomorrow night?"

"You know so much, you figure it out." Getting into his car, he grinned like he was challenging her to do so.

"I'll call you to find out."

Vinny laughed. "You ain't got my number, baby."

"I have your number, all right." A double entendre — she could read him like a book, plus…"You had to give your cell number to get on the *Chicago Heat* site. A friend of mine runs it." And she could also get whatever she needed from his employee records.

With a sour expression aimed at her, he started the engine, and Liz watched him drive off.

Chapter Seventeen

Thinking she'd better call Chase and tell him the game was over for the night, she started when she felt familiar arms wrap around her waist. Chase's breath against her ear sent a shiver through her. "I thought you were going to take him to a bar to get what you needed."

She turned to face him. "Didn't have to. He's primed. He'll tell Durant he found a client."

"You're sure of that?"

"I trust my instincts. I told him I would call him tomorrow."

"All right, then. Are you ready to go home?"

"Hell, no. I'm wide awake." Liz wasn't sure she was going to sleep tonight. "Too much adrenaline. Too much to think about."

"Then how about discussing what's haunting you over a drink that will relax you?"

"*Stewie's?*"

"*Stewie's,*" he agreed, leading her to the Jaguar and reaching past her to open the door. Cigar lounges didn't stay open as late as regular bars, so they'd have the place to themselves. Before she could turn to get into the car, he pulled her closer. "I've been wanting to kiss Desiree since I met her."

Though Liz tried to pull away, he was reluctant to let her go. She said, "You had plenty of time to kiss her at the Lavender Lounge."

Chase grinned and shook his head. "Not *that* Desiree." And kissed *her.*

Liz let her mind drift for a moment. Her heart was racing, and her knees went weak. Then a car horn blared at them and made her jump back against the Jaguar. Teenagers in a passing car waved at them and laughed.

"Little creeps." She couldn't help but grin. "Let's get out of here."

Chase opened the door for her, and she slid in.

They were both silent as he drove.

Liz was too busy thinking to talk, thinking about what the kiss might have meant to Chase. Pulling off the wig and the cap under it, she used her fingers to fluff out her real hair. Had he been kissing *her* or the woman she'd pretended to be tonight? And why did it matter so much to her?

Traffic was light at this time of night and, despite the start of a summer rain, Chase drove fast, so they arrived at *Stewie's* in less than ten minutes.

Slowing the Jag, he groaned. "Should have known. No parking. I'm going to take the car around back."

"There's parking in back?"

"Only Stewie's spot. He doesn't show until afternoon. I can always move the car in the morning before Stewie gets here."

The rain was coming down hard now. After Chase parked, he said, "Looks like we're going to get wet. No umbrella in the car."

"I'll give you a head start to get the back door open."

Grunting, Chase got out and moved fast. The moment he inserted his key in the door lock, she followed. They were both wet by the time they got inside.

Liz laughed. "That cooled me off. Now I'm chilly."

"Then let's get you a drink."

She followed him through the small kitchen area in back into the main room, not stopping until they hit the bar. Chase pulled a bottle of tequila from the shelf. "Have you ever tried it?"

"Nope. Years ago, I found a drink I liked and stuck with it."

"Hmm. How about trying something new? This is prime tequila."

"Sure, hit me."

Chase poured a jigger of tequila in a glass he set in front of her. And another for himself. "Here's to being adventurous." He downed his shot.

Liz took a sip of hers — "Okay" — then followed his lead. The tequila burned its way down her throat, but she shrugged. "Woo!"

"Being adventurous can have its setbacks."

She had the feeling he meant more than trying the tequila. "As in?"

"Danger."

"Wait. You think I'm putting myself in danger with the tequila? Or with Vinny?"

"Neither. But don't you believe Durant is dangerous? You don't think he would let this Vinny handle a sale on a classic, do you?"

"No way. He's going to damn well do it himself."

Chase poured them second shots. "So, that means you'll come face to face with Durant, right? Do you really think *he'll* buy you as Desiree?"

"He's greedy enough, so I expect he'll see the money he thinks he'll get rather than me. Besides you're going to be there up front and center. You'll be the guy supposedly *with* the money, so you'll be doing the talking, and he'll be all over you."

Surprised she wasn't feeling any effects from the first shot of tequila, Liz downed the second.

"Liz, I think you're fooling yourself."

"So you think I should just ditch the plan? You're the one who's going to be making the deal with Durant. I'll disappear in the background."

"You'll always be seen...at least by me." Chase downed his shot and poured them thirds. "Though I do think you should let me handle Durant from here on."

"Handle him how?" Liz clinked his glass and drank when he did.

"Not tonight." Chase reached for her. "Tonight I want to handle *you.*"

As he slid his arms around her, Liz finally felt the alcohol kick in. "Like drinking firewater," she whispered as she swayed against him. She was hot all over, eager for his kiss, for his hands on her back pulling her closer to him.

When Liz slid her hand along Chase's side, he gasped and jerked away from her touch. Pulling away, she realized she'd hit the wound Javier had given him. "Sorry!"

"Don't be. I'll live." Chase started to move in on her, but Liz backed off.

"You could be right about the danger thing," she said. "I don't want you getting hurt again on my account. Maybe we should involve Detective Turner now. Then if Durant tries to sell you one of the cars that supposedly burned, we'll have him. Kate O'Neal died in the fire, remember."

"How could I forget?" His voice deepened and his expression went dark. "But you can't believe Turner will go along with us involving ourselves in a dangerous situation."

"Why not? He can be there, with as many men as he wants out of sight. In addition to fraud and theft, Durant will at least be charged with manslaughter."

"If it *was* manslaughter." Chase looked like he didn't believe it was. "We need proof of exactly what kind of guilt Durant is hiding."

"But —"

Chase cut off her protest with another kiss that drove away thoughts of Durant. Liz felt his anger dissipate as the kiss deepened and she wrapped her arms around his neck. His arms secured her waist, his hands her butt. He lifted her and she wrapped her legs around his hips. He danced her into his dark temporary housing, but rather than the cot, he set her on the pool table.

Liz's mood shifted along with the move. "Now this is adventurous."

He hopped up beside her. "This is wider than my bed. And probably more comfortable than the lumpy mattress." He pushed her shoulder and went down with her, so they were both lying on the felt. "Besides, I wasn't thinking of playing…well, not pool."

Grabbing a loose ball, he rolled it into a table pocket near her head. Then slid his arms around her and pulled her tight against him.

Liz's mouth went dry, and her pulse kicked up. Chase kissed her again and her awareness suddenly shifted from this barely lit room to a deeper darkness inside her mind. She was here with Chase and yet not. The past crept closer, some unknown terror threatening to overtake her. She fought the potential memory, fought to stay in the present with the man she was beginning to care about.

Chase felt the shift in Liz. Something was wrong. Her breath came quick and hard, and she trembled in his arms. He would swear she wanted to be with him fully, yet she wasn't okay. Wasn't ready for more. Protective instincts coming to the fore, he slid his arms around her and simply pulled her against him and held her until she relaxed. Her body softened against his. Her breathing shifted.

She was asleep.

Had she passed out from the tequila? Had drinking shifted her mood? Or was there some deeper reason he knew nothing about?

The tequila would be the easy answer. Too easy, he suspected. Something had happened to her in the past to make her the woman she was now. Strong. Powerful at best. Determined to bring down Durant.

Durant.

Had the fuck done to Liz what he'd done to Katie?

Chase held Liz fast, determined that she wouldn't end up dead the way his sister had.

Thinking his brilliant plan was taking its time to pay off, Durant tapped his code to turn off security before pulling into the old Humboldt Park warehouse where a half-dozen classic cars were shrouded both by protective coverings and the darkness. An incredible haul, from a 1990 Ferrari Testarossa at just under three hundred thousand to a1932 Rolls-Royce Phantom II at two million plus.

Vinny had left him a message to get there as soon as he could. Durant sat in the dark, waiting for a minute, wondering where in the hell the little dick was. The security system would let the mechanic use a code to get in, as well. As Durant got out of the car, the shop lights came on, and Vinny raced across the garage to meet him.

Puffing, he said, "I was startin' to get nervous."

"I can smell you sweating. So what's so important?" Durant approached one of the shrouded cars.

"We got a bite."

"Through whom?"

"This broad I had a date with tonight. A hot number, a pro," Vinny told him. "Says a friend of a friend told her I might be able to hook her up with a classic Ferrari. Another *friend* is the buyer."

Vinny appeared and sounded a little too edgy for Durant.

"What's wrong with this picture? How would she know someone who knows about our undercover operation?" Had Vinny told someone about it? "I don't like angels showing up out of nowhere. Especially not a hot one." Who no doubt had already seduced Vinny mentally with some kind of promise if not with fact.

"So we'll be extra careful."

"If you're wrong…"

"Cut the crap, Durant. You ain't had a bite. I gotta feeling about this. It could really lead to a sale. And me some extra cash since I brought it in."

Durant glared at him. "Agree to a meeting. Both her *and* the buyer." That way, if necessary, they could both be taken care of together. Not the first time he'd had to get rid of a problem. "It's a big gamble, but one I suppose we'll be taking until all these beauties have new homes. Then I'll have the money to buy out Annelise."

"What if your tight-ass stepsister don't wanna sell?"

Durant clapped the mechanic on the back. "Ah, Vinny, sometimes you are naive. Women are weak creatures. Controllable. I already know her G-spot. All I have to do is stroke it at the right time."

Whether or not she agreed to it…

It was nearly five in the morning when Liz entered the garage and went straight up to her quarters. She'd slept in Chase's arms for hours. Still thinking about him, about how they'd seemed in perfect sync on the hard pool table until some damn memory tried to kick in, she was startled when she opened the door to a dark room. Odd, since she always left the light on when she went out. Sensing someone had been inside her room while she'd been gone, she flipped the switch and when the light snapped on took a good look around. The room was exactly as she'd left it…

…except for the folded piece of magenta-colored paper in the middle of the floor…

"What the hell?"

Pulse fluttering unevenly, Liz stooped to pick up the paper and unfold it.

I know where you live.

The message made her catch her breath. And then she muttered, "Fuck!"

Who else could it have been from other than Javier? The snake had her original driver's license which gave him her address. Now it had to be him trying to frighten her. First hitting the Mustang, then waiting outside, smoking his cigar in the greenery to spy on her. Undoubtedly he'd seen her come from the garage and had somehow found her quarters.

Had he jimmied her lock and let himself in? How could she be sure he wasn't still here? Crumpling up the paper and discarding it, she picked up an umbrella as a weapon. She checked the bathroom and closet. No one hiding in either place. Relieved, she took a big breath and made sure the entry door was double-locked.

Then she quickly undressed, washed her face, redid her hair and donned the clothes she'd been wearing earlier before changing to become Desiree. Checking her mirror, she looked like Annelise again.

Taking the umbrella with her, she unlocked the door — relocking it behind her — popped a secret panel in the nearby wall, slid through the opening and, head turning, eyes searching every dark corner, made her way down the stairs all the way to the underground tunnel. The passageway that would take her to the house was dank and poorly lit by a few bare bulbs. Surely the person who'd invaded her space didn't know about the tunnel. Even so, she remained aware, turning in a circle every few yards, ready to run or fight whoever might be waiting for her if the feeling of being watched was real.

A skittering noise made her jump and freeze. She stared deep into the shadows, heart racing. Then she spotted the rat scurrying into a hole in the wall where it disappeared. She shook off the spooky feeling and stepped around puddled murky water, the remnants of the night's rain.

Reaching another secret panel that would take her into the basement of the house — rather into a basement closet — Liz opened it and stepped inside where she waited a moment and listened. Nothing. But the feeling of being watched wouldn't dissipate. She left the closet and headed for the elevator to the second floor. No one to question her as she made for Annelise's room.

Once inside, she took her first easy breath…

…until she noted the charging cell phone and realized how much she had to share with her alter to bring Annelise up to speed.

Chapter Eighteen

"What was so important that you had to see me today?" the psychiatrist asked as she took her seat opposite the recliner. "As I said, I have a rule that I never see clients on Sunday, but the fact that *you* called for the first time, Liz...that you *allowed* yourself to sound frightened...I felt I had to break my own rule. You've never relaxed talking with me before, so I feared it might discourage you if I didn't agree."

"Thanks for breaking your rule." It had taken several phone calls throughout the day to get Marva to agree to this appointment. It was nearly six in the evening, and Liz had to meet Vinny at eight. "We both appreciate your time. It's not just me who needs you. So does Annelise."

"I agreed to see *you* because you sounded frantic, Liz."

Who wouldn't be frantic with a creep like Javier after her? "So you knew it was me who made the last call."

"Of course I did. The way you phrase things...you and Annelise sound like two different people.

A fact that Liz couldn't argue with and now made her feel a bit guilty that she hadn't trusted Marva from the first time they'd met. Just as she had been trying to physically protect Annelise for so long, the psychiatrist had done the same for Annelise's mental stability.

"A few days ago, Annelise and I started communicating by leaving phone messages for each other."

"Communicating? Why that's great progress!"

"And necessary. We're in a really bad situation, working together to take Durant down *now.* And he's not our only problem. We have a stalker, one who wants some kind of revenge. Dealing with two dangerous men…Annelise and I have to be able to communicate with each other faster. Starting tonight."

"Tell me about this situation."

"I already told you about Javier." Liz pulled out the rumpled magenta note. "That night I took him on at the bar, I dropped my bag, and the contents flew onto the pavement. I thought I'd retrieved everything, but when I got to the car, I saw Javier pick up something and then aim a malevolent smile at me." She handed the note to Marva. "I assume he was stoked because he had my driver's license and our address."

"*I know where you live.* Hmm, so you think he left this note to scare you?"

"To threaten me. It wouldn't be the first time. And now he's upped his game."

"What do you mean? What do you think this Javier will do to you?"

"More of what he's already done."

Liz brought the psychiatrist up to speed, telling her about Annelise being rear-ended and chased until she'd stopped in front of a cop shop. Then about the cigar smoke in the garden area and her sensing someone was there when she came out of the garage the other night.

"I think he was there watching. Waiting for an opportunity to get at me…"

"You didn't see his face?"

Liz shook her head. "I didn't spot him at all. I just felt him, and I got out of there as fast as I could. Annelise saw the guy who rear-ended her in her sideview mirror, but he was wearing a baseball cap, so she couldn't really see his face."

The psychiatrist waited for a moment as if absorbing all Liz told her. Then she said, "So now that you and Annelise are communicating, what do you need from me?"

"A way to communicate faster."

"Faster? Or instantly?"

Liz nodded. "Instantly would be safest. I need to know what Annelise knows, and she needs to know what I do at all times."

"So you want to integrate—"

"Whoa! I didn't say anything about that, Marva." The idea nearly choked Liz. She feared integration would mean she would simply disappear.

"All right."

Apparently the psychiatrist was backing off after hearing her reaction. Liz was relieved Marva wouldn't press them to jump into anything.

"Let's start with your being open to each other, to psychically hear what's going on at all times."

"Yes. Good. How would we manage that?"

"I can implant the imperative in both you and Annelise if you agree to hypnosis again."

A shiver shot through Liz as she considered the suggestion. If they were hypnotized again, Marva could do whatever she wanted to them.

"Don't worry, I won't try to force integration on you. It wouldn't work without you both agreeing. You both have to want to heal first."

To heal? She didn't even know from what. Still, Liz said, "All right, Marva, I'll put my trust in you."

"Good. Then get comfortable." The psychiatrist dimmed the lights as Liz reclined. "Take three deep breaths and close your eyes. Slow down your breathing."

Liz relaxed as best she could and concentrated on the psychiatrist's modulated, soothing tone.

"Notice how your breathing feels...how it has slowed...how it calms you..."

Her thoughts quieted as she relaxed each part of her body as

Marva suggested. Eventually, her mind began to float in a darkness which had no end.

"Liz, you came to me asking for help because you feel you and Annelise need a more direct contact than leaving messages for each other. Are you willing to let her know what is going on with you at all times?"

"Yes."

"Will you allow her to hear what you hear when you are in charge?"

"I will."

"Good. Then I'm going to ask Annelise to talk to me, and I want *you* to hear what *she* says. Do you agree?"

"I agree."

"Annelise, are you present?"

Liz *felt* her alter's presence, but now the time had come, and she could tell Annelise was uncomfortable. Hesitant. *Please, Annelise, don't be afraid to do this. Trust me. I won't let anything bad happen to you, I promise.* With that, she allowed her mind to slip back into the darkness...

"I'm here," Annelise said. "And I heard. This is important, Dr. Jackson. Liz and I need to figure out how to work together when we're not under hypnosis."

"I can help with your doing so. Do you agree when Liz is in charge, you will know what is happening with her, and when you're in charge, she will know what you do?"

Though the thought terrified her — what if she lost herself? — Annelise knew she had to seize the moment. She had to stop being cautious and afraid of change. "Of course I agree."

"You agree Liz can hear your thoughts?"

"I do."

"Then we're good for now. You have both agreed, so you will know all that is going on with each other. It's a start. We'll talk more about how it's working for you both next time. I'm going to count backward from three, Annelise, and when I get to one, you'll open your eyes...feel refreshed...and remember everything. Three...two...one."

Annelise opened her eyes.

"How do you feel?"

"Afraid." Definitely not refreshed. "I know you spoke to Liz about integration. I'm not ready for that, either."

"Not yet. You won't be ready for a real change until you deal with the trauma."

"Trauma? What trauma?"

"Whatever you went through to cause the dissociative identity disorder. I can help you go back ten years. You need to remember and accept the trauma that occurred to you back then and look at it from a distance, so while you recognize it, you don't keep re-experiencing it. We can work on controlling the memory next time, as well."

Annelise tightened with dread. "I don't remember what happened, and I don't want to think about it."

"Not now perhaps, but when you least expect it, the memory may come to you. If it happens, try to be open to the past. Don't push it away. Examine it. Use it. Knowing and dealing with what happened will give you purpose and help you heal. The memory may be accompanied by feelings of helpless-ness...betrayal...anger. But we can work through any negativity. You just need to give it some time."

Thinking about facing the past, Annelise could hardly breathe. "If I remember, it could be over for me. And for Liz."

"Over how? What do you fear will happen?"

Annelise couldn't take an easy breath. Panic threatened to overwhelm her as she said, "That it's my turn to die."

It was Annelise's turn to die?

Liz rode the thought all the way home as she drove the Mustang after Annelise psychically hid from her. Had something happened to her alter that she hadn't shared? Rather to them both, because they were parts of the same person. Even as she thought it, she remembered the dark memory she had picked up on when Annelise was struggling against Javier outside the bar. Did it have something to do with Lizzie's death?

Whatever it is, you can handle it. You might think you can't, but you're the strong one...

She would swear she just heard her dead sister! "Lizzie, is that you?"

Who else would it be?

Suddenly Liz felt like she couldn't breathe, and her hands tightened on the steering wheel.

The car behind her honked. Startled, Liz realized she'd let up on the accelerator. Rather than speeding up, she pulled over to the curb and stopped. A couple of deep breaths calmed her. Her imagination was running wild. She checked the time. It was already after seven. Turning on her cell, she called Chase, who could bring her back down to reality.

He answered on the first ring. "Liz. Finally. I've tried calling you several times. We have plans to make."

Right. She couldn't tell him about maybe hearing a dead woman. They both needed to be sharp to pull off this con that would prove Durant was guilty of causing the fire and who knew what else.

Liz took a deep breath. "Sorry. My cell was off. I had something important to take care of. And I got the information we need for tonight."

"Vinny's whereabouts?"

"Yep. North Branch Bowl at eight."

"He's going bowling? So he invited you to join him?"

"Nope. I did it all on my own when I called him. Hah, he was surprised to hear from me, but he didn't object. He said he wanted to know more about this friend looking for a classic Ferrari. We could discuss it over the phone, but I guess he wanted to see more of my Desiree."

"You're going in disguise. Good. For all we know, Durant could be with him."

"Durant in a bowling alley?" She snorted.

"Yeah, probably not. But *I* will be there."

They made plans. Vinny would be there at eight, so Liz would give him twenty minutes to wonder if she would show. Chase would arrive there before either of them. He would try to get one of the tables close to Vinny, though he had to wait to see what lane the mechanic would occupy.

"Take an Uber," Chase said. "I'll make sure you get home safe and sound."

His tone was so masculinely protective it made her grin. "Yessir! I have to get going. It's after seven already. Becoming Desiree takes some doing."

"Then I'll see her in an hour."

Liz hurried home and pulled the Mustang into the garage. Before going to her room, she stepped outside to make sure that no one was out there watching her from the garden. She saw nothing, heard nothing, smelled nothing. No cigar smoke tonight.

Relieved but with all senses on alert for trouble, she turned toward the garage only to hear "Miss Covington, I've been waiting to speak to you."

Recognizing the man's deep voice, she turned toward him wearing an insincere smile and, thankfully, Annelise's clothing. Detective Marcellus Turner was coming toward her from a parked car. What the hell was he doing here at her home?

"Detective Turner, do you have news on the fire?" she asked hopefully.

"Nothing I can share. But I have a question for you, Miss Covington. Do you know Javier Delgado?"

Javier? What in the world could this be about?

Frowning, she shook her head. "Name doesn't ring a bell with me."

Turner pulled out his cell phone and showed her the line-up photo. "This man — do you recognize him?"

Of course she did. So of course she said, "No. Why?"

He slid his cell into a pocket and pulled out something else. "Who would be using this driver's license?" He held out *her* license — the one Javier had picked up off the street — now encased in protective plastic.

She did her best to appear shocked when her stomach suddenly tied itself in knots. "Elizabeth Covington?" She shook her head. "But Lizzie is dead. I don't understand."

"Neither did I, especially since she died ten years ago, and this is a current license."

Liz told herself he couldn't have a clue about her real life. She shrugged. "Maybe someone paid to have that made. Identity theft. You hear stories all the time about a criminal taking over the life of someone who is dead."

He shook his head and pointed to the gold star in the upper right corner. "This license is REAL-ID compliant. Whoever had this made needed valid hard copy documents to get it."

Though her gut tightened, Liz kept her cool. "I assure you my sister is dead. Those documents could have been forged, too. It would seem that whoever approved it wasn't diligent enough in his or her duty." She held out her hand. "I'll destroy it."

Turner pulled back the driver's license and tucked it into his pocket. "So you have no idea where this came from?"

"I don't, but you must. Where did you get it? From that Javier guy?"

"Any idea of why he might have had it on him?"

"Not a clue." Liz's mind was racing. Javier had apparently been arrested. Had he explained the license had been in her purse? Was Turner trying to trick her into admitting it? "So you took it from a criminal. Did this Javier Delgado say where *he* got it?"

He gave her the cop stare. "If you have any thoughts on this license, you'll let me know?"

"Yes, of course."

Turner backed away. "Then you have a good evening."

"I'll try."

Taking a calming breath as Detective Turner left, Liz waited until he drove off before going up to her quarters. Her mind was still spinning. If Javier had been arrested, when had that been? Before or after he'd rammed the Mustang and had laid in wait for her in the garden? *If it had been Javier.* Not knowing when he'd been arrested or if he was being held in jail rather than released after a hearing as Joyce's brother had been, she couldn't be certain he'd been the guilty one.

She thought about the men she'd messed with recently who might like some revenge against her. Last month she'd kicked that Mark guy into the lake off a pier. He'd been trying to force a girl onto a boat parked in a docking slip when she didn't want to go with him. The girl had run like she was being chased. She remembered the nameless guy on the street corner who'd pressed himself up against the ass of a young woman who'd screamed. Liz had whacked the side of his neck with her fist to make him let her go. Then there was Scanlon and the damage she'd done to his life. But none of those men had a clue as to who she was or where to find her.

Relieved that she'd at least handled Turner without panicking, but with all senses still on alert for trouble, she went up to her hidden room without incident. Once inside, she took a quick shower, then stepped into a sexy red mini dress with long bell sleeves, a cut out between her breasts and another down her left thigh which had tie-up strings. Checking herself out in the mirror, she wasn't thinking of Vinny but of Chase. Wondering how long it might take him to do more than admire the look. The thought made her grin, and her stomach tightened a bit.

If the opportunity to get closer presented itself, she wasn't going to fall asleep on him tonight.

She spent the next twenty minutes on makeup and donning the blonde wig. When she was done, she didn't recognize her own reflection. Perfect. It was just about eight. Exactly late enough to get to the bowling alley to worry Vinny just a little.

Grabbing her bag and heading for the door, she sensed a worried Annelise was tuned into her.

"Lighten up, Annelise. It's going to be okay. I can handle Vinny DeLarosa. He'll play right into the plot we set up for him. With his help, we'll get Durant, soon enough."

Liz slinked into North Branch Bowl at 8:17. Perfect timing. She spotted Chase at one of the tables behind the lanes right away. He raised his beer in a salute and nodded at her.

It took her a minute to spot Vinny. He was picking up a red ball and setting himself up in the lane. Looked like he was with a couple of bowling buddies, one on the scorekeeper's seat, the other on the bench in back. Not a great start. She wasn't about to chat with him in front of his friends.

Vinny rolled the ball down the center of the alley and knocked down all ten pins. "Yeah!" Pumped, he gave the scorekeeper a high five.

Then his gaze connected with Liz in her disguise. She stood behind the bench, watching as he bent over and whispered something in his buddy's ear. He grinned at her and pointed to her and then in the direction of the bowling alley lounge.

She moved in that direction, and he was at her side in seconds, his gaze locked on her breasts. "You look a little tight tonight. Some booze will loosen you up."

"I could use a drink," she said agreeably, following him into the nearly empty lounge, dark but for multiple neon signs lining the walls.

A glance back assured her Chase was leisurely following, beer in hand, taking a seat at the front of the bar.

Vinny led her to a booth in the corner. "Sit. I'll get the beers."

"Okay with me, sweetie."

The moment he turned his back on her, Liz let her smile fade. So far, the ruse was going as she'd hoped, but she knew it could backfire at any time. She had to stay convincing.

So when Vinny came back with two bottles of beer, she gave him a sexy smile, winked and clinked her bottleneck against his. "To a successful sale."

"I knew I could count on you."

He could count all he wanted, but he wouldn't get what he no doubt expected of her. "The question is, can I count on *you* to set up this sale for my friend?"

"*Your* friend can count on *my* friend," Vinny said. He slipped her a piece of paper. "That's the location. My friend and I will be there tomorrow at midnight, and you be there with yours."

Liz glanced at the address, then slipped the paper into her bag. "He'll want to know a price."

"Can't give it to you."

"That's ridiculous, expecting him to just show not having the information about cost."

Vinny shrugged. "I can't give you what I don't have."

Realizing she would waste her time trying to pry it out of him — maybe he didn't have the information — she said, "My friend will be pumped."

"What about you?" Vinny asked.

"If the sale goes through, I'll be in ecstasy."

"Mm, I hope you plan on taking me with."

Enjoying reeling him in, Liz raised an eyebrow. "I'll take you on a ride you'll never forget." That was a promise, though not one Vinny would appreciate if he had a clue as to what was going down.

Grinning, Vinny toasted her with his beer and drained the bottle. He slammed it down and backhanded his mouth to wipe it dry. "You know, something's been bothering me."

"So you've been saying."

He stared intently, as if trying to see through her skin.

"Other than that. There's something about you. Something familiar."

Uh-oh, was he about to nail her as Annelise? She froze for a second.

Don't let him throw you, Liz. Pour it on.

Liz smiled and used her most come-on tone when she said, "Believe me, I'd remember if I met a man like you before."

Vinny swallowed her statement as if it was a compliment and preened. "If this transaction goes through, we'll celebrate, and I promise you'll never forget me."

She gave him a thousand watt smile. "Nor you me." She got to her feet.

"Hey, you're not going so soon, are you? Let the celebration begin."

Liz tsk-tsked. "The idea was to make arrangements for the possible sale tonight. Which we did. We don't have anything to celebrate." She winked at him. "Yet." And then walked off, straight past Chase as she headed for the exit.

Chase waited until Liz was outside of the bowling alley, then got up and followed. Once outside, he looked around and finally spotted her against a tree near the Jaguar. As he approached her, he glanced back to make certain Vinny hadn't come outside to follow Liz. No sign of the mechanic, so he quickly unlocked the passenger door. She got in while he went around to the other side.

Settling in his seat, he asked, "You got what we came for?"

"An address in Humboldt Park. It's a storage area for a lot of companies, so I assume this is some kind of garage. And a time tomorrow night. Ten-thirty. He said the Ferrari would be there and that his *friend* wanted cash."

"How much?"

"Didn't say."

Chase whistled and started the car. "We'll have to figure out how to handle this."

"Easy. You want to see and drive the product before you decide what it's worth."

He had a feeling she'd already devised a plan. "And then what?"

"You'll say you can meet him the following day with the money, in an area that *isn't* deserted for the exchange. Assuming you like the test ride, of course. We need to get out of the garage in Humboldt Park. Not exactly the safest place in the city."

"Good idea. Who knows what he has planned."

"A reason I think we should involve Detective Turner as I suggested before."

Chase shook his head. "No go. We'll record everything instead. You involve the police too early, and things won't go the way you think they will."

"They may not anyway."

"But we'll have a chance to do this the way we want without interference."

"All right."

Liz's voice was tight, making him think she was nervous about how this was all going to work out. He reached over and placed a hand on her thigh that was tight with tension.

"Working together, we'll see Durant pay for his crimes," he assured her, gently rubbing. "I swear." He felt the tautness of her flesh loosen up. "We should go over our plans together, make sure we've thought of everything."

"At *Stewie's?*"

"At *your* place."

"I don't have any tequila." She sounded a bit breathless at the idea. "I do have a bottle of wine we could—"

"All I want to taste tonight is *you.*"

"Ohhh."

When she let out a big breath and cleared her throat, he grinned. Didn't sound like she was going to fall asleep on him tonight.

* * *

"You need to look for a parking spot on another street. Turn here" Liz said a street early. "If Durant spots this Jaguar anywhere near the house, Durant will surely come looking for the owner."

"Which would ruin our plans for taking him down," Chase said. "Not to mention our plans for tonight."

The *tonight* part made her pulse kick up. Thoughts of spending a night with Chase left her a little conflicted.

Luckily, they found a spot halfway up the block. Chase slipped an arm around her waist as they backtracked to her family property. Liz kept an eye out for anyone who might be watching them. The street was quiet tonight. No smell of cigar smoke. Nothing that made the back of her neck crawl with apprehension.

Even so, Liz experienced some trepidation of a different type as they walked into the garage. Butterflies. She had feelings for Chase, was physically attracted to him, but she didn't know if she was mentally ready to take their relationship in the obvious direction it was heading.

Until Chase swept her into his arms and kissed her. Warmth shot through her, and she wrapped her arms around his neck. He made her feel whole, not just someone's alter. She had to admit that he might be something she needed in her life.

Ending the kiss, he kept her in his arms. "So how do we keep Durant from spotting us?"

"We're not going near the house. We're going upstairs to my FROG."

"Finished Room Over Garage?"

Liz grinned. "Right. Did you have one of those?"

"No. I wanted one, but Da thought I was nuts."

She led the way through the hidden door to the staircase, still with doubt whispering through her. His not getting why she wasn't always Liz wasn't fair to him. He was a man who cared about people. Plus, Chase wasn't just some guy who could give her physical satisfaction. He was someone who brought her out of herself, who could expand her world and make her feel alive again.

Whoa! Where had that last thought come from? She *was* alive. Of course she was, at least when she chose to be. When she wasn't on the off mode and Annelise was in charge.

As she unlocked the door to her quarters, Chase nuzzled the back of her neck. A thrill shot through her, all the way down to her toes, and she swallowed hard. This might be just for tonight, so what was she worrying about? Even so, she couldn't forget that he had a right to know what was going on with her and Annelise. She had no clue how to tell him so that she didn't come off sounding like she was making up some crazy story. What if she was honest with him and he didn't believe her?

Only one way to find out.

Once inside the room, she turned on the light but kept it low. Her pulse surged, and her mouth felt dry when she said, "We need to talk."

"About some kind of change in the plan?"

"About me."

Chase took her in his arms. "Are you going to tell me that you have another man in your life?"

"No." *Not exactly.* He had two women in *his* life. How was she going to explain dissociative identity disorder? And some trauma in the past that she didn't even remember? "About Annelise and me. My life is more complicated than you can imagine."

"I have a good imagination, and I like complicated." He tightened his arms around her. "Especially when that complication is *you.*"

Then he kissed her and thoughts of trying to tell him she was Annelise's alter fled from her mind. She wrapped her arms around Chase's neck and enjoyed the pleasure he was making her feel right now. No, more than simple pleasure. An unfamiliar happiness.

Backing away from him, she kicked off her heels and slowly started removing her dress.

Chase's brow furrowed. "Liz, you're sure?"

Her answer was to let the dress slide down to the floor. Then she helped him remove his shirt. His flesh was as hot to the touch as she was inside. She'd never felt so much attraction to any man.

Then, there had never been a Chase in her life before.

Dropping his pants, he pulled her onto the bed with him, where he removed her fancy lingerie. As he made love to her, she alternated between the feelings she'd never experienced before and the doubts still plaguing her.

What if his learning the truth about her and Annelise drove Chase away? Not that she expected that what they had was long term. Even so, what if the little time she might have with him was lost because of something she had no control over?

As waves of pleasure washed over her, there was no way she was going to tell him now.

Maybe she could get control if she stopped ignoring Marva's advice that she needed to face the trauma that had caused her to break.

Maybe then she could tell him...

Chapter Nineteen

Late the next morning, Annelise hung up the phone as Joyce entered her office with both arms full. "Mail call."

"Mail will have to wait." Annelise picked up some folders and got to her feet. "Durant just called another meeting."

Ignoring Joyce, she hurried from the room.

By the time she joined them, Durant and the two managers were already seated around the elliptical table. Both Dolhonik and Nakagawa appeared grim. What had Durant been telling them?

When Dolhonik realized she was standing there staring at them, he rapped his knuckles against the table and asked her, "You get some answers about the fire?"

"Who, me?" she asked, as she sat. "You probably have more answers than I do."

Nakagawa stared at her. "Actually, we have more questions. Like, how is it that our COO is consorting with the enemy?"

"What enemy?" Annelise asked.

Nakagawa looked from her to Durant, who aimed an ugly expression at Annelise. "Visiting Tully O'Neal," Durant said. "Going to his daughter's funeral and then to her apartment. Wasting time which has nothing to do with company work."

Though angry that the man she was certain was responsible for the fire was trying to stop her from getting answers, Annelise kept a calm demeanor. "You have someone following me?"

"I have my sources."

"Detective Turner?"

Durant shrugged. "Your actions have been anything but appropriate."

Annelise glared at him. "Are you saying you don't want to find the killer?"

"We're talking about arson."

"No, I'm talking about murder."

Dolhonik drummed his knuckles against the tabletop again. "I gotta agree with Durant on this one, Annelise. Talking to our own people is one thing. Getting chummy with the O'Neals is another."

"You just asked if I had information about the fire. How would you expect me to get it other than to talk to people who might know something?"

Nakagawa cleared his throat and stopped a confrontation between them. "No matter what, we can expect to be involved in a lawsuit. Anything you say to the deceased's family can be held against us."

Ah, the men were closing ranks on her. Annelise clenched her jaw. "That's ridiculous."

Durant shook his head. "As CEO of this company, I'm ordering you to cease and desist having anything to do with the fire immediately."

"*Acting* CEO," she reminded him. "And as the COO and one of the owners, I'm telling you I will do as I see fit." Annelise grabbed her tablet and stood.

"Sit down! We're not done here!"

"You might not be, but I am."

She hurried out of the room and back to her own office, where she took a deep breath to calm herself as she sat at her desk. Hoping to get her mind off Durant, she thought about Chase. What a contrast he was to her stepbrother. He'd been working with Liz, apparently out of the goodness of his heart. Maybe because he cared about her alter. She didn't want to think about the night before when she'd been fully aware of their physical encounter. Her own body responded anyway, tightening at the thought of his and Liz's lovemaking. Chase Donovan was a man she could appreciate. There had to be others like him out there. If Liz could find someone worth knowing, then perhaps she could, as well.

Determined to distract herself, she shook the thought away and started sorting through the stack of mail Joyce had left on her desk. Halfway in, a sheet of folded magenta paper popped out at her.

"Another one?" She stared at it for a moment, before unfolding it and reading: *I know where you work.*

Thinking about the note Liz had found, Annelise had trouble taking a deep breath. She was staring at the new message when Joyce entered. Holding up the piece of paper without letting her assistant see the contents, Annelise asked, "Do you have the envelope this came in?"

"You have all the envelopes right there."

"No."

Joyce moved closer. "Let me take a look."

Not wanting Joyce anywhere near her, Annelise put the paper facedown, leaving her hand on the note. "Listen, don't bother. I'll get to it. Right now I need some thinking time. Alone."

Joyce backed off, saying, "I need to leave early. At two. It's my brother. I have to pick him up and bring him home."

So Durant had gotten to the judge as promised. Clearly, Joyce's loyalties were solidly with Durant now.

"Fine. Until then, hold my calls."

"Of course." Joyce nodded and backed off. The moment the door closed behind her, Annelise concentrated hard on connecting with Liz. *Another note from our stalker in today's mail.*

Wondering if Liz could really hear her thoughts, Annelise was startled when she heard *Take it home with you when you leave. Keep it safe. Don't let anyone else have access to it.* Liz's thoughts or her own? Would she ever know for certain?

Annelise immediately slid the magenta note into her bag which she kept locked in a desk drawer these days. Then she got back to work, going over reports from each department about last week's events.

To her relief, Durant left her alone for the rest of the day. Was he here or had he gone to his Humboldt Park garage where he kept the classics that had supposedly been destroyed in the fire? It wouldn't be long before the drama played out between Durant and Chase. While she would love to be there in person, Liz was a better fit. Besides, she didn't have to be there. She would know what was happening through her and Liz's new connection.

Though she headed for home early, Annelise parked the Mustang in the garage and didn't go straight to the house. The damn *I know where you work* note was bothering her, and she wondered if Liz had gotten another message, as well. She stared out at the property from the entryway, quickly searched every inch within view but saw nothing to alarm her.

Moving deep into the garage, she stopped at the panel in the wall leading to the stairwell and took it up to the hidden room. Once inside, she started looking for another note Liz may not have shared, poking into drawers, sorting through Liz's things. The tablet that must have belonged to Liz's former boyfriend James was still in a drawer. Which is where she found the crushed *I know where you live* note.

She stared at the missive before shoving it into her pocket and slamming the drawer shut. Standing in the middle of the room, she wondered what Javier wanted from them.

But came up with no answers.

Durant paced the length of the garage, checking his watch every minute or two. "So where the hell are they, Vinny?"

"Got me. I gave Desiree your message, so she had the address and time. She tends to be late. Some kinda head game with her."

As he stared out the window into the dark, Durant caught movement. "There's a man coming down the street this way. Can't see what he looks like. Wearing a damn felt fedora with a wide brim." Wide enough to cast a shadow over his face. As the guy got closer, Durant recognized the brand from the silver-trimmed hat band. Expensive enough to tell him this had to be the guy. "He's alone. I told you I wanted both of them."

"Which I told her," Vinny insisted from the open doorway. "Maybe it's not him."

A moment later, the man stopped in front of the mechanic. "You Vinny?"

"Hey, where's *Desiree?* She was supposed to bring you!"

The man ignored Vinny and pushed his way in. As if he could feel Durant in the shadows, he looked straight in his direction. "I deal alone. I expect you do the same or I'm not interested."

Durant sized him up. "Vinny, get lost for a while."

"You sure?"

"Stay in shooting range."

Vinny reluctantly backed off into the bowels of the garage.

Durant looked over this supposed buyer. If he was expecting a suit, he didn't get it. The man was dressed in jeans and a sweater. Expensive like the hat maybe, but it put him off as did the way the man stood there as if this was his gig.

"Are we doing this?" the man asked. "If we are, then come out of the shadows."

Durant ignored the demand. "So what are you looking for?"

"A classic Ferrari Testarossa. I prefer red, but I'm not set on it."

"And you think I have a connection who can get you one of those?"

Shaking his head, the man turned to leave. "You find one,

get word to me."

"Wait. Maybe I can find one." The man turned and focused on the dark area where Durant remained so the prick couldn't see his face. He added, "For the right price."

"Name it."

"Three hundred and fifty thousand. Cash."

"How soon?"

"On delivery, of course."

"No. I mean how soon can you deliver?" The stranger's eyes narrowed as he stared into the shadows.

"I'll see what I can do," Durant said. "What did you say your name was?"

"Chase Donovan."

"I'll be in touch through Desiree."

The man saluted and left the way he came.

Durant shifted forward into a pool of light. "Hmm, Chase...Chase...unusual name...but familiar." His eyes narrowed on Chase's back as if he could get a better read on him.

Vinny stopped in the doorway, anxiously looking after the man, while Chase didn't give him a second glance. Vinny rushed to Durant. "So we got a deal?"

"We have to watch our backs!" Durant snapped. "You've been sloppy Vinny. You'll have to make up for your careless-ness."

"What's that? A threat. Don't even, not with what I got on you."

"Do I look like a man who doesn't believe in insurance?"

Durant grinned. For the first time, Vinny looked scared.

Just the way he wanted him.

Liz was leaning on the Jaguar, waiting for Chase when he got close enough to see her. Because he'd feared Durant might somehow recognize Liz, Chase had made her wait away from the garage entry.

"Well?" she asked.

"Durant expected you to be there. Oddly, he didn't press the issue."

If necessary, he would have led Durant to her where it was dark enough to help hide her true identity, but thankfully he hadn't had to take that chance.

He drove Liz straight home and came up to her hidden quarters with her. She stopped in front of the mirror, pulled off her wig and ran her fingers through her hair. Then she began removing the makeup.

"Other than his being an asshole, why do you hate Durant so much?"

"He's trying to steal our company."

"Uh-uh. That's only part of it. And not personal enough."

"I'd hate any man who forced a young woman into suicide."

He wasn't surprised by her accusation. "You mean your sister Lizzie. Is this why you've been playing her, Annelise?"

When she turned to face him, Liz shrugged. "How long have you known?"

"That you and Annelise are one and the same? That you like playing games? Long enough."

"How long have you known?" she asked again. "Since the beginning? Or before?"

"Now how could I have known before I met you? When I faced you in your office, I was a little surprised you didn't admit to knowing who I was."

Chase tented her with his body, wrapped his arms around her waist, nuzzled her neck, distracted her. Her throat arched, and a groan escaped her.

"I thought you were a different kind of man…but you aren't really."

"I thought you were enjoying me anyway."

She placed a hand in the middle of his chest and pushed him back. "I am. The problem is that if you want to change the subject, you do it with sex. Arthur used sex if in a different, disgusting way—to control Mama. No one controls me."

Chase moved closer and slid his hand down her hip to the hem of the short dress. "I'll stop if you want." He could tell she was fighting the attraction. "I just want to know what the hell else Durant is responsible for. What did he do to you?"

She shook her head and backed away from him. "I don't remember what happened, Chase. Truthfully, I don't know why. After my sister died, everything changed for me. I chose to play life safe. To be the Annelise everyone expected of me."

"And to spend your nights being your dead twin?"

Her expression of fear-laced anger got to him. He took her in his arms and held her close. She was trembling. Afraid. Unlike the Liz he thought he knew.

What had the creep done to make her so afraid that she couldn't remember?

Whatever Durant had done, Chase was going to make the bastard pay...

Curled on her bed, a sleepy Liz awoke alone only to hear the shower running. A glance at the clock told her it was nearly four in the morning. Chase had held her, comforting her until she fell asleep. She lay there for a moment, thinking. Worry tensing her. She had the feeling Chase wasn't going to stop asking her about the past until she remembered whatever it was her mind had buried. Slipping from the bed, she realized she was still dressed like Desiree. She quickly changed back into Annelise.

Chase's clothes decorated the floor on the way to the bathroom. The shower was still running.

Liz couldn't help herself. She scooped up the discarded sweater and held it to her face, mesmerized by his scent, then set it over the back of a chair mand picked up his jeans. A small notebook slid out of a pocket.

She picked it up and turned it over. What kind of information did it hold? If she went through it, would she find out more about him? Only, not here. She slipped it into her pocket and knocked on the bathroom door.

"Chase, I need to get back to the house."

The shower stopped. "Go ahead. I'll see you tonight."

Liz left the room and just outside the door, stepped on another piece of magenta paper. Staring at what was surely another threat — one delivered when she and Chase had been in bed together — her heart raced as she picked up the paper and unfolded it.

I know who you are. Maybe I'll tell.

Unnerved, Liz crumpled the paper and peered out the high window, searching the dark street for some sign of Javier. There was a man leaning against a car on the other side of the street, but she couldn't make him out in the dark before he slid into the night.

Frustrated, Liz made for the tunnel and the house. Once she entered Annelise's room, she threw herself across the bed. The lump in her pocket made her shift.

Chase's notebook.

She pulled it out, stroked it as if she were stroking him.

Her uncertainty about invading his privacy made her hesitate. But she knew he'd been keeping things from her, so in the end, she opened the book and flipped through it. Nothing but phone numbers and notes about some of the contacts. Seemingly a waste of her time. Even so, she continued flipping through the pages.

Then her eyes widened in horror: *Katie - 773-555-4763.*

Shock and betrayal tied up her gut, while her fingers tightened around the book. Chase had known the dead woman, but he hadn't said a word about it.

What the hell?

Who had Katie been to him? His lover?

Her cell beeped. Chase had texted: *Leaving now. Get a good night's sleep. Tomorrow we'll nail Durant together.*

A few minutes later, after checking to make certain Chase's Jaguar was gone, she got in Lizzie's Mustang and headed for the office. She was still wearing Annelise's clothes, though she doubted anyone would be there at four-thirty in the morning.

Indeed, the garage was dark when she pulled in. The old wooden door creaked as it dropped closed behind her. The area was a little spooky, but there was no sign of anyone else here. She found the flashlight under her seat and used it to get to her office without turning on building lights.

From one of her desk drawers, she took out the *Tully O'Neal* file Joyce had pulled from the morgue for her the week before.

Sorting through the contents, she got to the medical records and began looking through them for something about O'Neal's son. Tully had called him Donny.

Then she found a medical record which told her what she'd guessed: *Chase D. O'Neal - Broken arm.*

Liz could hardly breathe. Chase Donovan O'Neal had been playing her all along. Her eyes filled with tears. "Bastard!"

Broken-hearted, she got on her computer and typed in his name and searched for information on the man she obviously didn't know at all.

"Well this is certainly a twist hearing from you again so soon."

"I had to talk to someone who would understand, Marva. Thanks for seeing me." Still dressed like Annelise later that afternoon, Liz was pacing the office, venting. "I just learned Chase Donovan is really C.D. O'Neal, a top NASCAR driver, son of Tully O'Neal, brother of the dead Kate. When he talked about her, he even called her Katie like Tully did and I didn't get it. The clues to his real identity were there all the time, right in front of my nose, and I couldn't read him."

"Perhaps you didn't want to."

Ready to scream with frustration, Liz sank into the recliner.

"It's exhausting always being on guard, always being alone. I wanted to trust someone. I wanted to trust *him.*"

"Have you confronted him? Asked him why he didn't tell you who he really was?"

Liz shook her head. "He doesn't know I know."

"Why not? What are you waiting for?"

"Revenge."

"Against Chase? Has he done anything to hurt you? Other than not revealing his real identity and that he probably came to Chicago knowing his sister had just died. What is it you want to do to him? What kind of revenge?"

"I want him to know what it feels like to not know the person he's involved with, to be hurt and angry when he gets what he's missed."

"Perhaps he really cares about you."

"He's a liar! Like Arthur. Like Durant."

"Are you certain?"

"I was a fool. I can't trust anyone but myself. Not even Annelise."

"That's certainly an unexpected change. Do you feel Annelise has done something to betray you?"

Liz laughed, but the sound was one of hurt, of bitterness. "Remember Annelise wanted to get rid of me. She only agreed to work with me to give herself extra protection against Durant. How do I know that has changed?"

"You could ask her. Have you considered Annelise might want to know you because you're a part of her?"

"Or...maybe she still wants to get rid of me. Then there'd be no Liz." Her head began buzzing as if Annelise was trying to object. "It'll be as if I never existed!"

"As I explained before, if you choose to integrate, your consciousness will become one with Annelise's. You won't forget anything. You'll be one person. You can live a different type of life. A fuller life. Do you feel it would be so bad?"

Liz thought about it, but the situation was making her

desperate. "I'm the strong one, and I don't want to die. If one of us has to go, it's not going to be me."

She dug her nails into the chair arms and gave over to Annelise.

An exhausted, fragile Annelise exited the Mustang. She'd taken over from Liz, had finished the session with Dr. Jackson, then had gone to work as expected. She'd holed up in her office with so much thinking to do, it unnerved her.

About to walk up the front steps to the house, she changed her mind and circled the building into the rose garden, where she stood, silent and desperately trying to remember the trauma Dr. Jackson had warned her about.

A perfect-looking little Lizzie ran through the rain and into the safety of the garden, where the sun was shining. She plucked a rose, closed her ears to the crack of the strap and angry, incomprehensible voices.

The pieces of memory and the confusion they brought made Annelise press shaky fingers to her forehead. She feared learning the truth, but doing so was necessary to get her real life back. "What do I have to do to remember the trauma that split us?"

Maybe she had to leave it to Liz...

Chapter Twenty

Dark had fallen while Liz lay on the bed in her quarters, staring at the three threatening notes. She hadn't been any more successful in remembering the past than Annelise had. The phone rang. She checked her cell and stiffened as she answered. "Your dime."

"Surely I'm worth more than a dime," Chase said in a teasing voice.

"Who is this?"

"What kind of game are we playing now?"

She stared at the *Maybe I'll tell* note. "You tell me. *Donny.*"

He was silent for a moment, and she figured he was trying to come up with a believable lie, but instead, he said, "I can explain."

"I bet you can. Only I'm not buying."

Chase cursed under his breath. "Liz, don't do this. You know I care about you. What about our getting Durant?"

"The two of you can fuck each other over for all I care!" She turned off the cell and threw it across the room with teeth-rattling force. "And maybe I can help."

She crossed to a desk, dropped the threatening notes, took out the cell she'd taken from Jimmy-boy last week, checked to make sure she could still use it and changed his name on the phone identification to Desiree. Then she started a text. Durant was going to want to kill her for this when he figured things out, but the threat would be effective. He couldn't ignore it. She finished with *Meet us at the Walsh Garage on Elston tomorrow night at 10.* She didn't sign it. Let him think it came from Desiree writing for his mystery buyer.

Not in the least happy about what she had planned, she started a second text, this one telling Chase to be there, as well.

Durant opened the text within seconds after arrival.

We need to discuss terms. Agree to half of your asking price, or I'll go to the cops about the fire. Meet me at the Walsh garage on Elston tomorrow night at 10.

Durant's face froze for a moment, then he smiled.

Liz wasn't ready to relinquish control when she read Kyle's message which came in on Annelise's cell just after eleven the next morning. She knew Annelise had some guilt feelings about being attracted to Lizzie's boyfriend, but Liz didn't. An invite for lunch at his new Wicker Park Home sounded perfect. She wanted to see Kyle and his new home for herself. Wanted to know if there was still anything there. She convinced herself he would be a far better man for her than Chase. At least she didn't think Kyle lied about anything.

Set on a street with several refurbished old mansions — part of the Polish Gold Coast as this area was once called — Kyle's home was an incredible four-level turn-of-the-century Chicago Graystone with an architecturally well-preserved façade.

Kyle opened the front door before Liz had a chance to ring the bell. His handsome face was wreathed with a smile. "So glad you could make it. I thought maybe you didn't want to see me again."

When he hugged her and kissed her cheek, Liz felt a sense of loss she couldn't deny. "I might not be able to go to Indianapolis with you, but I did promise to take a look at your new place and see if I had any ideas about the decor."

"Let's start with a tour."

His hand behind her back, Kyle guided her through the main floor which had retained a classic interior style in the formal living and dining rooms, as well as the kitchen and family room in the rear. The furniture was all modern — no doubt from his condo — and looked out of place in the rooms.

"I can see why you wanted my help."

The same could be said of the second floor's retreat with a giant master bedroom and fireplace in the private library. They skipped the upper floor's bedrooms and baths, but Kyle wanted her to see the garden-level guest suite and wine cellar.

In her mind, his new home was as much a classic as the cars she loved. She gave him suggestions for furniture, artwork and greenery to make it all come together.

"There are quite a few really interesting Chicago antique shops where you can find just about anything you can imagine. You can have a pick of old fireplace mantels, stained glass windows and insets into doors, and lighting fixtures that have been renovated with safer modern electrical wiring. Try Urban Remains, Architectural Artifacts and Salvage One."

Kyle nodded. "Perhaps we could look through them together."

Liz smiled but didn't answer.

The dining room table was set with china and crystal. Kyle opened a bottle of wine. "How nice you could join me for lunch, Annelise."

But it was Liz who stared at him. "I'm not really hungry."

"Then we could talk over a drink first."

"Or do other things." Had he been doing other things with Annelise? She felt the need to find out. "Are you attracted to me, Kyle?"

"You know I am."

Wanting to know how he would react to her, Liz moved closer to him and slid a hand up his chest. With one hand around her back, Kyle pulled her closer and kissed her. Without breaking the kiss, he set down the wine.

Liz was left feeling nothing but sadness for the man.

Breathing hard, Kyle kissed her neck and whispered into her ear. "Oh, Lizzie."

Which made Liz jerk away from him.

"I'm sorry, Annelise. A slip, that's all."

Realizing she'd made a big mistake coming here, she shook her head and backed up. "I can't do this, Kyle. I thought I could, but I just can't."

"It's my fault. You were pretty clear about what you didn't want the last time we spoke. Sorry. I'm an ass."

"It's not you. It's me. It has always been me." Grabbing her purse, she rushed for the door, glancing back at the man Lizzie had loved.

He ran a hand through his hair. "Annelise, wait, please!"

Tears gathered in her eyes when Liz said, "It's ten years too late for us, Kyle."

Knowing he didn't understand, she left, slamming the door on any kind of relationship with a really decent man.

After Liz's failed lunch with Kyle, she bowed out, leaving the rest of the day to Annelise.

When the garage door opened, Annelise saw Durant and Vinny hovering near Durant's Cord Berline classic car in an apparently heated argument. What was going on there? She drove in and parked. Vinny appeared angry at whatever Durant was dishing out.

As she left the Mustang, Durant glared at her and muttered, "We're going to take care of the situation. Permanently." He gripped the piece of metal in his hand tight enough to bend it.

Annelise hurried past them without speaking. No doubt this had to do with Liz's plan to get Durant to sell one of the supposedly burned classics to Chase. Whatever Durant and

Vinny were cooking up, they weren't going to give explicit details with her around.

When she approached her office, Joyce looked up from her desk. "Have a good lunch?" Annelise gave her a questioning look, and Joyce added, "Kyle Zimmerman?"

"Oh, right. Nice. Very nice." Her empty stomach rumbled as she rushed into her office, feeling Joyce's gaze on the middle of her back.

Collapsing against a wall, Annelise wasn't feeling so hot. "Liz, what is going on? What the hell are you up to? I can feel something is wrong. Please, let me understand."

Her hand trembled its way to her forehead as an aura started and the room began to move without her. "No, not now!"

But the aura didn't progress into a migraine. Annelise realized Liz was trying to tell her something as she had during their session with the psychiatrist. She already knew Chase was Kate's brother. And Liz was angry with him for keeping her in the dark. She closed her eyes and concentrated on getting through to her alter. It only took a minute to get an answer.

I set up a meeting between Chase and Durant tonight. I'll be there to record everything, so we can finally nail Durant. Then we can go back to living our lives.

"But how can we assume it's possible without knowing what happened to us in the past?" Annelise asked.

Maybe not remembering will keep us safe.

Annelise wasn't certain if it was true, but obviously, Liz feared remembering as much as she did.

Later that night, descending the stairs to street level, carrying her bag with the wig and make-up, Liz was dressed to kill. She started for the secret panel, then changed her mind, went down to the underground tunnel and took it all the way to the house and the living room.

In his wheelchair before a fire, her stepfather Arthur stiffened as if he sensed her presence. Using his good hand, he turned his chair to face her.

Liz stared at him malevolently from the doorway.

Arthur's good eye widened when he saw her.

"No, you're not seeing a ghost, old man." She moved closer, her expression menacing as Arthur garbled some protest. "Lizzie's dead, remember? Afraid *I'm* going to hurt you like you did her? It would be so easy. You're the helpless one now, aren't you?"

Arthur made weird sounds and trembled as he tried to back up his wheelchair with his good arm. Liz stopped him by placing her hands on his armrests.

"I really could kill you for what you've done, you know. First you. Then the worm you call a son who you brought into this house and goaded into giving my sister and me hell."

Arthur made more incomprehensible sounds. Liz played with the lapels of his dressing gown, her long fingernails sliding to his throat.

"But if you were dead, I wouldn't have the joy of seeing you like this. Impotent. Durant's going to get his come-uppance, too. Soon. He may not survive the night."

Arthur continued to make weird noises as if he was calling her mother for help.

Liz smiled and turned away only to face Mama standing there, her expression shocked.

"Mama. Spying?"

"Don't do this. Don't put yourself in more danger."

"You're the one who put us all in danger by marrying this bastard. You chose to keep living with it."

Madeline ignored Arthur, who was trying to get her attention. Tears slid down her cheeks and her hand plucked at the material covering her breasts. "There was nothing I could do but try to protect you, Lizzie. I've been protecting you the only way I know how."

Mama appeared very, very frightened and suddenly far older

than her years.

Refusing to feel sorry for her, Liz stormed past her mother and went out the front door for the first time as herself rather than as Annelise. She entered the garage, slid into the Mustang and sat there for a quiet moment. The darkness surrounded her, tried to seduce her into stepping inside. To face the memory which had kept her trapped for the past ten years. Her heart thundered. The truth waited for her, but fear wouldn't let her go there. Liz shook off the creepy feeling trying to encase her. Claim her. Destroy her. She threw the bag with the wig and make-up into the back seat. Liz rather than Desiree would face Durant tonight.

She drove fast and made it to the Walsh garage in record time.

Chase's Jaguar was parked aways up the street, but he was nowhere in sight. He'd texted her Durant had contacted him. He'd suggested they go together. She'd said she would meet him instead. Though Liz didn't see him on the street, he was probably already inside.

Still, she hesitated.

The factory building seemed to be hunched, a behemoth waiting for her in the dark. Her pulse picked up a beat when she thought she saw Durant at a window. She blinked and he was gone. The garage door sat open. Her breath quickened as she pulled inside cautiously, her attention immediately drawn to the golden light pooling around the classic Ferrari sitting deeper in the bowels of the building, behind another car still shrouded in protective cloth.

She slipped her hand into the pocket at her right hip and started the mini-recorder she'd bought to record Durant.

As she got out of the car, a low male curse made Liz jump. She flipped around, backed up into the pool of light, appreciating Durant's stunned face when he saw her.

"What's wrong, Durant? Not happy to see me?"

"Trying to make me think I'm seeing a ghost? I didn't know

you had it in you, Annelise. I should have seen the potential." He tapped the button to close the garage door. "But after Lizzie and I had a great night of sex, all I could think about was her."

The Shadow Man — Durant — forcing himself over Lizzie, pinning her hands above her head so she couldn't fight him.

Startled by the repressed memory, Liz choked out, "Great night? For you, maybe. How much did you get off hurting Lizzie?"

Durant stalked Liz, who moved around the car to keep some distance between them. Where the hell was Chase when she needed him?

"Lizzie wanted me. And I wanted her. Only she was trying to make me jealous with Kyle. I couldn't let her keep doing the freak."

"Lizzie *loved* Kyle!" And had never had sex with the young man she really loved.

"She gave herself to him so I would admit how I felt about her. And it worked. I told her I was crazy about her. That's when we made love. Only afterward, she was angry. She said she'd see me locked up if it was the last thing she ever did."

The last statement hit Liz hard, and she stared at him for a moment. "When *exactly* did she threaten you?"

"Later. When she found me in the garage."

Emotions warred through Liz. Then the truth dawned on her. "My God, she didn't lock herself in the garage with the car running. You did!"

Durant shrugged. "She gave me no choice. I believed her when she said she would have me arrested. She would have *lied* about what happened between us."

"All this time, I thought it was suicide. You killed my sister!"

"Enough of the past. Time for *you* to take a last ride." He laughed. "Lizzie died from a car's carbon monoxide. Your car takes you for a dip in the lake. Apropos, considering the family business."

He pulled out a handgun. Liz wildly looked for Chase and

when she couldn't see him, an escape route.

"I'm not going anywhere with you. And if you shoot me, it won't look like suicide."

"I was going to buy you out, Annelise. Now Father will inherit your shares the way he did Lizzie's. Soon, they'll be mine anyway. He can't last much longer." He lunged at her, grabbed her arm and started dragging her toward the Mustang's passenger door. "How well do you swim...just in case you manage to get out of the car?"

Liz was stunned. Her vision suddenly went wonky, and she couldn't make her brain focus to find a way out of this. "Can't we make some kind of deal?"

"You should have thought about what would happen before you got involved in something over your head, Annelise."

Liz almost felt hypnotized. As if she couldn't move. Her brain felt ready to explode. Annelise was trying to get in!

Yeah...*Annelise*, not her.

She was the strong one, Liz thought in a panic. Not Annelise. She could survive anything, but not with Durant. Not again. Maybe she should let Annelise take over.

"You're shaking with fear, little sister," he said. "It will all be over soon."

Liz couldn't focus, and though she fought it, her thoughts went blank as she felt Annelise getting stronger...

...then Liz's mind simply blinked out.

Leaving Annelise stranded with a murderer.

Chapter Twenty-One

Annelise looked down at her flashy clothing, then at Durant. And knew yet again she'd picked the wrong time to subvert Liz.

Now she was in real trouble.

Staring at the gun Durant held on her, she ripped her arm free of him and backed up. "Stay away from me, Durant."

"C'mon, little sister, it's time we ended the game."

As he moved toward her, she searched for an escape, looking for Chase, thinking fast, but holding her ground. Liz's recorder in her pocket was still running. Hoping for another confession, she asked, "Like you did with Kate O'Neal?"

"She showed up at Parts and Storage at the wrong time. She already suspected what I was up to. She said if I married her, they couldn't force her to testify against me. I don't blackmail well."

Marry? What the hell had Durant done to Kate that the poor woman might have had to testify? And why would she want to marry the creep?

Moving in on her, Durant reached out to grab her arm again. Annelise pulled a protector cover off the other classic car parked there — spare Ferrari in case Chase didn't like the first one? — and threw the cover over Durant.

The gun went flying, hit a work bench and flew away into the darkness.

While he struggled to get the cloth off, she got into the Mustang. As she turned the car to get out, she saw Durant free of the cover and diving for his gun.

Annelise put the Mustang in gear and backed up, trying to run down Durant, who flew out of the way, yelling, "Bitch! You're dead and you just don't know it yet!"

Before she could escape, he grabbed onto the convertible's side door and aimed the gun directly at her.

Go! Get out of here!

Lizzie's prompt made her stomp the accelerator. Then she caught her breath when a shot went off behind her, and she saw the closed garage door in front of her. Her sideview mirror told her Durant was gaining on her. She hit the gas pedal harder, driving Lizzie's Mustang straight through the old wood, shattering it.

A piece of flying garage door debris flew over the open top and smacked her in the face. Stunned, Annelise braked and put her hand to her bleeding forehead.

The driver's door opened, and Annelise screamed and tried to beat off Durant. Except it wasn't Durant. Chase had come to her rescue. He took the car out of drive, shoved her over the low center console into the passenger seat and got behind the wheel. Annelise checked her sideview mirror to see Durant run to his own car.

"I put Vinny on hold," Chase said. "What the hell's going on, Liz?"

"I'm Annelise, not Liz. Durant killed Kate. Wants us dead, too."

Durant zoomed past them, banging into the Mustang as he fled the garage. Chase took after him like a madman. Annelise held her head trying to stop the mother of all headaches, trying to concentrate.

After all her promises, Liz had somehow blocked her from knowing what she was up to now.

Chase's attention was on Durant, both men driving hi-speed down Elston Avenue, the industrial street deserted at this time of night. Suddenly Durant careened around a corner. Chase missed the cut-off...turned on two wheels and took the corner too fast...slowed only slightly as he hit the side street before picking up speed again.

Durant popped out on another main thoroughfare.

Chase gunned the engine and closed in on him until a couple of tattooed gangbangers tussled out from between cars. Chase braked with a screech. "Out of the way!"

One laughed. "Hey, getta load of the great wheels. I always wanted a convertible." He began stroking the hood like he thought he owned it.

The other yelled, "Out of the car, asshole!" and pulled out a handgun.

"Carjack!" Annelise croaked.

"Not tonight!" Chase backed up, then stepped hard on the gas. The tires spun until they caught, and he zoomed straight toward the threat. The gangbanger let off a wild shot as he flew away from the car.

Searching the area for Durant, Chase couldn't see him. "Shit! The prick disappeared!"

Annelise took a good look around. "We're near Walsh Scraps. Make a right at the intersection."

Chase turned through a red light without stopping. Horns blared after them. Tires screeched.

Annelise saw Durant's car in the distance. She pointed. "There!"

"I see him!"

Annelise's features pulled tight as she tried to retrieve a missing memory. *Liz, let me in. Tell me what you kept from me!*

The Mustang flew by six-foot chain link fencing. Chase stomped the brakes and backed up. She saw Durant's car turn into a parking lot, and he cut his running lights. He threw open his door and left the car, then unlocked the gate and made a break for one of several large piles of metal scrap.

Chase pulled the Mustang into the lot. Annelise saw Durant with his gun in hand before her sister's murderer slipped into the shadows.

Getting out of the Mustang, Durant said, "Stay here, Liz."

"Annelise!"

"Whoever you are today, I don't want to see you hurt."

Then he ran after Durant through the opening in the chain link fence.

Her face screwed up in pain, and she fisted her hands in frustration as she concentrated. *Liz, what the hell did Durant tell you? Cooperate once in your life! Maybe we can beat him together!* She took a big breath and was startled when she swore she heard *Lizzie...he admitted he killed Lizzie...*

Fumbling with the car door, she threw it open in rage and ran to the gate. As she flew through the opening, she was shaking inside but kept pushing herself. Durant had just admitted to killing her sister...her twin...her other half! Then telling herself to be cautious until she found Chase, she slowed and peered around a scrap pile.

Nothing.

She wanted to be there when Chase took on Durant, so she started moving again. Small noises shot at her from every direction. A rat ran across her foot. She flipped back and stifled a scream. Catching her breath, she visualized Durant lying dead on the pavement and continued circling into a darker space. The wind picked up and scrap metal settled with an echo that cut through her. Were those footsteps? Chase or Durant? She couldn't tell which. Her throat went dry, and she held her breath. Fear tightened her gut, but she wasn't about to stop and miss Chase's takedown of Lizzie's killer!

Not until she identified a loud click and the metal of a gun pressed to her temple. Feeling as if her blood had just run cold, Annelise froze in place.

Durant laughed. "You always were the stupid one." Then louder, "C'mon, Donovan. I've got your slut!"

* * *

Unarmed, Chase hid in the shadow of a scrap heap, watching Durant as he started down one aisle, Annelise in tow, stopped and then changed direction. Chase couldn't help but wonder what the hell was going on to make the normally bold Liz switch to the fearful Annelise. Whoever she was, he cared about her and wasn't going to let her die.

Durant spat out a threat. "I'm going to blow her fucking brains out if you don't show yourself, Donovan!"

"Don't do it, Chase!" Annelise yelled. "He'll kill me anyway! My sister didn't commit suicide any more than your sister burned in her own fire! He killed them both!"

Chase saw Durant back up, but where did he think he would be safe? Nowhere he could hide from Chase, and if he hurt the woman Chase loved, Durant would be dead meat.

Circling a scrap pile, Chase listened hard and heard heavy breathing.

Annelise...

He inched forward, and through the dark saw Durant holding a gun to her head. Then Annelise suddenly swung her free arm and smacked Durant in the throat with her elbow. He stumbled a bit, but seconds later he responded by hitting the side of her head with the gun. Even so, the two scuffled across the pavement in a struggle Chase knew Annelise could never win.

Desperate to keep her alive, Chase picked up a rusty sheet of metal and threw it to the side to distract Durant. He spun around, losing his edge slightly, enough for Annelise to shove him, break free and run.

Chase was on Durant in seconds and shoved a foot into the back of his knees. That brought him down to the ground, and Chase pummeled him in the face and chest, wanting to end him right there. Then he suddenly felt something hard slam in his gut.

Chase froze and looked down at the gun in Durant's hand.

Durant slid back and got to his feet, the weapon still aimed at Chase. "So Kate was your sister."

Chase wondered if he could take a bullet and still stop the murderer for good. "Katie told me she was in love with you! How could you do what you did to her and then kill her?"

"She couldn't keep our secret? *Tch-tch-tch.* Good thing I torched her mouth shut for her."

Chase lost the little control he had left. He'd warned Katie about Durant from the beginning when she first told him he'd asked her out. He'd shared horror stories about Durant that he'd heard from girls in high school.

"Katie was pregnant with your kid because you tricked her into thinking you were someone decent! When she let you know you were going to be a father, you told her to go fuck herself!"

"She thought I would marry her! As if I would demean the Walsh name by bringing her spawn into the family! Then she thought she could blackmail me!"

Katie simply hadn't believed him. Not until after Durant forced himself on her. And she hadn't told Chase about the pregnancy and betrayal until their last phone call the day before she'd died. She'd sworn she didn't love Durant anymore, but having her family thrown in the street without a home when Durant's father had fired theirs, she'd felt it was comeuppance time. Her baby didn't deserve to be thrown away, too. He or she deserved a place in the Walsh world with all the privileges it offered.

Durant still aimed the gun at him but now stood less than a yard away. Chase lunged forward and jumped the murderer, got his hands on the gun and kneed him in the groin. Durant cursed him as they tripped over scrap metal, Chase's hands locked over his, struggling to get the weapon from him.

Behind Durant, Chase saw Annelise slowly edging away, her gaze focused on the rusted sheet metal he'd used to distract the prick.

She reached down...

Durant laughed. "First Lizzie, then Kate. How appropriate

you and Annelise should die together."

…and got her hands on the metal as Durant swiped Chase's legs, and he crashed to his knees.

"Now that's the way I like seeing you," Durant said, pulling away from him and aiming the gun in the middle of his forehead.

Chase saw a screaming, rage-filled Annelise lunge toward Durant, sheet metal in her hands.

Durant turned to face her…and she swung.

The jagged metal slashed into the front of Durant's neck, splitting it open. Blood sprayed from the wound, covering Annelise, who appeared even more terrified, eyes wide, face frozen, mouth opened in a silent scream.

Chase got to his feet as Durant staggered and put a hand to his throat as if he could stop the bleeding. Then he fell forward and landed face down, continuing to lose more blood in spurts. Chase didn't think anything was going to save Durant now. Before he could check to see if Durant's heart was still beating, his body jerked once and then stilled.

And a panicked Annelise dropped the weapon and raced for the exit.

"Liz, wait!"

"I told you, I'm not Liz!"

Through the open gate, she headed for the Mustang. Chase had left the keys in the ignition so he knew she would be gone in a minute.

"Annelise!" Running after her, he quickly narrowed the distance between them.

With a last look at him, she scrambled into the car, locked the doors and started the engine. Chase banged on the window. Annelise appeared frozen except for her shaking hands as she grabbed the steering wheel, gunned the Mustang and sped out of the lot.

Chase stood there, watching her drive away like a maniac. Then went to Durant's car, found his cell phone and dialed 9-1-1.

"I'm reporting a death. Connect me to Detective Marcellus Turner in Violent Crimes."

Waiting to talk to the detective, Chase thought about Katie, certain he could have helped calm her anger and see the light. He'd made plans to come back to Chicago after the NASCAR race that weekend. But the motherfucker had killed her before he'd had a chance.

He focused on Durant and the blood pooled around him. Annelise had been defending herself. Defending them both.

He only hoped Turner would believe him.

Chapter Twenty-Two

Coming to a stop in the driveway, Annelise stumbled out of the Mustang and hit the button to close and lock the garage door. Splattered with blood, she shoved her hair back from her face. She was sobbing in broken gasps, but she couldn't stop. Dear God, she'd just killed a man. Durant was a vile creature, and she'd wanted him punished, but she had never planned to take his life. She'd hoped that he would be arrested, tried, found guilty and locked up forever.

An aura was building. Everything seemed to be moving around her while she somehow felt her way to the secret panel and took the stairs up to Liz's quarters.

To her shock, the door was unlocked, and the lights were on as she stumbled inside, crying, "Oh, God, oh, God! What have I done?"

The sandy-haired stranger who stepped in front of her made her catch her breath. "A good question, Liz. That is blood all over you, isn't it? What *have* you done now?"

Backing up, she asked, "What do you want?" She tried to stare into his pale blue eyes, but she couldn't focus. "Who are you?"

"Another game? I think you're going to lose this one." He closed the door behind her.

She swallowed hard. "Look, I really don't know who you are. And I'm not Liz! I have to call the police."

Dazed, she pulled her cell from her pocket, but the man grabbed it out of her hand. "It's time for you to pay, Liz."

Silent tears rolled down her cheeks. "You don't understand that I'm not Liz!"

"I understand, all right." His gaze lowered from her face to her blood-soaked chest. "You're a prick tease. Looks like you busted someone's balls for good tonight. Fitting I showed up just now, isn't it?"

"Who are you?" she choked out as her vision suddenly shifted and the room seemed to be moving around her. Fighting the aura was useless. Her stomach churned and she resisted throwing up. "What do you want from me?"

"Only what you promised the night we met."

He pulled something out of his pocket and *snick*, a flame shot upward. She did her best to focus. Some kind of fancy torch lighter with a long blue flame.

"Then I'll fix your face so you can never trick another poor sap like me, you slut!"

Annelise wheeled toward the room's door and opened it to get away from him. Hearing banging on the outer door below slowed her for a second. The man tried to grab her, but she knocked his arm with the lit torch lighter upward toward him. The blue flame touched his shirt and ignited the cloth. He screamed, "Bitch!" as he hit the flames on his chest with the other hand to put out the fire.

"Liz? Annelise? Let me in!"

Chase's voice...downstairs...locked out of the garage...

"Chase, help! He's going to kill me!" Annelise raced for the secret panel, but her vision wasn't stable, and she was exhausted and tripping over her own feet.

The intruder followed and the distance between them quickly narrowed.

A last glance back before entering the stairwell to the tunnel — Annelise saw Chase through the door's window as he heaved his shoulder into the wood. When it didn't give, he smashed his elbow through the glass.

Halfway down the stairway to the tunnel, the intruder caught up to her and grabbed Annelise's hair. Terrified, she dropped to her knees, and they fell together, rolling down the remaining stairs. Struggling to her feet, she staggered into the tunnel, using a wall to support herself, but she didn't get far before he caught her again and threw her to the murky ground.

He stood over her, waved the torch in her face, restarted the long blue flame and laughed. "Now we can finish what you started."

Terror coursed through Annelise as the aura intensified and there was nothing she could do to stop it from flipping her back into the past...

Durant on top of Lizzie, moving off her.

In shock, she stared at him through unseeing eyes.

What the hell? A horrible image, just like the one frightening Annelise. Her attacker was climbing over her. Terror engulfed her, and she fought him even as her head whirled. She finally realized Liz was trying to take over.

Annelise gasped in sheer relief and let it happen.

Coldly furious, Liz kneed Scanlon in the groin, and as he screamed, she shoved him away from her, then got to her feet.

"So you're the one who's been leaving the party notes." James Scanlon, the skirt chaser she'd obviously ruined after he'd screwed with the waitress in the cigar bar the week before. So he'd been the one to ram Annelise in the Mustang and wait in the garden smoking his damn cigar while watching her. Even knowing he was dangerous didn't stop her from taunting him. "What's the matter, Jimmy-boy? Can't get it up so you have to use another kind of weapon? Poison pen notes do seem more your style."

"Ramming a smart ass woman in her car is more my speed." Scanlon struggled to get upright. "Shut your mouth or —"

"What? You'll do it for me?"

So he'd been the one to ram Annelise in the Mustang and hide somewhere in the garden smoking his damn cigar when she came from the garage without a car. Then he must have spent some time finding the path to her hidden quarters.

A crash and feet running through the coach house told her Chase was on his way. Her heart thumped faster.

Now on his feet, Scanlon sounded threatening. "I wouldn't mess with me if I were you."

Liz laughed. "I could say the same. You haven't come out on top yet, have you? What kind of man needs a weapon to score with a woman?"

"Maybe you're right." Grinning, he tossed the still flaming torch onto the ground.

The distraction gave Liz seconds to take off, with Scanlon right behind her.

She could hear Chase crashing down the stairs and calling, "Annelise! Liz!"

Hitting an uneven spot in the ground, she stumbled.

Then Scanlon was on top of her, throwing her to the ground, putting his hands around her throat. Liz shrieked and clawed his face until her nails were bloody..."Not happening!"

Scanlon clubbed her in the side of the head with a closed fist, but though it left her dizzy, she was filled with too much rage to let it stop her. She kneed him again. He yowled in pain, then rolled as he tried to whack the side of her head again.

She went for his eyes, but he jumped off her just as Chase caught up to them, twirling her attacker around. Chase wasn't fast enough to duck Scanlon's fist, but he recovered fast. The two men moved in a circle and sized each other up. There was no doubt in Liz's mind that she and Chase together could take the bastard. She got to her feet and looked around for a weapon.

Scanlon slipped a hand toward his back, where Liz could see part of a flat blade knife handle and horizontal leather holder.

Scanlon withdrew it from its holder and aimed it at Chase. Chase heaved a sigh, held out his hands and backed up as if retreating.

Liz looked from him to Scanlon, who grinned and let down his guard.

In a flash, Chase took a step forward and kicked, knocking the weapon from the other man's hand. Scanlon went for him, landed on top of him, knee in his groin, hands around his throat.

Breathing hard, Liz flew to grab the knife and aimed it at the threat. "Better let go, Jimmy-boy, or I'll carve out the little brains you possess."

Cursing her with a "Fuck you, bitch!" Scanlon let go.

To Liz's relief, Chase then delivered what looked like the punch of his life. Scanlon flew backward, bounced off the wall headfirst and was out before hitting the ground.

Liz picked up the torch from the muck underfoot.

Chase grabbed her arms and stared into her face. "Liz?"

She nodded. He slid his hands around her back and held her in a fierce grip, saying, "Thank God I got here in time. I'd better call Detective Turner. He'll be wondering what the hell is going on."

"You called him from the scrap yard?"

He nodded. "I called 9-1-1 after I knew Durant was dead. Then realized you might not get my help if I was there when the police arrived."

"So you came after me?"

"I did and called Turner from the car. He got the short version of what happened. I told him I needed to go after you and would call to let him know what happened."

"That's how you were here so soon after Annelise arrived."

"Right. Annelise. If not for her bravery, Durant would have shot me. I can't imagine what she was feeling when she killed him."

"I know. I wasn't there, but I felt her horror and fear.

Annelise and I have been sharing...well, not everything but most of what's been going on the last couple of days." When Chase's expression told her he was confused, Liz said, "I'll try to explain everything, once we get this mess settled." She indicated Scanlon, who was still out for the count. "As for Durant..."

She reached into her pocket and withdrew the recorder which miraculously was still activated after all the physical trauma she'd been through. She handed it to Chase.

"What's on this?" he asked.

"Proof of murder. Durant confessed to killing Lizzie."

"And if it was still recording, Scanlon trying to harm you."

Liz nodded. She'd given Scanlon reason to want revenge, but she'd just made a few phone calls to make him look bad both professionally and personally. Nothing life-threatening.

Chase kept one arm around her and pulled out his cell with the other. When Turner answered, he said, "It's Chase O'Neil. We have a complication to deal with." Chase explained where he was and why. He listened for a minute and clicked off the cell. "Turner said he would be here with backup as soon as the medical examiner removed Durant's body."

More than an hour later, a uniform gripped a handcuffed Scanlon and got him out of the garage to his squad car. Chase stepped back into Liz's not so hidden room where she sat silent and unanimated, seemingly lost, while Detective Turner finished a call and pocketed his cell. When the detective had arrived, Chase had told him everything.

Now Turner grimly stared at Liz. "Some night's work."

"Yeah, some night," Chase muttered, giving Liz a concerned look. Or was it Annelise? He wasn't certain. She'd retreated into herself well before the police had arrived, and he hadn't been able to get through to her. What was she thinking about? Worrying she might be arrested?

Turner held out the recorder Chase had turned over to him. "Thanks for this. If it has Walsh confessing and threatening to murder you and Miss Covington, you'll be in the clear. Same with her and Scanlon. He's taken care of for the moment, but I'm going to need your official statements, both for Walsh's death and for Scanlon's attack on Miss Covington."

"Of course. She's not doing too well at the moment. It's been a terrible night for her. Give me some time alone with her so Annelise can collect herself," Chase said. No need to confuse things by calling her Liz when Turner knew her as Annelise. "I'll bring her to the station if she can deal with it."

"Tomorrow is soon enough." Turner handed Chase his card but looked squarely at Liz. "We have a lot to talk about, including that driver's license for Elizabeth Covington." Then he turned to Chase. "It seems to me there's more here than you've let on. Call me directly when you're ready to come in." He left, pulling the door closed behind him.

Realizing the detective wouldn't stop asking questions until he learned that Annelise was also sometimes Liz, Chase stood over her, touched her hair gently. She was staring at the fists in her lap. "You okay, Liz?"

Her fists softened, opened. She looked up at him with a sorrow-filled expression that belonged neither to Liz nor to Annelise.

She shook her head. "No, I'm not okay. And I'm not Liz or Annelise. I'm Lizzie."

Chase shook his head. "You told me Durant killed her, remember."

Lizzie met his gaze and shook her head again. "Durant killed the wrong twin. He thought it was me, but he actually killed Annelise."

"You're confused." Chase sat next to her and put an arm around her back to comfort her when she tried to suppress a sob.

"Not anymore. I finally remember. And I know who I am."

Chapter Twenty-Three

Lizzie turned inward, finally recounting the trauma which had ruled her life for the last decade...

She'd arrived home late, tucking her beloved Mustang in the garage and then just sitting there smiling, thinking about the most perfect evening she'd ever had. The most perfect date, a picnic on the lawn at a Ravinia concert. Kyle had somehow gotten a small bottle of champagne and luckily no one had stopped them from drinking it even though they were both underage. Nor had anyone stopped them from making out. Then Kyle had told her he loved her. Lizzie had loved him like forever, for at least a year, but he hadn't seemed to notice her until two months, one week and three days ago. Now he had all kinds of plans for them in the coming weeks before he had to go back to college in the fall. At least until then, they would be inseparable.

Sighing, Lizzie slid out of the car, but rather than taking the walkway to the house, she decided to spend a little dreaming time in the hidden room that Daddy'd had built for her before he died. Well for her and Annelise, but it had been her idea, and she was pretty much the only one who used it. If she went to the house, Arthur or Durant would find some way to make her miserable. They couldn't stand seeing her happy.

She'd only gotten a few feet from the car when she realized she wasn't alone.

The flesh on the back of her neck pebbled, and she whipped around to see Durant behind her, his face set in an angry if familiar scowl.

"You were with him tonight, weren't you? That Kyle prick!"

Though the bitterness of his words worried Lizzie enough to make her breath catch, she tried to keep the encounter peaceful. She didn't want an argument to ruin her evening. "Yes, we went to a lovely dinner and concert at Ravinia."

"Is that where you fucked him?"

Lizzie gaped at him, stunned by the words delivered in a demanding, angry tone. "Goodnight, Durant."

She turned to go to the house, but he grabbed her shoulder and spun her around, making her stomach clench and her pulse kickstart.

"You know I'm crazy about you—"

Crazy, yes! "Omigod, you're my stepbrother!"

"But not related. And you're just trying to make me jealous," he spat out.

"Why would I do that?"

"Because you want me, and I'm not an easy target."

"Target?" The tightness inched upward toward her throat. His words were making her heart thunder, but Lizzie shrugged and tried to make her "Get over yourself" sound like a throwaway.

She moved toward the exit to the walkway. Before she could get halfway to the door, he had both hands on her shoulders. And she could feel his hot breath on the back of her neck, making her want to wrench herself away and flatten him.

If only she could.

That was the problem, the difference in their size and strength. They weren't kids anymore. Even then she'd never been able to win a fight, though she had given him a shiner once. She could fight him now but knew she would lose.

He moved his mouth to her ear. "You're always taunting me with insults because you want me, and I haven't taken you up on it. But I give up, Lizzie. Tonight you can have me."

Still trying to keep her temper in check, Lizzie said, "Let go of me, please," and attempted to pull away from him, but Durant's disgusting hands were locked around her upper arms.

"You're not going anywhere until I'm finished with you."

Finished with her?

Now furious, she stomped on his foot, digging her high heel into him as hard as she could. In return, he punched her in the lower back so hard her muscles spasmed, and she couldn't move. Could hardly take a breath. He punched her back again. Dropping fast, she could do nothing to stop the fall.

The moment she crashed into the pavement, Durant was on her, rolling her flat on her back. She screamed in frustration and pain. The back spasm tightened as she tried to push him away. She was paralyzed by the pain as well as with fear that, this time, he was going to kill her.

"Hey, are you okay?"

Thrust back into the present, Lizzie stared into Chase's face and realized he was worried about her.

"Lizzie, tell me what's bothering you. You're safe now with me."

She shook her head. "I remember Durant attacked me..."

And slipped back in time.

"Durant, please..."

He ignored her whispered words as he undid his zipper, then pulled her skirt up. Lizzie tried to stop him, wanted to tear out his eyes with her nails, but her arms weren't working right. And the garage felt like it was moving around her. Even though it was as dark as night, she swore she saw the secret door to the tunnel open and someone slip inside. A swirl of colors filled her mind, obliterating whoever was there. When Durant shoved himself into her, she screamed, but his hand covered her mouth and absorbed the sound.

She felt somehow removed, watching from outside her body and looking in.

Flashes of light and strange whispering voices penetrated her mind.

"Don't fight him or he'll hurt you more!"

"Don't listen to that crap!" *A second voice.* "Grab him where the sun don't shine!"

"No! Try not to think about what's happening!"

"Don't ever forget what he's doing to us!"

Us? The two voices distracted her so that, for a moment, Lizzie couldn't see or feel anything at all.

Then Durant rolled off her. "Man, I needed that!"

Lizzie lay there, her body on fire, raw with pain, stunned as if in some other universe, while Durant got to his feet and secured his pants.

"Well, you finally got what you wanted," *he said, moving to the walkway door.* "You're mine now whenever I want you and don't you forget it."

Though still in that weird untethered mental state, she didn't miss the threat. Whenever he wanted her? Dear Lord, what could she do to stop him?

"You'll find a way to ignore him," *the first voice said.*

"No! Find a way to get even." *The second voice sounded as furious as she was feeling.* "Make the motherfucker wish he was dead!"

The opposing voices in her head confused her, and she thought she was simply imagining an argument between her and Annelise.

Then she heard, "Lizzie, what did I just see? What's going on?"

Opening her eyes, she realized her twin was standing there, over her. Though she recognized Annelise appeared freaked out, Lizzie felt lost and alone and couldn't explain. The next thing she knew, her sister was helping her sit up.

"My back!" *she cried. The pain reminded her of the way Durant had brought her down.*

Annelise put a supporting arm around her. "Just sit for a few *minutes and I'll help you get to your feet, then take you upstairs."*

Pulling out of the horrific memory, Lizzie locked gazes with Chase and whispered, "When I was seventeen, Durant raped me, and Annelise came in the garage in the middle of things. By the time she realized I wasn't with Durant because I wanted to be, it was too late to stop him. If she could have. After he was done with me, she got me up to our hidden room, helped me take off my clothes and got me into the shower."

The memory sucked her back in...

Still crying, Lizzie ran the water and lowered her head, so the heat hit her sore back. What was she going to do now? How could she ever protect herself from Durant? How could she ever be with Kyle after this?

"Annelise cried and cried," Lizzie told Chase. "Said she should have done something, that it was her fault. She should have realized I didn't want what was happening sooner. She undressed after helping me into the shower, then said I should put on *her* clothes so I wouldn't have to put mine back on ever again."

Lizzie numbly rubbed soap over herself as Annelise went back to the main room. Lizzie glanced at the doorway and saw her twin had dressed in her discarded clothing.

A sob broke Lizzie's story. Chase took her in his arms and held her tight.

"Durant killed Annelise. He said she gave him no choice. She was wearing my clothes when she faced him and said she would have him arrested. He told me that she would have *lied* about what happened between us because we had made love. He must have knocked her out, put her in the car and turned on the engine. Durant thought he was killing *me.*" A sob escaped her. "And I'm the one who found her dead behind the wheel of my car! I assumed she killed herself! I screamed and screamed until people came running to find out what happened."

"What made you think your sister committed suicide?"

"Guilt because Annelise couldn't save me? Or maybe she feared she would be next."

He nodded. "I'm so sorry you lost her. But why did you pretend to be her afterward?"

"I was afraid of Durant. He said he could have me whenever he wanted." Tears seeped through Lizzie's lashes. "After all those years of defying Durant and his deranged father…" She shook her head. "Annelise wasn't like me. Didn't stir anyone's passions. Or anyone's real cruelty. When Mama and her husband rushed to the garage, Arthur called me Annelise. I guess because I was wearing her clothes. Then I thought maybe I should *be* Annelise, that I would be safe from him and his horrible son. I guess I was fooling myself. We never were safe." Lizzie stared at him, her regret laid open for him to see.

"Lizzie —"

"I vowed I would never let a man use sex to control me or any woman again. And then there was you."

Chase's expression held both guilt and regret. "I had to trap Durant. I was the only one my sister confided in. Katie told me about their affair. I knew Durant in the old days, remember, first in high school and then because of Da's job. I had his number. I tried to convince Katie to stop seeing him, but she wouldn't listen to me. I didn't try hard enough. He forced sex on her and got her pregnant, and when she told him, he had no use for her."

"She cared about him. She was a fool in love."

"Not at the end, she wasn't. Am I a fool, Lizzie? Because I care about *you*."

Lizzie laughed. "Then you care about a woman who doesn't exist."

He cupped her cheek. "You exist. And I also care about whatever women you've had to become to protect yourself. Can you forgive me for using you to find out why Katie died?"

Though she hadn't taken charge, Lizzie had drawn closer to Chase through Liz's connection with him in the past week, but she was in no shape to try on a real relationship with anyone.

How could she with a man who didn't truly know her? She couldn't. Not now. Not yet.

Maybe someday...

The coming weeks were difficult but rewarding. Detective Turner turned Lizzie inside out. He'd gotten the truth from her about Durant killing Annelise rather than her — the reason for the Elizabeth Covington driver's license. Mama had known which daughter had lived all along, and Lizzie realized Mama really had been trying to protect her by keeping her secret.

The story made the papers and the news every night for a few weeks before it died down. In the meantime, someone had to run Walsh Motors, and Lizzie already had a lawyer working on getting the company control taken away from Arthur, who wasn't capable of controlling his own body. The first thing she planned to do when she took charge of the business was to change the name back to Covington Classics.

Lizzie and her alters already had something of a peace accord, brokered by sessions with Dr. Marva Jackson. Both Liz and Annelise feared she would one day make them disappear. Lizzie wanted to reclaim her life as it should be, but they had kept her hidden and safe for a decade, and she wouldn't force integration on them.

Chase had stuck around as promised, but for backup until she was ready for more. He still drove for NASCAR, but Chicago was now his home base again. Thankfully, he'd started rebuilding his relationship with his father. He was so steadfast, so willing to spend time with her, never putting pressure on her for more than friendship.

Finally freed from the shadows of her mind, Lizzie knew there was still work to do when it came to her mental health. And Chase needed the truth about how she'd spent the last decade, something Lizzie feared she would never be able to properly explain herself. Promising to help her, Marva suggested she bring Chase to a session. He readily agreed.

The psychiatrist's office was as deeply shadowed as Lizzie's mind had been for the last decade. When she introduced them, Marva smiled and shook Chase's hand. "So glad you were willing to take the time to do this with Lizzie."

Marva indicated an extra chair next to the recliner, where Lizzie sat, relaxed, breathing with an unfamiliar inner peace, finally free of some of the tragedies that life had dealt her. And ready to talk with Chase about how the past had changed her.

Marva turned to him. "I'm aware that you know about Annelise and Liz. Has the fact that Lizzie has been more than one person troubled you?"

"No. I understand she needed to present herself as Annelise to protect herself from Durant," Chase said. "On the night he died, she told me about what he did to her, and that when she was mistaken for Annelise, she chose to let everyone believe that to protect herself."

"Lizzie, would you like to add something to that?" Marva asked.

Lizzie's pulse was racing. "I broke, Chase. Swaths of time went by when I wasn't in the real world, and Annelise became a separate entity from me. What's called an alter. She didn't think she was pretending. She thought she *was* Annelise." Chase's brow furrowed and Lizzie forced herself to go on. "The blackouts started soon after, and then I lost *myself* when Liz was born through my anger. Liz got me through the nights, and I simply disappeared from this world."

He said, "I get the feeling I'm missing something really big here."

Exactly what Lizzie had dreaded. "I feared being in Durant's world, so I just let Annelise and Liz share the life I should have led."

"Let me explain." Marva leaned into Chase, her eyes locked with his. "Dissociative identity disorder is a coping mechanism when dealing with trauma. Lizzie's past so horrible that she developed the disorder. Meaning she split into different identities — Annelise and Liz — and let them live her life for her."

"While I simply watched from what I thought was some safe place," Lizzie added.

Thinking this was enough to scare any man away, she was relieved when Chase seemed to accept Marva's explanation.

"With her stepbrother gone for good, Lizzie is getting well," Marva told him. "She's broken out of the darkness she's lived in for years. She's rebuilding her life."

"But I'm not banishing Annelise and Liz. They have to trust enough to integrate with each other. And with me."

"Is integration really possible?"

"It's not usual," Marva said, "but yes, people who had dissociative identity disorder for years suddenly managed voluntary integration. That means all the fears and hopes and memories of the various alters are combined into one person."

"But what if my alters never integrate with me?" Lizzie asked.

He shrugged. "We'll wait to find out."

Chase didn't sound like he was going anywhere. Maybe *someday* was now.

ACKNOWLEDGMENTS

I want to thank my International Thriller Writers critique partners Joel Burcat, Janet McClintock, Gregory Wilson Taylor, Dani M. Brown, Carol Barreyre, Julie Johnson, Rosemary Simpson and Todd Cohen—and my local critique partners Sherrill Bodine, Cheryl Jefferson and Jude Mandell—for their help to make this a great read.

New York Times and *USA Today* bestselling author Patricia Rosemoor has had more than one hundred novels with eight publishers and nearly eight million books in print. Always fascinated with "dangerous love," Patricia combines romance with crime in her stories. She has won a Golden Heart from Romance Writers of America and two Reviewers Choice and two Career Achievement Awards from Romantic Times BOOKreviews, and in her other life, she taught Popular Fiction and Suspense-Thriller Writing at Columbia College Chicago.